THE EPIC CRUSH OF GENIE LO

A NOVEL BY **F. C. YEE**

THE EPIC CRUSH

OF GENIE LO

AMULET BOOKS
NEW YORK

Cataloging-in-Publication Data has been applied for
and may be obtained from the Library of Congress.

ISBN 978-1-4197-2548-7

ABRAMS The Art of Books
115 West 18th Street, New York, NY 10011
abramsbooks.com

for

ABIGAIL

1

SO I DIDN'T HANDLE THE MUGGING AS WELL AS I COULD HAVE.

I would have known what do to if I'd been the victim. Hand over everything quietly. Run away as fast as possible. Go for the eyes if I was cornered. I'd passed the optional SafeStrong girl's defense seminar at school with flying colors.

But we'd never covered what to do when you see six grown men stomping the utter hell out of a boy your age in broad daylight. It was a Tuesday morning, for god's sake. I was on my way to school, the kid was down on the ground, and the muggers were kicking him like their lives depended on it. They weren't even trying to take his money.

"Get away from him!" I screamed. I swung my backpack around by the strap like an Olympic hammer thrower and flung it at the group.

The result wasn't exactly gold medal–worthy. The pack, heavy with my schoolbooks, fell short and came to rest at one of the assailants' heels. They all turned to look at me.

Crap.

I should have made a break for it, but something froze me in place.

It was the boy's eyes. Even though he'd taken a beating that should have knocked him senseless, his eyes were perfectly clear as they locked on to mine. He stared at me like I was the only important thing in the world.

One of the men threw his cigarette on the ground and took a step in my direction, adjusting his trucker cap in a particularly menacing fashion. *Crap, crap, crap.*

That was as far as he got. The boy said something, his words lost in the distance. The man flinched like he couldn't believe what he was hearing, and then turned back to resume the brutal pounding.

Finally my legs remembered what they were good for. I ran away.

I should have been worried that the assault and battery would turn into outright homicide, but I kept going without looking back. I was too freaked out.

The last sight I had of that kid was his gleaming white teeth.

■　■　■

"You shouldn't have bothered in the first place," Yunie told me in homeroom. "He was with them."

I lifted my head up from the desk. "Huh?"

"It was a gang initiation. The older members induct the new ones by beating the snot out of them. If he was smiling at you the whole time, it was because he was happy about getting 'jumped in.'"

"I don't think there are gangs that hang out in the Johnson Square dog run, Yunie."

"You'd be surprised," she said as she thumbed through her messages. "Some areas past the Walgreens are pretty sketch."

Maybe she was right. It was easy to forget in the bubble of

Santa Firenza Prep that our town wasn't affluent. A competitive school was really the only thing it had going for it. We were hardly Anderton or Edison Park or any of the other pockets of Bay Area wealth where the venture capital and tech exec families lived.

On the other hand, that kid couldn't have been a gang member. It wasn't the kind of detail you focus on in the heat of the moment, but looking back on it, he was wearing rags. Like a beggar.

Ugh. I'd run across a group of assholes beating a homeless person for kicks and wasn't able to do anything to stop them. I groaned and dropped my forehead to the desk again.

"Flog yourself some more," Yunie said. "You told a teacher as soon as you got to school and spent all morning giving the police report, didn't you?"

"Yeah," I muttered into the veneer. "But if I wasn't such an idiot, I could have called the cops right there." The skirts on our uniforms didn't have pockets. So of course I was carrying my phone in my backpack. That is to say, I'd *been* carrying it.

It was going to be a long haul, re-creating the notes from my AP classes. My secret weapons—all of the practice exams that I'd hounded my teachers into giving me—were gone. Studying by any method other than active recall was for chumps.

And my textbooks. I wasn't sure what the school policy on replacements was. If the cost fell on me, I'd probably have to sell my blood plasma.

But while I'd never admit it, not even to Yunie, what hurt most wasn't losing my phone or my notes. It was the fake-gold earrings I'd pinned to the canvas straps. The ones my dad had bought me at Disneyland, even though I'd been too young for piercings back then—too young to remember much of the trip at all.

I'd never see them again.

The bell rang. Something heavy fell past my head to the floor, and I bolted upright.

"Hey, jerk!" I yelped. "That could have hit me in the—*whuh?*"

It was my backpack. With all my stuff still in it. Minnie Mouses unharmed.

Mrs. Nanda, our homeroom teacher, stood by her desk and rapped her EDUCATOR OF THE YEAR paperweight to get our attention, punctuating the air like a judge's gavel. Her round, pleasant face was even more chipper and sprightly than usual.

"Class, I'd like to introduce a new student," she said. "Please welcome Quentin Sun."

Holy crap. It was *him*.

2

"GREETINGS," HE SAID, HIS ACCENT THICK BUT HIS VOICE LOUD and clear. "I have arrived."

Now, I'd done my best to describe this guy to the police. They pressed me hard for details, as apparently this wasn't the first group mugging in recent weeks.

But I'd let Officers Davis and Rodriguez down. Nice eyes and a winning smile weren't much to go by. I was too frazzled to notice anything before, which meant this was my first decent look at the boy without the influence of adrenaline.

So a couple of things.

One: He was short. Like, really short for a guy. I felt bad that my brain went there first, but he wasn't even as tall as Mrs. Nanda.

Two: He was totally okay, physically. I didn't see how anyone could be up and about after that beating, but here he was, unbruised and unblemished. I felt relieved and disturbed at the same time to see there wasn't a scratch on him.

And his mint condition just made Point Three even more obvious. He was . . . *yeesh.*

Nothing good could come of our new classmate being that handsome. It was destructive. Twisted. Weaponized. He had the cheekbones and sharp jawline of a pop star, but his thick eyebrows and wild, unkempt hair lent him an air of natural ruggedness that some pampered singer could never achieve in a million years of makeup.

"Argh, my ovaries," Yunie mumbled. She wasn't alone, judging by the soft intakes of breath coming from around the room.

"Arrived from where?" said Mrs. Nanda.

Quentin looked at her in amusement. "China?"

"Yes, but where in, though?" said Mrs. Nanda, trying her best to convey that she was sensitive to the regional differences. Fujianese, Taishanese, Beijingren—she'd taught them all.

He just shrugged. "The stones," he said.

"You mean the mountains, sweetie?" said Rachel Li, batting her eyelashes at him from the front row.

"No! I don't misspeak."

The class giggled at his English. But none of it was incorrect, technically speaking.

"Tell us a little about yourself," Mrs. Nanda said.

Quentin puffed out his chest. The white button-down shirt and black pants of our school's uniform for boys made most of them look like limo drivers. But on him, the cheap stitching just made it clearer that he was extremely well-muscled underneath.

"I am the greatest of my kind," he said. "In this world I have no equal. I am known to thousands in faraway lands, and everyone I meet can't help but declare me king!"

There was a moment of silence and sputtering before guffaws broke out.

"Well . . . um . . . we are all high achievers here at SF Prep," said Mrs. Nanda as politely as she could. "I'm sure you'll fit right in?"

Quentin surveyed the cramped beige classroom with a cool

squint. To him, the other twenty-two laughing students were merely peons on whom his important message had been lost.

"Enough wasting of time," he snapped. "I came to these petty halls only to reclaim what is mine."

Before anyone could stop him, he hopped onto Rachel's desk and stepped over her to the next one, like she wasn't even there.

"Hey! Quentin!" Mrs. Nanda said, frantically waving her hands. "Get down now!"

The new student ignored her, stalking down the column of desks. Toward mine.

Everyone in his way leaned to the side to avoid getting kicked. They were all too flabbergasted to do anything but serve as his counterweights.

He stopped on my desk and crouched down, looking me in the eye. His gaze pinned me to my seat.

I couldn't turn away. He was so close our noses were almost touching. He smelled like wine and peaches.

"You!" he said.

"What?" I squeaked.

Quentin gave me a grin that was utterly feral. He tilted his head as if to whisper, but spoke loud enough for everyone to hear.

"You belong to *me*."

3

"HE'S GOING TO SUE YOU, GENIE," JENNY ROLSTON SAID WHILE we were changing in the locker room. "Once he learns that's how we do things in America, he's going to find a lawyer."

I slammed my locker shut. It immediately bounced back open, more than a year of my rough handling having misaligned the latch. It took the weight of my shoulder to close the dented gray door for good.

"Hey, *he* got in *my* face," I said, my head still buried under my jersey.

"Yeah, he was rude. And crazy. But you totally overreacted. He's probably blind now."

"Big Joe from SafeStrong would have approved of my reflexes. And my use of thumbs."

Jenny sighed. "If they suspend you for gouging out the eyes of a transfer student and I have to use a sub during regionals, I'm going to murder you."

I let the team captain have the last word. After today's double-dose of unpleasantness I just wanted to focus on practice. I had better things to worry about than a wackjob new student who'd latched on to me like a newborn duck. I laced up my sneakers, tied my hair back, and joined the rest of the girls on the court.

Jenny's death threat had been a compliment, sort of. I'd been pretty instrumental to the SF Lady Sharks' sudden surge of victories in the last year and a half. But it's not because I'm the greatest athlete in the world. I have no illusions as to why I've been on varsity volleyball since I was a freshman.

It's because I'm tall.

Ridiculously tall. Grossly tall. Monstrously tall.

Tall like a model, Yunie says. She's allowed to lie to me.

Jenny had her eye on me from day one. She didn't have to twist my arm to recruit me; it's safe to say this has been a mutually beneficial arrangement. I lead the league in career stuffs despite only having half a career, and I can probably get the attention of a college coach for a few minutes come admissions time. At least until he or she realizes I have the jump serve of a walrus.

The one thing I'm not too keen on is being nicknamed "The Great Wall of China." But then again, there are too many Asian students here to make it a minority slur. I'm pretty sure one of them came up with it in the first place.

My feet squeaked against the hardwood as I took my position in middle blocker. The time flew by as I sweated and grunted and spiked out the minutes in the echoing gym. Our only audience besides Coach Daniels were the shoddily painted murals of fall and spring sports athletes covering the walls.

At first I'd only joined this team to look well-rounded. I didn't have Yunie's gift for music, and I needed some extracurriculars. But over time I really came to love the game. When people asked why, I told them I thrived on the camaraderie.

In reality, though, I liked destroying people. Single-handedly.

I liked ruining the carefully crafted offensive schemes of the other team simply by existing. For five sets a week, the world was unfair in my favor. That didn't happen very often.

I was in the zone today, carrying the rookies that had been intentionally loaded on my side. Until I saw *him* standing in the bleachers.

"What the hell?" I said. "Get him out of here!"

"Can't," said Jenny. "Practice is over and we're in extra time. We don't have claim on the gym anymore. Just finish the scrim."

I grunted angrily and turned back to match point. I could still feel his eyes burning into the back of my head.

"Someone's got an admirer," Maxine Wong said from the other side of the net.

"Shut up."

"I heard all about it from Rachel," said the girl whose starter spot I'd taken. "You wigged out because he wanted to have an arranged marriage right there in class? I thought FOBs were into that kind of thing."

My eyes widened. The serve from my side was bumped and set for her.

"Shut UP!" I screamed as I went for the block.

Maxine wasn't beyond playing mind games. She was the same year as Jenny, but she crossed the line way too often with the sophomores and freshmen, at least in my opinion. I didn't like her at all.

Her taunts worked this time. She was better at playing while trash-talking than I was. I was off-balance and didn't have enough off the jump. She was going to get the winning kill—

"Gah!" Maxine yelped, landing hard on her butt. The ball bopped her on the head and rolled over the sideline.

"Dang, girl!" Jenny shouted from behind. "I wanna see that come game time!"

I looked at my hands, puzzled. I could have sworn I didn't have that block.

"Freak," Maxine said, as she got to her feet.

I glanced toward the bleachers. Quentin was gone.

Damn it. That scumbag was throwing me off so much that he was throwing me on.

■ ■ ■

"All right, this has gone too far," I said. "You crossed the border into stalker territory a long time ago. I don't mind talking to the police twice in one day."

Quentin was "walking me home." Or at least that's what he'd asked to do as I left school. I should have told him off right away instead of giving him the silent treatment. Now any uninitiated observers would think we were hashing out a misunderstanding like civilized people.

"Go ahead and call them," he said. "I'm told it's a free country."

Wait, had his English gotten better?

"I don't know what kind of game you're playing," I said, picking up the pace so that he fell behind and hopefully stayed there. "But it stops now. I don't know you. I don't want to know you. Just because I found you getting your ass kicked doesn't mean a thing. And you're welcome, by the way."

He snorted. "A lot of help you were. You didn't even tell anyone at school it was me you saw getting beat up, did you?"

I growled in frustration. There were actually a bunch of things I wanted to ask—like how he'd healed up so quickly, or what had happened to his old raggedy clothes, or how his speech seemed to randomly fluctuate between a Bay Area teenager and a Confucian bard—but I didn't want to encourage him.

"You dream of a mountain," Quentin said.

I stopped in my tracks and turned around. We were completely alone on the block, a splintery picket fence hemming us in on one side, and an empty lot with more abandoned bicycles than grass across the street.

"You dream of a mountain," he repeated. "Green and full of flowers. Every night when you fall asleep, you can smell the jasmine blossoms and hear the running streams."

He said this with real drama. Like it was supposed to hit home for me. Forge some kind of a connection between us.

I smirked. Because it didn't.

"Last night I dreamed I was floating in space and watching the stars," I said, feeling smug. "But you should keep trying that pickup line. I know at least a couple of girls at school like cheese."

Quentin didn't respond for a second. Apparently I was the one who'd floored him.

He broke out into a gigantic, ear-to-ear smile. Under better circumstances it would have been gorgeous.

"That's it!" he said, hopping in excitement. "That proves it! You really *are* mine!"

Okay. That kind of talk had to stop right here and right now. I inhaled deeply to unleash both a torrent of verbal abuse and a refresher in women's history over the last century.

But before I could give him what he asked for, Quentin jumped onto the neighboring fence, taking five feet in one smooth leap as easily as you'd take the escalator. He laughed and hooted and *cartwheeled* back and forth on the uprights, balancing on a surface that must have been narrower than a row of quarters.

My head began to spin. Something about his uninhibited display made it feel like there was a light shining behind my eyes, or like I was breathing in too much oxygen. I felt all the nausea that he should have, flipping around like that.

He wasn't normal. He must have been a gymnast or parkourista or whatever from online videos. Maybe a Shaolin.

I didn't care. I kicked the fence in the hope that he would fall and crotch himself, and I ran straight home.

∎ ∎ ∎

A few minutes later I crossed the finish line into my driveway, gasping for breath.

I hurried with the keys to my house, my hands clumsier than usual. The click of the lock never sounded sweeter. Finally, finally, I slipped inside and sighed.

Only to find Quentin sitting at the kitchen table with my mom.

4

I CHECKED BEHIND ME AS A REFLEX AND BANGED MY FACE against the door in the process.

"Genie," Mom said, beaming like we'd won the lottery. "You have a visitor. A friend from school."

I pointed at Quentin while holding my nose. "How did you get inside?"

He looked puzzled. "I knocked on the door and introduced myself to your mother? We've been chatting for a while now."

I had taken the shortest route home and hadn't seen him pass me. Given that I was a decent runner, he must have sprinted here like a bat out of hell. How was he not winded in the slightest?

"Quentin is so nice," Mom said. "He explained how you rescued him this morning. He came over to say thank-you in person." She pointed to a fancy-wrapped box of chocolates on the kitchen counter.

"I had to ask around for your address," Quentin said. "In case you were wondering."

I rubbed my eyes. I felt like I was going crazy. But I could figure out his little magic trick later, once he was gone.

"I don't know how you got here before me," I said to Quentin. "But get the hell out."

"Pei-Yi! Rude!" Mom snapped.

Quentin made eye contact with me. Maybe he thought I'd stay quiet in front of my mother for the sake of decorum. That a boy's good name was more important than a girl's safety. If so, he was dead effin' wrong.

"Mother," I said slowly. "While this person seems like a nice young man on the surface, he threatened me during class this morning. He's not my friend."

My mother looked at him.

"I'm so sorry!" Quentin cried out, his face stricken. He shot to his feet and lowered his head. "I came here to apologize. And to explain my horrendous behavior."

"I'd love an explanation," I said. "Starting with what happened in the park."

"That was a misunderstanding that got out of hand," he said. "Those men weren't even bad people, just ordinary folk I tried to make conversation with. But I accidentally insulted them to such a degree that they sought to teach me a lesson. I can barely even blame them."

I frowned. At the time, the beating had seemed a bit extreme for a misunderstanding. But then again, I hadn't turned the other cheek in class myself. I guess he had a knack for pissing people off to the point of violence.

"After they left I picked up your bag, cleaned myself off, and brought it to school," Quentin said. "I knew you went to the same one as me because I recognized your uniform."

"It was just a fortunate coincidence I was assigned to your class on my first day," he went on. "I was so happy when I saw the person who saved my life this morning that I lost my head and made the same error all over again. My English is from a book, and I still don't know how things really work in America."

Mom sniffled like she was watching a soap finale.

"I'm sorry to have spoken to you so personally," Quentin said, his voice cracking.

I bit the inside of my cheek. I wasn't inclined to believe any of his BS, but he said it in such a heartfelt way that I was actually considering giving him the benefit of the doubt. Maybe he was just a really, really awkward transplant with no sense of personal space.

That's when the bastard winked at me.

Fine. Two could play at this game.

"You know what would be great?" I said, putting on a coy expression. "If we could have you and your parents over for dinner. Let us welcome you to the States."

Quentin raised a black, regal eyebrow.

Got you, jerk. Let's see if you can handle me blowing your creepstory to the real *authorities.* If I let his parents know about his behavior, there'd be no way he'd get off scot-free.

"Oh, how lovely," Mom said, clapping her hands. "That's a wonderful idea."

"Uh . . . okay," said Quentin, looking unsure of himself for the first time ever. "They would also want to give their thanks . . . I guess."

"But for now you must be going," I said. "You promised the chess club you'd go out with them to try your first real American hamburger."

"Yes!" he said. "I am most interested in this thing that you're talking about."

As Quentin laced his shoes up in the hallway, Mom pulled me aside.

"Be nice to him," she said. "Not so harsh, like you always are."

Ugh. My mom is of the generation that believes the male can do no wrong.

"I should be nice like you were?" I said. "You took his side over your own daughter's pretty quickly. Did he tell you exactly what he did at school?"

She looked up at me sadly. "It's hard, coming to this country," she said. "You were born here; you never had to experience that. Of course he's going to make some mistakes."

Then her eyes gleamed. "Plus he's so handsome. And rich, too, probably. Like a prince. I can tell these things."

Ugggghhhhhh.

I showed Quentin out, mostly because I wanted to make sure he walked the hell away and didn't sneak into our bushes or something. Once I'd closed the door behind us, I stared him down.

"You picked the wrong girl to bully, asshat."

"I said I was sorry!"

"No, you lied about being sorry to my mother! There's a difference!"

"What, do you want me to grovel in front of your dad, too? Where is he? Still at work?"

At the mention of my father my teeth clenched so hard they almost turned to shrapnel.

"You don't have the right to talk to any of my family!" I said. "You have no right to anything of mine!"

"I don't understand why you're so upset!"

I poked him hard in his chest. It was like tapping granite.

"That doesn't matter," I hissed. "You are not entitled to my thoughts, emotions, or any other part of my life unless I say so.

What you get from me is jack and squat, regardless of whether or not you understand. *Ming bai le ma*, dickhead?"

Quentin opened his mouth to retort but nothing came out. He stood there, failing to turn over, like a car with a faulty ignition. I could read his face as plain as day. He just couldn't believe that I, an actual human being, was talking to him like this.

Finally he just scowled and stomped away.

I watched him go. I waited till he was out of sight.

The tension in my body left with him. I nearly toppled over with relief. He'd been banished, out of sight and out of mind. Hopefully for all time.

Then I remembered he was in my homeroom, where I'd see him every day.

5

A LITTLE MORE THAN A DECADE AGO THERE WAS SOME KIND of brainwave, some kind of collective spasm, some bug in the water, that induced every single Asian couple with a newborn daughter in America to name her Eugenia. Or Eunice. Something with an E-U. Seriously, these two vowels together had a base rate of next to nothing in the broader population and then BAM! An epidemic of Eumonia.

Eugenia Park has been my best friend ever since we made a deal in second grade to split the name we both hated like a turkey. She got the front end and was forevermore "Yunie." I got the back, "Genie." There was even a third girl in our class to whom we'd hopefully offered "Eugie," but we turned out not to like her, so she's not part of the treaty.

"You're gonna hate me," Yunie said during our study hall in the computer lab. "But I have to bail on the Read-a-Thon."

I made a face. "Your children will serve me in hell for this."

"I'll find a replacement. I'm sure there's someone else who wants to wake up extra early on Saturday and wrangle twenty screaming kindergartners. I'll tell them—"

"Hold on a second."

I glanced behind me across the room. Michael and his posse

were at it again, crowding around the workstation that Rutsuo was using.

Rutsuo Huang was one of the ultrageniuses at our school, a programming prodigy who was miles ahead of everyone else. I mean, I've only been able to wrap my head around introductory JavaScript. But Rutsuo had blown through our school's electives in a semester and could probably work at a startup right now if he wanted to. He was also painfully awkward and shy, and at SF Prep that's saying a lot.

He was working on what must have been a personal project, as there weren't any assignments left for him. But every so often while he was typing, Mike Wen or one of his two gym-rat flunkies would reach over his shoulder and press a random bunch of keys on the keyboard.

"Boop," Mike said as a series of complex statements turned to gibberish.

It was perhaps the nerdiest form of harassment ever invented, but still. Rutsuo kept plugging away without telling them to stop, fixing his code over and over. I could tell he was bothered, but he wouldn't say anything. And the teacher on duty was in the bathroom.

"Anyway, it's because we're celebrating my cousin's MCAT results," Yunie explained. "Apparently she did well enough that my aunt needs to force the entire bloodline to stop and congratulate her."

"Boop," said one of the other guys around Rutsuo.

"I think the only reason my parents are going is so they can pull the same move if I win my *concours,"* Yunie went on. "It's like, gee, thanks for the additional pressure."

"Boop."

I wasn't listening. I slammed my palms down hard on the table as I stood up to put an end to this.

But someone else beat me to it.

"This game looks like fun," Quentin said, his fingers tight around Mike's wrist. "How do I play?"

Mike tried to yank his hand away, but he was caught fast in Quentin's grip. There was an audible balloon-rubbing sound that promised the mother of all friction burns on Mike's forearm when this was over.

"Back off, shrimp," he said, his face turning red. But even with both arms he couldn't get Quentin to let go.

"Am I winning yet?" Quentin wondered.

One of Mike's friends, John or something, threw a sucker punch at Quentin's head. I saw it coming but couldn't say anything fast enough.

Quentin turned his head just enough to let the punch slide by and clasped John's fist under his chin. I didn't see how it was possible, but he had the other boy held just as tight as Mike, using only his *neck*.

The third one whose name I couldn't remember also tried to hit him, but Quentin swung his leg up like a contortionist and clamped the guy's fingers in the crook of his knee, squeezing hard enough to make him howl in pain. All four of them were wrapped up together like a human octopus. The way he was stretched out it should have been Quentin screaming, but he just laughed at the writhing, shrieking goons he'd trapped.

"Boop," he said, pressing Mike's nose hard with the heel of his free hand.

21

"The hell is going on here?" Androu bellowed as he stormed into the room.

It wasn't a teacher intervening. But it was the next best thing. The whole school, even the punks like Mike and his crew, respected Androu Glaros.

Androu was a senior, but it wasn't like he was the student council president or the captain of anything. He just had a natural charisma that made people listen to him. Admire him. Nurse a secret crush on him ever since he gave me the new student's tour on my first day of school.

Hey, it's not my fault. He's one of the few guys around who's actually taller than me.

Androu was naturally an imposing presence, his impeccable posture and steely eyes giving him the air of a poorly-disguised reporter who was always ducking in and out of phone booths when disaster struck. But Quentin looked up at him, nonchalant as can be.

"We are having the fun times together," said Quentin, regressing his English in a manner I now knew was more intentional than not. "Would you like to also?"

"Oh, drop the newcomer act, Quentin," Androu snapped. "This isn't acceptable anywhere."

Quentin's grin held but became a little more rigid. He unwound his limbs from his victims, who ran off while spewing a bunch of curses. No one paid them any mind. They didn't even qualify as a sideshow to the epic staredown going on.

"You are late to the scene," said Quentin. "But somehow still early to judgment."

"I know what I saw," said Androu. "And I heard what you did to Genie."

I nearly jumped at my name. While the whole school knew about Quentin's first day, and had spent a good week pointing fingers at me and laughing, I didn't think Androu cared enough to get upset about it.

"It doesn't matter whether you're 'adjusting,' " he said. "Pull this crap again, and we're gonna have a talk with the faculty."

With the last word firmly in hand, he exited stage left, continuing his journey onward to wherever it is heroic hot guys go during Sixth Period.

Quentin rolled his eyes and turned to Rutsuo, who'd been curled up in his chair the whole time. He whispered something in the quiet boy's ear and then punched him jovially in the arm. It was way too hard and nearly knocked him off his seat, but Rutsuo just blushed and smiled.

Yunie eyed Quentin, and then me.

"You two are a lot alike," she said.

"Don't even."

"I'm going over there," she said.

"I said *don't* even!"

Very little could prevent Yunie from doing what she wanted to. She marched right up to Quentin and tapped him on the shoulder.

"That was very good of you," she said.

Quentin shrugged. "I have always hated people like that."

"Yeah, Mike and his friends are assholes."

"No," said Quentin. "I mean the big one with curly hair."

"Huh? Androu?"

"Yes." Quentin's face darkened. "*Bai chi* like him care only for order, not justice. They'll let banditry run free right under their nose so long as no one raises a fuss."

Even Yunie had a hard time keeping a straight face at that. Calling our school douchebags a pack of bandits seemed like an upgrade they didn't deserve. She fought back a giggle and glanced across the room at me.

"Good thing we have one more fuss-maker around now," she said.

I gave her both middle fingers.

6

WAKING UP THIS EARLY ON SATURDAY WOULD HAVE SUCKED any time of the year, but today was a high-pollen-count day. My eyes burned at the beautiful weather outside, even though the window was shut tight. Lush green foliage, crisp breezes, chirping birds: Allergy apocalypse.

I sat up and rubbed my face until my room came into focus. It had been tiny for a very long time. Even though I kept it clean, it was covered in a thick layer of grade-school knickknacks that I never bothered to clear out—art projects that were mostly glue, dolls with bad haircuts, works of fiction that spanned from *Dick and Jane* to *Great Expectations*.

You could have dug a glacial core in my room and pinpointed the exact moment I stopped caring about anything but escaping it. That was where the textbooks and extra study materials and supplementary lessons took over the fossil record. That was when the comet had struck my family. My personal Chicxulub.

The news from the shower radio promised no respite from the assault on my eyes. The wildfires raging unchecked in the hills on the other side of the Bay could be sending us a welcoming embrace of particulate at any time. The governor was calling for a state of emergency due to drought conditions. California! What a paradise.

After I dressed, I made myself a pot of coffee and downed the whole thing while packing my lunch. I knew some of my classmates didn't drink it, but I could replace my blood with the stuff. It wasn't like it was going to stunt my growth at this point. Plus any magical liquid that makes you study harder was A-OK by my mom.

As lame as it sounds, this was no different from my weekday routine. I just left my house in a different direction, for the center of town instead of toward school.

It wouldn't have made a difference in the scenery. The houses in this part of the neighborhood had a chronic case of sameface. Garage-less brick boxes with lawns too small to make snow angels. And this was the "more livable" part of town. The rest of Santa Firenza by the office parks was a prairie of concrete and asphalt that grilled your optic nerves from reflected glare. Sure there were a few trees, but they didn't commit. This was a land that was hot, flat, and almost entirely without shade.

A far cry from the glorious playground of gleaming aluminum and primary colors that everyone thinks of when they imagine Silicon Valley. That image only holds up in the campuses of the two or three truly giant tech companies, the lone islands drifting in a sea of reality. The rest of the Bay Area is, unfortunately, the Bay Area.

The one thing we do have down here, more so than green spaces or the changing of the seasons, is education. We gobble up as much of it as we can, in forms both cheap and expensive, from bank-breaking Montessori preschools to flannel-wearing college kids paid under the table for tutoring. Whatever each of us can afford, really. Call it a side effect of our Asian-ness, whether genetic or absorbed through proximity.

Today I was doing my part to perpetuate the cycle of violence to the next generation. Every so often the library closes to the general public and holds an all-day event for children where older students read aloud to them. The kids get points for how long they last and how many books they sit through, with the winner at the end of the year receiving I don't remember what. A trip to Great United amusement park maybe.

The readers, on the other hand, get a big ol' badge of VOLUNTEERS and GIVES BACK TO THE COMMUNITY.

Yunie and I have been doing the Read-a-Thon ever since Ketki Pathpati graduated and unofficially passed the torch to us. Technically anyone can help, but it's sort of our thing now. I only wish we had invented it ourselves—the colleges would have given us a lot more points.

Mrs. Thompson, the town librarian, was waiting outside the building for me. "You didn't get my email?" she said. "We had to start half an hour earlier than normal."

"I don't have anything from you," I said. I'd checked my messages during breakfast.

Mrs. Thompson smacked her forehead. "I must have sent it to just Yunie."

"I'm going to kill that girl. I'm so sorry, Mrs. Thompson. The kids must be bored out of their minds . . ."

"Actually, they're doing fine," she said brightly as we walked inside. "She found a wonderful replacement."

"Replacement?" I thought Yunie had been joking before, so I assumed I'd be alone.

"Right in here," said Mrs. Thompson.

I'M GOING TO KILL THAT GIRL, I thought.

"Ready?" Quentin shouted from underneath the pile of laughing, squealing children. "One, two, three!"

He rose to his feet, kids clinging to his back, hanging off his biceps, sitting on his shoulders and using his hair as a grip. He made a slight bounce as if to throw them off, but they just shrieked with delight and hung on tighter. He was even stronger than he looked.

"*Raargh!*" he play-screamed, slowly spinning around underneath the toddler mountain until he faced me. "*Raaaaa* . . . oh . . . hello."

"He's been a treasure," Mrs. Thompson said adoringly. "I've never seen them take to anyone so quickly."

"Teacher's here, you little apes," said Quentin. "Quiet down and get to your spots. Or else I'll smash your heads open and eat your brains."

I thought someone would have an objection to that, but the kids all laughed and scrambled into neat rows at his behest. They plopped down onto musty blankets and cushions on the floor. Some were still talking and shoving each other.

"Change to stone!" Quentin shouted, wiggling his fingers like he was casting a spell. The children immediately straightened up and closed their mouths in intense concentration, sucking in their cheeks and biting their lips.

Call me a hypocrite, but I genuinely didn't want to make a scene here, of all places. I decided to just power through it. Plus the kids really did seem to like him. Kids could smell evil like dogs, right?

"How did you get them to behave like that?" I whispered as I slid onto the reader's bench. Yunie and I had never been able to rein them in so quickly.

"Mind control," he said. He sat next to me and handed me a book. "You can begin any time now, *laoshi*."

That was a little more respectful than necessary, but whatever. *"Father was eating his egg,"* I read. *"Mother was eating her egg. Gloria was sitting in a high chair and eating her egg, too. Frances was eating bread and jam."*

"Omnomnom slurp slurp gulp," said Quentin. *"Burp."*

I was about to glare at him for going off message, but the kids giggled and rolled in their seats.

"'What a lovely egg,' said Father." I read on. *"'It is just the thing to start the day off right,' said Mother. Frances . . . did not eat her egg."*

Quentin gasped as if the fate of the world rested on that little badger eating that egg. The kids did the same.

He was like a goofy morning show puppet. I smiled in spite of myself and went on. *"Frances sang a little song to it . . ."*

We settled into that rhythm, where I did the word-for-word reading, and Quentin made sound effects, spot-on animal noises, and embellishments that kept everyone awake.

"HOW hungry was that caterpillar?" he'd shout.

"VERY!" twenty young voices would respond.

It worked. It was a lot more raucous than normal, but a lot more fun. We almost didn't want to break for lunch.

The librarians herded the kids toward the pizzas that served as the bribe to get them here in the first place. The picnic tables outside the library were reserved for the readers, to give them a moment's peace.

Quentin sat down at the far end of the table from me as I took out my lunch. He glanced at the distance between us as if to say, *See? What you wanted.*

"Your friend asked me to help her, and her alone," he said. "She didn't tell me you'd be here."

I believed him. Only because I knew how much Yunie delighted in trolling me at every possible opportunity.

I noticed he was empty-handed. "You didn't bring any food? This is an all-day thing."

"I didn't think to. I'll be fine."

Yeah, right. He could play tough all he wanted, but I saw him give a long look at the fruit I'd packed.

"Here," I said, handing it over. "Just take it."

"Thanks!" He held up the gift for a brief moment with both hands like a monk accepting alms. "Peaches are my favorite food in the universe. But this one looks different?"

He took a nibble and his eyes grew as big as plates.

"It's a peach hybrid," I said. "Crossed with a plum or apricot or something. You like it?"

"It's amazing!" he mumbled through massive bites, trying to keep the juice from dribbling far and wide.

I watched him eat, completely absorbed in his treat. It was cute. If he had a tail, it would've been wagging like a puppy's.

I decided that small talk was acceptable. "You handled Mike and his gang pretty well," I said. "Where did you learn wushu?"

"Didn't," said Quentin. "Never took a single lesson in fighting."

"Oh? What about babysitting? You're a natural at that, too?"

"I've got a lot of little cousins and nieces and nephews back home that I used to take care of. I like kids. I was happy to volunteer for this."

He shifted the peach stone into his cheek like a gumball and stared accusingly at me. "From what I could gather from your friend, however, the two of you are only doing this to gain access to a magical kingdom called Harvard."

"*Pfft.* Yale would also suffice."

He didn't appreciate the joke. In fact, he grew downright serious.

"It seems to me that you are jumping through many hoops to please some petty bureaucratic gatekeepers," he said.

I laughed. I'd never heard the admissions process described like that before.

"That's how the system works," I said. "You think I care about my grades just because? You think I enjoy working on my essays for their own sake?"

His naïveté was strange. A transfer student from the mainland shouldn't have been this clueless. Most of them were only here in the first place to improve their shot at a top-tier school.

"I'm doing this because I don't want to be poor," I said. "I don't want to stay in this town. I want to move forward in life, and that means college. The more prestigious the better."

I wadded up my paper bag and chucked it into the recycling bin. "If you're a *taizidang* like my mother thinks you are, then you wouldn't understand. You probably had everything handed to you."

He looked disappointed in my response.

"I hope you have better luck with the system than I did," he said.

Quentin had a troubled, faraway look on his face, like he was remembering his own long-ago ordeal in academia. He must have gone to one of those cram-factories where they spanked you with abacuses. Maybe that was how his English seemed to be improving at an exponential rate.

I sighed. "You want half of my sandwich? It's ham and Swiss."

"Thanks," he said. "But I'm a vegetarian."

. . .

We went way over our allotted time. At the close of the Read-a-Thon, there was a whole crowd of parents just as enthralled as the kids they'd come to pick up.

"*George didn't say a word,*" I read. "*He felt quite trembly. He knew something tremendous had taken place that morning. For a few brief moments, he had touched with the very tips of his fingers the edge of a magic world.*"

"*The End,*" said Quentin. Somehow the difficulty level of the books had risen over the course of the day. The two of us got up and took a bow at Mrs. Thompson's insistence while everyone clapped.

The room began to clear out slowly, the adults lingering to chit-chat with each other and the children running around to enjoy their last moments of freedom.

"How soon can we have you two back?" Mrs. Thompson said with a smile. "After today's performance, I'd be willing to make this an every week thing."

An adorable little cherub tugged at Quentin's trouser leg.

"Where's the pretty girl?" the kid said to him. "You should read with the pretty girl instead of *her.*"

"Beth!" Mrs. Thompson gasped. "Your mother's calling. Get along now." She shooed the towheaded child away from the awkward-bomb she'd just dropped.

Yunie and I spent so much time together it was only natural that people would refer to us as a pair. And no one thinks she's gorgeous more so than me. She's petite, slender—the natural beauty.

Which means I'm the . . . *not.*

If she's the small one then I'm the big one. If she's the friendly one who's on good terms with everyone, then I'm the rough one with a sharp tongue and bad temper. If she's the attractive one, then, well, it's pretty obvious what's left over.

"Yeah . . . so, uh . . . this was a one-time arrangement," said Quentin.

"Aw," Mrs. Thompson said. "But the two of you have such good . . ." She waved her index fingers crisscross at him and me.

"Comedic contrast?" There was way too much edge in my voice. "Yeah, we're a regular Laurel and Hardy. I'll see you next month."

I spun on my heel and went out the back of the library, avoiding the crush of parents and children in the front lobby.

1

I DIDN'T HEAR FOOTSTEPS AS I BEGAN THE WALK BACK TO MY
house, or see a shadow trailing mine, but I spoke anyway.

"Are you going to tell me I was rude?" I said. "That I shouldn't
have spoken to an adult like that?"

Inside I was kicking myself. I *was* rude. Mrs. Thompson didn't
deserve any guff from me. She was like Mrs. Claus and Maria von
Trapp put together.

"I'm not going to tell you anything," Quentin said from behind.
"Except that you're going the long way."

I turned to face him. "Okay, how much of a stalker are you that
you know more than one way to my—"

Standing behind Quentin, perfectly and unnaturally stock still,
was a huge man.

The hugest one I'd ever seen. He had to have been at least eight
feet tall.

He was wearing a suit made out of silk so black it looked like
human hair. His bulging eyes didn't seem to point in the same
direction, and there was something crooked about his massive
arms, almost as if they had an extra joint he was hiding.

Quentin noticed my surprise and glanced behind him. In the blink
of an eye he was by my side, shoving me away from the stranger.

"Ho, little one," the giant said to him. "You've gone soft to let me sneak up on you. What happened to that famous vision of yours?"

"Hunshimowang!" Quentin shouted. "So it was *you* I sensed lurking about this town! How did your sorry ass get out of Hell?"

"Oh, wouldn't you like to find out?" the man in black said with a laugh. "Let's call it 'good behavior.' What really matters is that I, Hunshimowang, the Demon King of Confusion, am finally back in the world of the living." He fanned the air toward his egg-size nostrils and breathed in appreciatively.

Oh god oh god. Yunie was right. Quentin was a gangster and this was some Tong friend of his from prison. I fumbled for my phone to call someone, anyone, but the sweat pouring out of my palms cost me crucial seconds.

"Mmm, is that the smell of human child?" said the man. "After I kill you I'm going to have to follow the trail back and have myself a celebratory meal. It's been ages since I've tasted flesh of any kind."

"You make one move toward her and I'll feed you your own liver!" Quentin snapped.

"Always such concern for mortals." One of the man's eyes, just the one, swiveled toward me, and he licked a strand of drool off his lips with a tongue as thick and knotted as a two-by-four. His nauseating appearance and bizarre threats robbed me of the ability to respond quickly. Maybe I could have gotten over my confusion, and maybe I could have powered through my fear, but not both together.

"I notice you haven't told the girl to run yet," he said to Quentin. "Could it be that you're scared to face me without her? Surely you haven't become that weak?"

Quentin bristled. "You don't know who she is! And I don't need anybody's help to beat you to death a second time!"

He snatched my phone out of my grasp before I could hit the second 1 of 911.

"I'm sorry, Genie," Quentin said, crushing it to glass and metal splinters with a single squeeze. "But we can't involve anyone else."

The man in black grinned. And grinned. And kept grinning. His smile parted his face and sliced toward his ears, exposing a mouth that went nearly all the way around his head like a crocodile's.

Quentin snarled, his flawless looks contorting into a mask of rage. I could see his canines bared, much longer than they should have been. He gave me a hard push to the side, sending me through the air. I landed on the grass as he launched himself at the giant.

The force from their collision nearly popped my eardrums. Quentin was telling the truth before. Whatever he and the man in black were doing, it wasn't wushu. They attacked each other like rabid animals, clawing and biting as much as they punched and kicked.

I scrabbled backward on my heels and hands, trying to get away from the radius of their malice. My heart hadn't beat in the last minute. I was looking at two people trying to kill each other. The sight was an infection that I couldn't allow to reach me.

I heard a sharp wooden *crack* across the street like a tree had split and fallen, and suddenly Quentin was gone from sight. He must have been thrown off into the distance.

The giant yawned in pain and rolled his shoulders before turning his attention to me. He walked over and crouched down, slamming his hands against the ground on either side of me, blotting out the sun above.

"It's strange, meeting you for the first time under these circumstances," he said, his foul, raw-meat breath descending over me.

"Let's see if I can get a taste of you without cracking my teeth."

His saliva spattered against my cheek. I shut my eyes, screamed my lungs out, and kicked him as hard as I could.

It felt like I completely whiffed, which should have been impossible given how big he was. But the stench abated. I looked up to see an expression of complete shock on the man's face as he back-pedaled away, a foot-size chunk missing from his flank. Black goo dripped from the wound onto the sidewalk.

He and I must have shared the same bewilderment at that moment. *Look buddy, I'm as confused as you.*

"Don't touch her!" Quentin roared, taking advantage of his opponent's distraction to make his flying reentry. He dropped from the sky onto the man's platform-like shoulders and the two of them spiraled away into the street.

Despite their injuries, the fight wasn't over by a long shot. The giant managed to get Quentin at both arms' length and smashed him into the ground repeatedly like he was trying to open a coconut. I thought Quentin was dead from the first impact alone, but his legs snaked out and wrapped around the man's neck. He pulled the man's head into his abdomen and began strangling him with his whole body, all while being bounced against the pavement so hard I could see an outline of his shoulders on the ground where they blew away the dust.

The giant kept ramming Quentin into the earth, but his strength started to flag, especially since he was still bleeding heavily from his side. His knees buckled and he fell to the ground like a chain-sawed oak. Quentin maintained the chokehold until the man in black stopped moving, and then some.

Finally he scooted out from under his opponent. Then, without hesitating, Quentin clambered onto the man's back and grasped his chin and the top of his head.

"Wait, no!" I shrieked once I realized what he was going to do.

With a twist of his arms, he broke the man's neck.

■　■　■

Quentin looked up at me, breathing heavily.

"Are you okay?" he said.

"No," I whispered. "No no *no*."

"Genie, please," he said, reaching toward me. "I can explain—"

I wasn't listening. I was too busy staring at what was happening to the giant's corpse.

It was dissolving. Into the air. The dead man's body suddenly resembled a still-wet painting dunked into a tank of water, the colors and hues that made up his existence bleeding away into a surrounding liquid.

His body silently burst into a great splash of ink. Spouting swirls of his former mass chased each other in all directions like calligraphy strokes until they faded into invisibility.

Nothing remained of him. Even his blood, including the half that had been splattered all over Quentin, was gone.

Quentin waved his hand over where the body had been. "I, uh, can explain that, too."

No he couldn't.

I didn't waste another word. I just ran, and ran, and ran.

8

I ARRIVED HOME IN A DAZE, TRYING TO FIGURE OUT WHAT to do.

Mom wasn't going to be any help in this situation. I passed her in the kitchen without a word. That little slight would probably snowball into a future screaming match between us at a time yet to be determined.

I climbed the stairs to my room. Once I got there I sank into my desk chair, my head in my hands.

Taptaptap.

I could have tried to call the cops again on our landline, but what was I going to say? That my classmate fought with some kind of runaway circus experiment, *killed* him in cold blood, and that I helped? That I had no evidence any of this happened, because the victim self-liquefied somehow?

Taptaptaptap.

The bigger problem was Quentin. I didn't know if I was next on his list of people to murder, or if he had a list, or if he was trying to initiate me into his gang. I mean, if he'd just stop knocking on my window for one second, I could think straight—

Taptaptaptaptaptap.

I fell out of my chair. Quentin hovered outside the glass with a pleading look on his face. The worst part was that in my current state I couldn't even remember if we had a tree there for him to stand on.

He slid the window up and clambered inside. *"Silence,"* he said.

"Mom!" I shouted, crawling backward on my butt. "Help!"

"This isn't what you think! Let me explain." He got down on his knees to look at me on my level. It was more terrifying than reassuring.

"Mom!" She was just downstairs. Why wasn't she answering?

Quentin began kowtowing in submission, knocking his skull against the floor. It only added to the commotion in my room.

"Please," he said. "I'm not a danger to you, and I can prove it. Give me a chance. If you don't like what you hear, you can do as you will. You can even take my head if you wish."

"I don't want your head!" I said. "What is it with you and murder? You killed a man back there!"

"That wasn't a human being. That was a demon. A *yaoguai.* If the two of us weren't there to stop him, he could have slain this entire town!"

I was going to tell him that was stupid, but remembering the man in black's hulking form and monstrous visage made me seize up in post-traumatic fear. He could very well have been right on that point.

Quentin sensed my hesitation. "And I didn't kill him in the sense you're thinking of. I only sent his evil spirit back to *Diyu,* where it belonged."

"Diyu? You mean Chinese Hell? That doesn't make any sense!"

"It will once I tell you my real name!"

So he'd been operating under a false identity this whole time to boot? Wonderful. I couldn't wait to see how much deeper he was going to dig this hole.

"Go ahead," I said, groping behind me for any heavy, hard object I could find to clock him with. "Tell me your real name and we'll see if that makes it all better."

Quentin took a deep breath.

"My true name," he said, " . . . is *SUN WUKONG*."

A cold wind passed through the open window, rustling my loose papers like tumbleweed.

"I have no idea who that is," I said.

■　■　■

Quentin was still trying to cement his "look at me being serious" face. It took him a few seconds to realize I wasn't flipping out over whoever he was.

"*The* Sun Wukong," he said, scooping the air with his fingers. "Sun Wukong the Monkey King."

"I said, I don't know who that is."

His jaw dropped. Thankfully his teeth were still normal-size.

"You're Chinese and you don't know me?" he sputtered. "That's like an American child not knowing Batman!"

"You're Chinese Batman?"

"No! I'm stronger than Batman, and more important, like—like. *Tian na*, how do you not know who I am!?"

I didn't know why he expected me to recognize him. He couldn't have been a big-time actor or singer from overseas. I never followed mainland pop culture, but a lot of the other people at school did; word would have gotten around if we had a celebrity in our midst.

Plus that was a weird stage name. Monkey King? Was that what passed for sexy among the kids these days?

Quentin let go of his temples and began unbuttoning his shirt.

"What are you doing, you perv?" I shut my eyes and bicycle-kicked the empty air between us.

When he didn't say anything I glanced between my fingers to make sure he was keeping his distance, and *oh my god* I shouldn't have looked.

I wasn't sure how anyone could get muscles like that without eating meat. He had the kind of body-fat percentage where he could have done it for a living.

"See?" he said, brandishing his tanned, professional-grade torso at me.

"Like that means anything!" I said, throwing my elbow back over my face. "So you've got abs. Big deal. I've got abs."

"Not my body, you dolt! My tail! Look at my tail!"

With great reluctance, *great reluctance I tell you*, I ran my gaze down his stomach. The last two cans of his rippling eight-pack were partly covered by a fur belt running around his waist. I thought it was just a weird fashion statement until it twitched and pulled away from his body, unraveling behind him.

Quentin, it would appear, had a monkey's tail.

∎　∎　∎

I gaped at the fuzzy appendage dancing in the air.

"Go see a doctor," I said, holding out my finger between us. "Have your weird mutation somewhere other than my room. Somewhere other than my life."

Quentin seemed moderately disappointed with the way this conversation had gone, like he had the right to expect better than a raging dumpster fire. He got up and put his shirt back on but neglected to button it up.

"You've been through a lot today," he said, using the same tone as a country gentleman who recognized that his lady's corset was too tight. "I suppose I shouldn't have sprung this on you all at once."

"Get out."

He smiled gravely at me. "Take some time to think. We can pick up where we left off tomorrow."

I found a stapler and threw it at his head.

"Pei-Yi!" shouted my mother. She clomped up the stairs. "Where are you?"

Dear god, finally. I didn't care how bad it would look to have an undressed boy with an abnormal pelvis in my room. I just needed not to be alone with him anymore.

My mom threw open the door to my room without knocking, her usual practice. She stood over me, judgment raining down from her birdlike frame. Her square, ageless face was a carved-in-marble ode to perpetual indignation.

"What are you doing on the floor?" she said to me. "You look like a city bum."

I glanced back to see Quentin gone.

He must have jumped out the window. I popped up and stepped to the sill, leaning into the air to look around. Not a trace of him anywhere.

"What's the matter?" my mother snapped. "You sick?"

I pulled my body back inside and bumped my head against the window hard enough to make the glass rattle, but the pain was

43

inconsequential right now. "No, I . . . I just needed some fresh air."

She squinted at me. "Are you pregnant?"

"*What!?* No! Why would you even think that?"

"Well then if you're not sick and you're not pregnant then ANSWER ME WHEN I CALL YOUR NAME!"

Mom began screaming at me since she'd apparently been telling me to come down for the last five minutes and not ignoring me asking her to come up. This kind of crazy I could take. I almost sobbed with relief, her banshee song as soothing and familiar as a lullaby.

9

I HAD A WHOLE SLEEPLESS NIGHT TO FIGURE OUT WHAT TO DO.
I couldn't talk to anyone without proof. But at the same time, I
needed to protect myself. I would have to take matters into my
own hands.

I was ready when Quentin approached me after school the following day.

"Genie," he said. "Please. Let me expl—*moomph!*"

"Stay away," I said, mashing the bulb of garlic into his face as
hard as I could. I didn't have any crosses or holy water at home. I
had to work with what was available.

Quentin slowly picked the cloves out of my hand before popping them into his mouth.

"That's white vampires," he said, chewing and swallowing the
raw garlic like a bite of fruit. "If I was a *jiangshi* you should have
brought a mirror."

I wrinkled my nose. "You're going to stink now."

"What, like a Chinese?" He pursed his lips and blew a kiss at me.

Instead of being pungent, his breath was sweet with plum blossoms and coconut. Like his body magically refused to be anything
but intensely appealing to me, even on a molecular level.

I tried to swat away his scent before it made me drunk.

"Stop it with the tricks," I said. "I don't know why you and your giant buddy needed to stage a magic show in front of me yesterday, but your act sucks and I never want to see it again."

"Genie, I am telling you, that was a yaoguai."

"Yaoguai don't exist!" I was firm in my conviction, but that hadn't stopped me from looking them up online last night. "They're folk demons, and I bet no one has believed in them for hundreds of years!"

"That's because no one has seen them in hundreds of years. They're not supposed to be walking the earth anymore. Especially not *that* one." Quentin looked chagrined, as if his disposing of another living being were akin to being caught double-dipping at a party.

"I came to this town because I felt a demonic presence stirring in the human world for the first time in centuries," he said. "I knew modern people weren't equipped to deal with yaoguai, so I hunted down the source myself. I didn't expect to find *you* of all people here as well."

There were many things I was not okay with in this explanation. The way he said *human world* like he had been hanging out somewhere else. His loose use of time signifiers. The way he still talked to me as if he knew me intimately.

"So you're only stalking me as an afterthought," I said.

"Yes. I mean no!" Quentin closed his eyes and pinched invisible threads from the air, trying to figure out which ones were connected to the end he wanted.

"Look," he said. "What happened yesterday was impossible."

I was about to violently agree with him in a general sense, but he kept going down a weird path.

"The Demon King of Confusion should not have been up and about," he said, seemingly more concerned about *which* monster we'd seen, like a fanatic who believed in Bigfoot but was shocked by the Abominable Snowman. "I personally rid the mortal world of him a very long time ago. The fact that he showed up alive means that there's something funny going on here, and until we find out what it is, the two of us have to stick together."

"*You* are the funny thing that's going on," I said. "You and your ... demons, yaoguai, whatevers. I don't want any part of it. In fact, if you ever trot this horse crap out in front of me or my family again I will make it my life's mission to see you regret it."

I turned away and walked halfway down the block before stopping.

"That wasn't a cue to follow me!" I screamed at Quentin, who was trailing only a few steps behind.

"Well, tough. We're heading to the same place, regardless of whether or not you believe me about yaoguai."

"Oh you have got to be kidding me."

"Yup." He grimaced like a man condemned. "Tonight is when I promised your mother we'd have dinner."

■ ■ ■

One of the reasons I didn't have friends over for meals very often was because of how seriously my mother took the occasions. Eating at our table was like some kind of blood pact for her. If the get-together went well, you were *in*. For life. You could sleep in our cupboard if you wanted to and she wouldn't bat an eye.

If you did not hold up your end of the bargain in terms of being

F. C. YEE

good company, or if, god forbid, you *flaked*, then you were cast into the lake of fire for eternity. Quentin, who must have picked up on Mom's peculiarities in this regard, was right in that we were locked in for one last dance. The Apocalypse couldn't have prevented this dinner.

I could smell food even before entering our driveway—a deep, savory promise of good things to come. My mother must have been at the stove all day. For someone who gives me such a hard time about my weight, you'd think she wouldn't cook so goddamn much.

"Remember," Quentin said as we went inside. "This was your idea."

His parents were already there, sitting at our table. "Pei-Yi," Mom said. "Come and meet the Suns."

Mr. Sun was tall and reedy with wiry hair, most of the resemblance to his son coming from the mischief in his eyes that his banker's suit failed to tamp down. Mrs. Sun was the picture-perfect image of a young *taitai*. She was a straight-backed beauty resplendent in tasteful fashions, the kind of woman Yunie would turn out to be in a decade or two if she dropped the punk-rock look in favor of European couture.

"Eugenia," said Mr. Sun. "We've heard so much about you."

To their credit, they didn't flinch at my height. Quentin must have warned them that I was a *kaiju*.

"We're forever in your debt," Mrs. Sun said. "Our boy can be so careless. It was a miracle you were there to save him."

Having seen what I'd seen, I seriously doubted Quentin was in any sort of trouble when I'd first run into him at the park. I wondered if his parents were in on his weirdness. They had to have been aware of his extra limb at least.

"You two are just in time," Mom said. "Dinner's ready."

The table was decked out with more food than my entire volleyball team could have eaten in two sittings. Red wine chicken. Steamed white radish with *conpoy*. *Misua* swimming in broth.

"Wait a sec," I said, tilting my head at Quentin. "He's a vegetarian."

"It's all mock meat," my mother said proudly. "It took me a few tries."

Of course she would kill herself over an attempt to impress. The Suns were everything she wanted our family to be. Rich. Refined. Whole. Quentin's parents even had British accents when they spoke in English, like they'd learned in an overseas grammar school or owned property in London. If there was one group of people my mother idolized more than the wealthy, it was the British.

"This looks absolutely delicious," said Mr. Sun.

He was not wrong. Mom was a spectacular cook. But I already knew that very little of this dinner was going to be touched. Mr. and Mrs. Sun were too genteel to finish the massive quantities that had been prepared, and if I had anything more than a "ladylike" serving in front of guests, my mother would have lasered me to death with her eyes.

Quentin alone had license to eat. He began chowing down with delight, scarfing the mouthwatering grub as fast as he could.

Over the course of the conversation I learned that his dad worked in international shipping and logistics, coming up with new route calculations based on incidents like storms and pirates. And his mom ran her family's charitable foundation, which spread basic technology like flashlights and cell phones to undeveloped areas around the world.

Now both of those jobs were actually really, really cool. I'd gone into this dinner eager to harness my class resentment and write Quentin's parents off as useless gentry, but both of them were genuinely interesting. I could have coasted on them talking shop all night.

Instead of going on about themselves, though, his parents kept turning the conversation back to me. I hated talking about myself to other people. It was why I had such a difficult time with my application essays.

But what really caused my gears to lock up was the way, whether through prior research or on-the-fly Holmesian deduction, they continually managed to avoid bringing up my dad. Not even a question about where I got my height from, since it clearly wasn't maternal. Their collective inquiries left a father-shaped hole in the conversation, like snow falling around a hot spot. I would have felt less on edge and defensive had they not been going out of their way to be tactful.

"So Genie," said Mr. Sun. "What are your plans for the future? What do you want to do with your life?"

"I don't know yet," I said, with what I hoped was a demure smile. "I guess one of the reasons why I study as much as I do is to keep my options open."

There. A better answer than screaming *I just wanna be somebody!* like a chorus member from a forties musical.

"Do you have a favorite subject?" Mrs. Sun asked. "Sometimes that can be a big life hint."

Jeez, let it go already. "I like them all about the same."

"Really?" said Quentin. "Rutsuo told me you once got pretty excited about computer science."

"That was an elective that didn't count for credit," I said. "And I only jumped on the table to celebrate because my code for a binomial heap finally compiled after fifteen tries."

"Passion's passion," said Mr. Sun. "Ever thought about being a programmer?"

I had. And no.

We lived in the epicenter of the tech industry. I'd paid enough attention to the news to know that all the good programming careers were concentrated right here in the Bay Area, not even fifty miles from where we were sitting. I wasn't going to work my ass off only to end up right back where I started in life, within shouting distance of my mother.

I racked my brain for a more polite way of saying that I felt zero obligations to the place where I grew up. Santa Firenza wasn't a quaint bucolic suburb where happy families were grown from the rich earth. Santa Firenza was a blacktopped hellscape of bubble tea shops and strip-mall nail salons, where feral children worshiped professional video-game streamers. The major cultural contribution of this part of the country was recording yourself dancing alongside your car while it rolled forward with no one driving it.

"Well, I'm sure that once you decide what you want, you'll get it," Mrs. Sun said in response to my silence. "You have so much determination for someone so young."

"She's always been like that, even as a baby," said Mom. "She used to watch the educational shows with the puppets and get the questions for the kids right. But then there would be a joke for the adults that she couldn't have possibly understood, and she'd get so *angry* that she'd missed something. That she didn't get a 'perfect score.' She was such an angry little girl."

"It's not like you got the *Masterpiece Theatre* references inside *Sesame Street* either," I snapped. "I remember asking you to explain them, and you never could."

The only person to smell the change in the wind was Quentin, who glanced up at me while chewing a mouthful of noodles.

"There was also the time you cracked that boy's rib for pushing Yunie into a tree," Mom said. "The only reason you didn't get suspended was because he was so embarrassed he wouldn't admit the two of you got into a fight. You should have seen yourself standing up to the principal, saying over and over that you *did* hit him and you *deserved* your proper punishment. The teachers didn't know what to make of it."

"Ah, so she has a sense of justice," Mrs. Sun said admiringly. "If only our boy were the same way. He was such a little delinquent when he was young."

"Now look at him," said Mr. Sun. "He pretends to be good but it's all an act. He thinks he has us fooled."

I did look at Quentin, who was busy slurping the last of his soup. He didn't seem at all bothered by his parents' put-downs. In fact, he gave me a little wink over the edge of his bowl.

"I also hear that you're the star of the volleyball team," Mrs. Sun said to me. "Their secret weapon. Have you always been stronger than other people?"

"Yes," said my mother. "She's always been big."

Oh boy. The gates were open.

"Oh, I meant in an athletic sense," said Mrs. Sun. "Skill-wise. Good *gongfu* at sports."

The distinction was lost on my mother. All those words meant the same thing to her. Masculine. Ungirly. Wrong.

"She's always towered over the other girls," Mom said. "The boys, too. I don't know where she got it from."

"Oh yeah, like my height is under my control," I responded. "There was a button you press to grow taller and I got greedy and hit it too many times."

"Maybe it was my fault," she added, turning martyr mode on. "Maybe I fed you too much."

"Okay, the implications of that are horrifying." I raised my voice like I'd done a thousand times before. "You're going to say you should have done the reverse and starved me into a proper size?"

"Why are you getting so upset?" Mom said. "I'm just saying life would be easier for you if you weren't . . ." She waved her hand.

"Thank you!" I practically shouted. Okay, I was flat-out shouting. "I well and truly did not know that before you said it this very moment!"

"I think Genie's beautiful," Quentin said.

The air went out of the room before I could use it to finish exploding. Everyone turned to look at him.

"I think Genie is beautiful," he repeated. "Glorious. Perfection incarnate. Sometimes all I can think about is getting my hands on her."

■ ■ ■

"*Quentin!*" shouted Mrs. Sun. "You awful, horrible boy!"

Mr. Sun smacked Quentin in the back of the head so hard his nose hit the bottom of his empty bowl. "Apologize to Genie and her mother right now!" he demanded.

"No," said Quentin. "I meant it."

His parents each grabbed an ear of his and did their best to twist it off.

"Ow! Okay! Sorry! I meant that I like her! Not in the bad sense! I mean I want to become her friend! I used the wrong words!"

"Sure you did, you terrible brat," Mrs. Sun hissed. She turned to us, crimson. "I am so, so sorry."

My mother was stunned. Torn. While that display by Quentin was definitely improper by her delicate standards, she also had wedding bells chiming in her ears. The sum of all her fears had just been lifted from her shoulders.

"Oh, it's all right," she murmured. "Boys."

I could only stare. At everything and everyone. This was a car accident, and now burning clowns were spilling out of the wreckage.

"Who's Sun Wukong?" I blurted out.

I had absolutely no idea why I said that. But *that* was anything but *this*, and therefore preferable.

"Sun Wukong," I said again, talking as fast as I could. "Quentin mentioned him earlier at school and I didn't get the reference. Everyone knows I hate it when I don't get a reference. Who is he?"

My mother frowned at me and my one-wheeled segue. "You want to know? Now?"

"Yes," I insisted. "Let me go to the bathroom first, and then when I come back I want to hear the whole story."

My outburst was bizarre enough to kill the momentum of the other competing outbursts. While everyone was still confused, I stood up and marched out of the room.

■ ■ ■

I hadn't even filled my hands with water to splash my face when Quentin appeared behind me in the mirror.

"Gah!" The running faucet masked my strangled scream. "What is wrong with you? This is a bathroom!"

"You left the door open," he said.

I could have sworn I heard his voice twice, the second time coming faintly from the dining table. It must have been my mind deciding to peace out of this dinner, because if not, Quentin was casually violating time and space again.

"*Who's Sun Wukong?*" he repeated in a mocking tone. "Smooth."

"You don't get to criticize after what you did!"

"I was trying to . . . how does it go? 'Have your back?' "

"Your English is perfectly fine," I snapped. "Or at least good enough to make your point without being lewd."

"I'll work on it. Anyway, the situation is turning out perfectly."

That was in contention for the dumbest comment made tonight. "In what *possible* way?"

Quentin reached behind me and turned the faucet off. "You'll hear the story of Sun Wukong from someone else, so you'll know I'm not making it up."

Before I could question his logic, he slipped out the bathroom door.

■ ■ ■

When I came back to the table, Mr. Sun was unwrapping a gift. It was a huge urn of horridly expensive *baijiu*, big enough to toast the entire Communist Party. It probably cost more than our car.

"The legend of Sun Wukong can get pretty long," he said. "We should hear it over a drink." He winked at me, willing to run with the diversion I'd handed him. Bless his heart.

Mr. Sun poured us all a bit, even me and Quentin after getting a nod from my mom. I took a single tiny sip and felt it etch a trail down my throat like battery acid.

"All right, so Sun Wukong," I said. "What gives?"

"I tried telling you these stories at bedtime when you were young," said Mom. "You never wanted to listen back then. But here goes . . ."

10

SO TO PARAPHRASE MY MOTHER'S STORY . . .

A long time ago, in a galaxy far, far away, there was China. Ancient China.

Here, in a long-lost place called the Mountain of Flowers and Fruit, all the wisdom and splendor of the sun and the moon poured into a stone until—crack!—out popped a monkey.

When the monkey was born, a light shone from his eyes all the way up to the Heavens. But the Jade Emperor who ruled the universe from atop the celestial pantheon ignored the obvious sign of greatness, and the monkey was left to fend for himself on the lowly Earth.

It didn't go so badly. The monkey was much stronger and braver than the other apes of the mountain, and he became their king. But he wanted more than to feast and frolic with his subjects until he died. He wanted to keep the party going forever. He wanted to become immortal.

He left the Mountain of Flowers and Fruit and searched the lands of the humans until he found the Patriarch Subodai, an enlightened master who had transcended death. Subodai was so impressed with the monkey's grasp of the Way (the Way being one of the many things that Asian culture refuses to explain but vigorously condemns you for not understanding) that he taught him the Seventy-Two Earthly Transformations, spells of kickass power that allowed one to change shape, split into multiple bodies, and leap across the world in a single somersault.

Subodai also gave his star pupil a name. Sun Wukong. It meant Monkey Aware of Emptiness.

Once he achieved these new abilities, Sun Wukong wasted no time in getting kicked out of school for bad behavior. He left Subodai and went home to his mountain, only to find that it had been taken over by a monster known as Hunshimowang, the Demon King of Confusion—

I nearly dropped my glass when my mother got to that part. I whipped around to look at Quentin. He just tilted his head and motioned me to keep listening.

The Demon King of Confusion had been terrorizing the other monkeys in their king's absence. Sun Wukong defeated the hulking monster with his bare hands, but he was dissatisfied that demons should think of him and his kin as easy targets.

What he really needed was a weapon. A big, threatening, FU kind of weapon that would show everyone the Monkey King meant business.

He paid a visit to Ao Guang, the Dragon King of the Eastern Sea. Ao Guang was willing to let Sun Wukong take a gift from the armory, but what the Monkey King really wanted was the great pillar from the old dragon's underwater palace.

This beam of black iron, end-capped with bands of gold, had once been used to measure the depths of the celestial ocean and anchor the Milky Way. It glowed with heavenly light as Sun Wukong approached, much as his own eyes had when he was born. Ao Guang thought the pillar couldn't be lifted and was unusable as a weapon, but at Sun Wukong's command it shrank until it became the perfect staff. That was how the Monkey King got his famous weapon, the Ruyi Jingu Bang. The As-You-Will Cudgel.

The first thing that Sun Wukong did with the Ruyi Jingu Bang was to march straight into Hell. It turned out that Subodai hadn't actually taught him immortality, and that his name was still in the big book of people scheduled to die. Sun Wukong threatened the horse-faced and ox-headed guardians of Hell with the Ruyi Jingu Bang, and out of fear they let him strike his name from the ledger.

So that was how Sun Wukong became immortal. Not through mastery of enlightenment. But by carrying the biggest, baddest stick in the valley.

The Jade Emperor didn't take kindly to monkeys subverting the laws of life and death willy-nilly. On the advice of his officials, he invited Sun Wukong into the celestial pantheon in order to keep an eye on him. And hopefully a tighter leash.

The Monkey King was pleased to be in Heaven at first, rubbing elbows with noble gods and exalted spirits. But he was repeatedly humiliated with low-status assignments in the Thunder Palace, like grooming the divine horses in the stables, and kept from attending the great Peach Banquets. Sun Wukong got fed up with his treatment and went AWOL from Heaven after trashing the joint like a rock star on a bender.

The Jade Emperor sent a whole army of martial gods to Earth after him. And Sun Wukong beat the tar out of them all. The only one who could take him down was the Jade Emperor's nephew, Erlang Shen, Master of Rain and Floods.

The duel between the two powerhouses shattered the scales. Erlang Shen chased Sun Wukong down through many forms as they fought and shapeshifted all over the Earth. The rain god finally got the upper hand, but even then securing the win took the combined effort of Erlang Shen's six sworn brothers, a pack of divine hunting hounds, and an assist from Lao Tze, the founder of Daoism.

The celestial pantheon dragged Sun Wukong to Heaven and tried to execute the Monkey King by throwing him in the furnace used to create elixirs of longevity. It didn't work. The dunking only gave Sun Wukong even more strength, plus the ability to see through any deception. Sure, his now-golden eyes also developed a lame Kryptonite-like weakness to smoke, but that didn't matter. He broke free from the furnace, grabbed his Ruyi Jingu Bang, and began laying waste to the heart of Heaven.

All the gods hid from Sun Wukong's rage. He was actually close to seizing the Dragon Throne of Heaven for himself, deposing the Jade Emperor to become ruler of the cosmos, but at the last minute a ringer, an outsider, was called in to help.

Buddha. Sakyamuni Buddha. *The* Buddha.

Even Sun Wukong would spare a moment to listen to the Venerable One. Buddha proposed a challenge—if the Monkey King could leap out of the Buddha's outstretched hand, then he was free to overthrow Heaven. If not, he'd have to chill the eff out.

Sun Wukong took the bet and sprang forth from the Buddha's palm. He leaped to what looked like the End of the Universe where five pillars marked the boundary. But those were nothing more than the fingers of Buddha's hand. Buddha grabbed Sun Wukong, slammed him to the Earth, and dropped an entire mountain on top of him. The prison was sealed with the binding chant *Om Mani Padme Om*.

Sun Wukong, who had struck fear into Heaven itself, was trapped. . . .

11

AFTER DESCRIBING THE MONKEY KING'S IMPRISONMENT BY
the Buddha, my mother leaned back into her chair.

"I don't get it," I said. "Is Sun Wukong a good guy or a bad guy?"

"He's an anti-hero," said Quentin. "He doesn't play by anyone
else's rules."

"He sounds like a tool," I said.

Quentin gave me an angry squint. My mother didn't know that
particular phrase, so she didn't yell at me for being vulgar.

"He redeems himself later by becoming the enemy of evil spirits and protecting the innocent," she said. "That was only the first
part, and the story is really long. I mean *really* long. A lot of English
translations leave out whole chunks."

"So then what happens after he gets stuck under the rock?" I
said. "How does he get out?"

"I'm not telling anymore," she said, making a face. "You have
this book somewhere in your room. Go read it."

"How long ago did all of this happen?" I said without thinking.

It's not often that I'm the one making the verbal blunder in a
conversation with my mom.

"Genie," she said, looking at me like there was something growing out of my forehead. "It's a folk tale."

"But it's one that's very important to our culture," said Mrs. Sun. "If you live in Asia, there's probably some TV show or movie playing any given time of day that either tells the story of Sun Wukong or is based off it in some form."

"It was always Quentin's favorite," said Mr. Sun. "I'm sure our last name helped. It would be like an American child being named Bruce Wayne. You bet he'd love Batman."

Quentin gave me a look. *See? They know Batman, but you don't know Sun Wukong?*

He yawned and stretched his arms, sending thick bundles of trapezius muscle skyward. "Genie, before I forget, can I take a look at your bio notes from today? I mean, I did mine, but I zoned out in class and missed a section."

"They're in my room." I waited, and watched.

He glanced toward our parents. Mr. and Mrs. Sun gave him threatening glares, but my mother shooed at him with her hands.

"It's okay," she said. "You two can go upstairs."

. . .

I led Quentin to my room. It felt way too intimate, doing that. His footsteps were heavier than mine up the stairs, a mismatched thump-thump that I could feel in my bones.

He closed the door behind us, shutting out our parents' laughter, and looked into my eyes. I don't know what he thought of mine, but his felt like they went all the way down to the bottom of the universe.

Dark brown, I thought to myself. Not shining gold. Just a very dark, drinkable chocolate.

"Yo, so those notes?" he said.

Ugh. The baijiu must have gotten to my head.

"Very funny. So that's the story of Sun Wukong? You're that guy?"

"More or less."

"Well, I don't believe it," I said. "Any of it. You're crazy and you've latched on to a story because you happen to bear a resemblance to the main character."

Quentin gave me a dry stare like he was puzzling something out. What to say next.

"Your mom's a great cook," he offered. "I can tell how much she cares about you. I'm jealous."

"Huh?" I was thrown off guard. "Why? Your parents are awesome. They're smart and they're rich and they're relevant!"

"They're not real," said Quentin.

"Wait, what?"

"Didn't you hear your mom's story? I came from a rock. I don't have a mother or father. Never did."

"Then who are those people downstairs? Actors? Con artists?" I was starting to get indignant at being lied to again.

"They're no one."

He reached into his hair and yanked a couple of strands out of his scalp. He tossed them into the air where they poofed into a white cloud like road flares.

"Goddamnit Quentin!" I waved my arms and prayed the smoke detector wouldn't go off.

"Look."

Once I finished coughing and fanning the vapors away, there, in my room, were Mr. and Mrs. Sun. They beamed at me as if we were meeting for the first time.

Downstairs, Mr. and Mrs. Sun and my mother laughed raucously at some joke, probably at my expense.

"Wha—what *the hell IS THIS*?" I half-yelled through clenched teeth.

"Transformation," he said. "I can turn my hairs into anything. I needed parents to bring over for dinner, so I made a couple."

He gestured at his mother and father and they disappeared with another puff of smoke.

■   ■   ■

This was . . . this was . . .

"Hoo," I said without knowing what I meant. "Hoooo."

I sank to the floor and began to furiously rub my eyes. Partly out of disbelief and partly because the faint white dust the Suns left behind was making my tear ducts itch. When my fingers wouldn't cut it, I began scraping my face against my knees.

"Sorry," said Quentin. "But I did promise to explain everything."

I took a couple of Lamaze breaths.

"What," I said as steadily as I could, *"do you want with me?"*

Quentin scanned my room before walking up to my shelves and plucking a book out. He took a seat on the floor in front of me, cross-legged. He could pull a full lotus with ease.

"Do you believe in reincarnation?" he asked.

"No," I said flatly. That was the truth. Compared to some of the girls at school, I was about as spiritual as a Chicken McNugget.

"Well, it doesn't matter," he said. "It's something that just happens. All creatures live their lives, and then they die. If they've built up enough merit through good deeds and conduct, they're reborn in another time and place, in more fortunate circumstances. If they've done evil then they'll suffer in their next life. They might even end up in Hell."

"What about you?"

"I'm immortal," he said. "I freed myself of the Wheel of Rebirth because I liked being who I was. I didn't want to have to struggle through who knows how many different versions of myself just to gain standing in the cosmos. I accumulated enough power within my first life to become unstuck in time, like a god."

I could hear his words but couldn't bring myself to allow them any quarter inside my head. How could any of this be true?

"I've seen people come and go over the ages," said Quentin. "And rarely, very rarely, I see them come back. I knew you in your past life, Genie."

He handed me the book. It was the one my mother was talking about. *Journey to the West*, it said, the big black letters covered by a thick layer of dust. If I had ever read it, it had been ages ago.

"Here," he said. "This is the second half of my story."

I took it with an air of suspicion even though it had come from my own shelf. "Why is this important?" I said.

"Because you're in it."

I swallowed my jitters and attempted to pry open the book, but the glossy, child-friendly covers were stuck from years of compression. The sudden crack as they pulled apart rattled me like a gunshot, and I slammed it back shut before any of its contents could leap off the page and melt my face.

I frisbeed the book to the side. The stiff cardboard backing allowed it to sail through the air and land on my bed.

"No," I said. "Nope. All the nope. I'm done. I'm done with tonight."

"Genie, you can't ignore what you've seen with your own eyes."

Sure I could. "If your parents are fake, then your demon could be fake, and I bet your tail is fake, too," I said. "Animatronic or something."

Quentin looked personally insulted by that last accusation. "You *saw* my tail. It's as real as can be."

"Prove it."

He scowled and untucked his shirt, wiggling on his butt to free up some room around the waist of his pants. I caught a brief glimpse of the muscled crease running down his hip before the smooth skin was blocked by fur. The thick brown rope came loose and stood up behind him.

"There," he said. "See?"

Not good enough. I held my hand out and wagged my fingers, demanding. He looked hesitant but brought it forward anyway, gingerly laying it across my palm.

This was beyond weird.

His tail was alive and warm. It wasn't too gross. In fact, it was strangely comforting to hold. An elongated Tribble. I rubbed the soft, silky fur into crisscross patterns with my thumb.

I must have squeezed too hard at some point because Quentin made a strangled noise from deep in his larynx. At the exact same time his mother entered my room.

"Quentin," Mrs. Sun said. "It's getting late. We should be lea—"

We scrambled to our knees. Quentin wrapped up his tail again, quick as a whip. But the lingering image was still him with part of his shirt undone, and me pulling my hands away from his lap. Not the most innocent diorama.

"QUENTIN! *NI ZAI GAN MA?!?*" Mrs. Sun shouted.

"What has he done now?" roared Mr. Sun from downstairs. "You're dead once we get home, you hear? Dead!"

"Whatever it is, it's okay," Mom called out.

Quentin's mother stormed in and hauled him downstairs like a milk crate while apologizing to me all the while. She was stronger than her delicate build suggested.

The Suns gave their hurried, mortified thanks to my mother and left, yelling at Quentin all the way. Only the slamming of their car doors silenced the smacks, slaps, and scoldings heaped upon his head. It made me smile to hear such familiar sounds, to the extent that it wasn't until after they were long gone that I remembered Mr. and Mrs. Sun weren't real.

Quentin's trick must have endowed them with some kind of independent AI, to better serve the illusion. If there was a flaw in their behavior, it was that they hadn't blamed me for the compromising situation and accused me of corrupting their precious little emperor, like actual Asian parents would have. Or Western ones, for that matter.

∎ ∎ ∎

My mother stood next to me in the doorway, looking out into the street.

"I haven't had that much fun in a while," she said quietly. "I was so worried they'd look down on us. But they're lovely people. Some folks are just good in everything. Luck, character, everything."

She looked so relieved that I thought she might cry. I was struck by the fact that she hadn't talked to anyone besides me in a meaningful way for a very long time. She had no family in California, and her adult connections had been mostly Dad's friends.

I put my arm around her shoulders, and we went back inside.

12

"SO HAVE YOU TAPPED THAT SWEET ASS YET OR WHAT?" YUNIE asked me the next day in the school library.

"Oh come on! We could be talking about literally anything else. Didn't you win your *concours*? Doesn't that make you the best violinist in the state now?"

"It was only a qualification round," my best friend said as she doodled over my oxidation-reduction equations. "But yes, I crushed everyone so hard even the woodwinds went home crying. And as my victory prize, I want a full report on whether you're getting any."

"First of all, there is nothing between us. *Nothing.* Second of all, do you know how ridiculous Quentin and I would look as a couple? It'd be like Boris and Natasha chasing moose and squirrel."

A massive grin spread across Yunie's face. "So he's bite-size. Doesn't mean he's not tasty. Rachel made a run at him. So did Charlotte, Nita, Hyejeong, both Vivians, and Other Eugenia. Greg and Philip, just to touch all the bases. Even Maxine, though that was probably an attempt to screw with you. That girl is a psycho, by the way."

"And you?"

I wasn't asking her seriously, but she totally took it seriously, putting her hands up. "Sister Code," she said. "I don't have dibs. You should have seen the way the two of you looked at each other the first day you met. I could swear you were both glowing like a pair of heat lamps."

Yunie got up to go to her next class. I was the only one of us who was supposed to be in the library for study hall; she was just habitually late for everything.

"By the way," she whispered into my ear. "I was talking about Androu at first. You're the one who brought up Quentin."

I pushed the lead in on my mechanical pencil so it was less pointy. Then I hurled it at her as she retreated through the door, laughing all the way down the hall.

As much as I loved her, I was glad to be alone. I needed the peace and quiet to continue my study-bender.

Tearing through my homework put me at ease like nothing else. It got me ready—or at least readier—to think about what I'd seen recently. By crushing my assignments, it felt like I was putting deposits into the First National Bank of Sanity. Confronting Quentin's craziness was going to require one gigantic withdrawal.

I pushed aside my chem papers once I was finished and pulled out a book from my bag without stopping for a break. It was the one from my room. The continued legend of Sun Wukong.

It felt safer to read it here, in the light of day, away from my home. Just to be sure, though, I moved to the table in the back alcove, near the last row of shelves. The library may have already been empty, but I still wanted to isolate myself like a responsible bomb technician.

I was able to get the book all the way open this time. There had to be something in it that would make my life fall back into place . . .

. . .

The Tang Emperor of China, as emperors are wont to do, looked around him one day and decided that everything sucked. His lands were filled with greed, hedonism, and sin. What he needed, he reasoned, was for an ambassador to travel to the West and retrieve the holy scriptures that would bring his people back to right-mindedness.

The man he found for the task was a pure-hearted monk named Xuanzang. Xuanzang was a learned and earnest man, beautiful and dignified of appearance, talented in both preaching and the arts. He was eager for the monumental task. Unfortunately he was also weak and hopelessly naïve.

Xuanzang needed a bodyguard. Someone who could handle the vicious bandits and flesh-eating demons that lay in wait on his journey. Someone who needed a difficult quest to atone for defying Heaven.

It wasn't a difficult search. The gods had the perfect candidate lying under a rock.

The Bodhisattva Guanyin made the introductions. She freed Sun Wukong from his mountain prison and ordered him to serve Xuanzang on his trip. The Monkey King refused, forcing Guanyin to place a magic band around his head that would tighten whenever Xuanzang said the words *Om Mani Padme Om*. If Sun Wukong didn't want to suffer excruciating pain, he would have to obey his new master to the letter.

Because it wasn't enough to be accompanied by the beast who scared the crap out of every god in Heaven, Xuanzang was assigned a few more traveling companions. The gluttonous pig-man Zhu Baijie. Sha Wujing, the repentant sand demon. And the Dragon Prince of the West Sea, who took the form of a horse for Xuanzang to ride. The five adventurers, thusly gathered, set off on their—

"Holy ballsacks!" I yelped. I dropped the book like I'd been bitten.

"How far did you get?" Quentin said.

He was leaning against the end of the nearest shelf, as casually as if he'd been there the whole time, waiting for this moment.

I ignored that he'd snuck up on me again, just this once. There was a bigger issue at play.

In the book was an illustration of the group done up in bold lines and bright colors. There was Sun Wukong at the front, dressed in a beggar's cassock, holding his Ruyi Jingu Bang in one hand and the reins of the Dragon Horse in the other. A scary-looking pig-faced man and a wide-eyed demon monk followed, carrying the luggage. And perched on top of the horse was . . . me.

The artist had tried to give Xuanzang delicate, beatific features and ended up with a rather girly face. By whatever coincidence, the drawing of Sun Wukong's old master could have been a rough caricature of sixteen-year-old Eugenia Lo from Santa Firenza, California.

■　■　■

"That's who you think I am?" I said to Quentin.

"That's who I know you are," he answered. "My dearest friend. My boon companion. You've reincarnated into such a different form, but I'd recognize you anywhere. Your spiritual energies are unmistakable."

"Are you sure? If you're from a long time ago, maybe your memory's a little fuzzy."

"The realms beyond Earth exist on a different time scale," Quentin said. "Only one day among the gods passes for every human year. To me, you haven't been gone long. Months, not centuries."

"This is just . . . I don't know." I took a moment to assemble my words. "You can't walk up to me and expect me to believe right away that I'm the reincarnation of some legendary monk from a folk tale."

"Wait, what?" Quentin squinted at me in confusion.

"I said you can't expect me to go, 'okay, I'm Xuanzang,' just because you tell me so."

Quentin's mouth opened slowly like the dawning of the sun. His face went from confusion to understanding to horror and then finally to laughter.

"*mmmmphhhhghAHAHAHAHA!*" he roared. He nearly toppled over, trying to hold his sides in. "HAHAHAHA!"

"What the hell is so funny?"

"You," Quentin said through his giggles. "You're not Xuanzang. Xuanzang was meek and mild. A friend to all living things. You think that sounds like you?"

It did not. But then again I wasn't the one trying to make a case here.

"Xuanzang was delicate like a chrysanthemum." Quentin was getting a kick out of this. "*You* are so tough you snapped the battle-axe of the Mighty Miracle God like a twig. Xuanzang cried over squashing a mosquito. *You*, on the other hand, have killed more demons than the Catholic Church."

I was starting to get annoyed. "Okay, then who the hell am I supposed to be?" If he thought I was the pig, then this whole deal was off.

"You're my weapon," he said. "You're the Ruyi Jingu Bang."

I punched Quentin as hard as I could in the face.

13

I WILL ADMIT TO BEING AN ANGRY PERSON. CERTAIN THINGS I get upset about. Certain things are worth getting upset about.

But never in my life had I felt as furious as when Quentin called me the Ruyi Jingu Bang.

The volcanic surge of bile rising in my throat collided with a skull-cleaving headache going in the opposite direction. I was bisected by the pain of my anger. Blinded by it. My vision went.

The best way I could describe it was like my life's work had been doused with gasoline and set on fire. I didn't have a life's work yet, but that's how I felt.

"Genie," Quentin said from a million miles away. I could barely hear him.

"Genie," he said again, tapping me on my wrists. "Let up a bit."

He was coming in garbled, on helium. The lights gradually turned back on.

I had bodily thrown him onto the table. My hands were wrapped around his neck. I was strangling him so hard that I could feel my fingernails beginning to bend.

"Please stop doing that," he coughed. "You're one of the few things in the universe that can hurt me."

"Good." I squeezed harder.

I couldn't explain why I was behaving this way. Calling me the Ruyi Jingu Bang should have meant nothing. It should have been a non sequitur, like walking up to a stranger and saying, "Hello my good fellow, did you know you are a 1976 Volkswagen Beetle?" I was overreacting in a way that lent credence to a zero-percent scenario.

Quentin managed to loosen my grip on his throat enough for his face to return to its normal color. "Can we talk about this?"

He slid off the table and got back to his feet. I only let him go because I didn't want to give my impending speech to a corpse. He wanted to talk? Sure. I was going to go Supreme Court on his ass and hammer home an articulate, lengthy, and logical rebuttal to his claim of me being the reincarnated Ruyi Jingu Bang.

"I hate you," I said instead.

I poked my finger into his chest as hard as my joints would take.

"I hate you," I said again. That was all I was capable of, it seemed.

He slowly put his hands up and began backing away. "Why?"

I wouldn't let him get away so easily. "Because," I said. "I don't need a reason. People don't need a reason to hate things. And I am *people*."

I kept jabbing him over and over as he retreated, trying to drive home the message like a spear point.

"I am a human person," I snarled. "I am not the Ruyi Jingu Bang. I am not a freaking stick, do you hear me?"

"Um, Genie," Quentin said, looking down awkwardly.

I hadn't noticed that I'd been continuously poking Quentin in the chest from where I stood, even though he'd now backed all the way across the room.

My arm had stretched out to follow him. My arm was twenty feet long.

. . .

There's a moment when you realize that you've never been truly scared before. It wasn't when I'd met Quentin, and it wasn't when I'd been introduced to the Demon King of Confusion. Those times were apparently just practice.

"AAAAAAAAA!" I screamed. "WHAT DID YOU DO TO ME?!"

"I didn't do anything!" Quentin screamed back. "Put it back before someone sees us!"

I was too terrified to move my elongated arm for fear that it would shatter under its own ridiculous proportions. "It's too big!" I said, waving at it with my other hand. "Make it smaller! Make it go down!"

"I can't! You have to do it yourself!"

"I don't know how!"

By now footsteps were coming down the hall toward us. I could hear teachers' voices. If they sounded upset now, they hadn't seen anything yet.

Quentin realized I wasn't going to do much other than hyperventilate. He ran over and grabbed me by the waist. Then he rolled up the window behind us and jumped straight out of it. I could feel my arm accommodating his trajectory by bending in places where I didn't have joints.

I saw nothing but cloudless blue sky as Quentin hauled me up the sheer brick side of the building. It didn't fully register that he was dangling me two stories off the ground as he scampered up the school walls. I had, believe it or not, even worse things to worry about.

The ascent was over in a split second. Quentin reached the roof and unceremoniously dumped me onto the asphalt. We were safely out of sight for the moment.

I squeezed my eyes shut so I wouldn't have to look at my arm trailing away like the streamer on a bike handle.

"I can't be stuck like this!" I wailed. Visions of having to gnaw it off like a jackal in a trap flooded my brain.

Quentin knelt before me and put his hands on my trembling shoulders.

"You're not going to be stuck," he said, his voice low and reassuring in my ears. "You are the most powerful thing on Earth short of a god. You can do absolutely anything. So believe me when I say you can certainly change your arm back to normal."

He held me firmly, the way you'd brace someone trying to pop a dislocated joint back into place. "Just relax and breathe," he said. "It'll happen as you will it."

I took his advice and focused on calming down. Focused on nothing. Focused on him.

I couldn't really feel my arm retracting. And I certainly didn't want to look at it happening. I just . . . remembered how I was supposed to be. I kept quiet, kept at it for what must have been a good ten minutes, until I could feel both of my hands firmly on Quentin's broad back.

"There you go," he said.

I opened my eyes. My arm was normal again. I was aware that we were sort of hugging.

I buried my face in his chest and blew my nose on his shirt. "I'm a human being," I muttered.

"I never said you weren't."

I raised my head. Quentin looked at me with a smile that was free of any smugness. He didn't even mind my snot on his lapel.

"Reincarnation as a human is practically the highest goal any spirit can achieve," he said. "It's considered the next best thing to enlightenment. If anything, I'm proud of you for what you've accomplished."

I'm not sure why, but the rage that had been so palpable before seemed to float away at his words. Like I could have been angry with him forever had he said anything different.

I was mildly relieved. It was a hell of a one-eighty on my part, but right now I didn't think I wanted to hate Quentin until the end of time.

"Genie Lo, you are unquestionably, undeniably human," he said. "You just . . . have a whole bunch of other stuff going on as well."

"Tell me about it."

14

"WAS THERE EVER ANYTHING WEIRD ABOUT ME AS A BABY?"
I asked my mother at the breakfast table.

The soles of her cheap slippers scraped against the linoleum of our kitchen as she put a steaming bowl of porridge in front of me. Only then did she consider my question.

I was all ready for her to say, *What, besides the fact that you weren't a boy? Besides your size?* There was always a certain amount of thorny jungle I had to pass through in order to arrive at a straight answer.

But today was different, for reasons unknown. She shuffled around the table and sat down even though she hadn't prepared any food for herself.

"No," she said.

She pulled her legs up into one side of her chair, the kind of thing that young girls did. I'd yelled at her in the past for it, afraid she'd risk hurting her back.

"You were perfect," she said matter-of-factly. "We'd had such a hard time having you that I didn't know what to expect when you were born. But the doctors told me you were the healthiest child they'd ever seen. They showed me the chart of your vitals. It was the first perfect score you ever earned."

"There was nothing out of the ordinary at all? What about coincidences? Full moons? Solar eclipses?"

She shrugged. "There could have been an earthquake and I wouldn't have noticed. I only had eyes for you at the time. After the labor I was just so . . ."

"Exhausted?"

She smiled at me. "Grateful."

I looked away. It was best not to think of all the times in the past few years that she and I had proved incapable of a simple conversation like this—where one person spoke and the other listened. It would have been a difficult thing to tally the waste.

"Come on," she said, nudging the bowl toward me. "It'll get cold."

■ ■ ■

It was a good thing the route to Johnson Square, where I first met Quentin, was so ingrained into my memory. I nearly sleepwalked there, not having gotten any rest last night. I had been too busy reading *that* book.

It was a bizarre story, Sun Wukong's journey to the west. As I got further and further into it, the only lesson I could take away was that everyone in Ancient China was a gigantic asshole. Xuanzang's traveling circus was constantly beset by yaoguai who wanted to eat him.

In addition to monk flesh apparently being the filet mignon of human beings, nearly every demon thought it would gain Xuanzang's spiritual powers by consuming his body. They were so desperate for this leapfrog in personal growth that even when their schemes were caught by Sun Wukong, they'd resort to open combat instead of running away.

The Monkey King managed to outsmart or defeat most of these adversaries, but what came afterward was rather galling. If the demon at hand wasn't killed and sent back to Hell immediately, it was often revealed to be an animal spirit from Heaven who had gained magic powers and used them to terrorize people on Earth. After Sun Wukong's victory, a Chinese god would show up and be like, "Sorry, bruh, that ogre was actually my goldfish. I'll take him back now."

And then that would be that. No mention of all the little farmer children said goldfish-ogre had eaten before being defeated by Sun Wukong. No retribution for any damages. Not even a slap on the wrist for trying to chow down on Xuanzang.

Compared to the "regular" evil demons that Sun Wukong killed, the fallen animal spirits suffered the same punishment as a rich kid on a DUI charge. None. Having a god in your corner was the ultimate get-out-of-jail-free card. Nor did anyone ever call out the various divinities on their negligence. You would think that after the fifteenth time their pet ferret or whatever escaped and caused a whole mess of human suffering they'd accept some responsibility.

And Xuanzang himself. Woof. Dude did nothing but cry all the time. Like he'd literally cry at having to cross a stream. I kept hoping he might be able to pull out some badass exorcisms, being a holy man and all, but spirits seemed to be able to tie him up at will. And he kept using the band-tightening spell on Sun Wukong in ways that were exceptionally cruel. If Sun Wukong attacked a demon disguised as a human, Xuanzang would torture him instead of, you know, trusting the member of the party who has all-seeing golden eyes of Detect Evil.

Maybe I was missing a deeper message. I could ask the guy who supposedly had been there.

．．．

I found him in the square in a secluded little spot masked from the surrounding huddle of commercial properties by a row of shrubs. The smell of cut grass and gasoline still lingered from a dawn mowing. It was still early enough that I'd arrived before the old-timers who used the space to practice tai chi.

Quentin, however, had me beat. I caught him checking me out as I approached, his eyes roaming up and down my legs.

I was surprised he'd even bother. "Stop that, you skeez," I said.

He blinked and shook his head. "I'm not used to the way people dress these days."

"This is yoga gear," I said. "And it's perfectly acceptable for outdoors."

"I'll take your word for it."

Quentin might not have been kidding about lacking a sartorial sense. He was still in his school uniform, the only concession being his sleeves rolled up for our "training" session.

Guh. His forearms were like bridge cables. My spine twitched at the sight of them flexing in the breeze.

I blinked and shook my head. "You said you were going to teach me how to manage my limbs so they don't go wonky again."

"It would be a crime if that were the only thing I taught you," he said. "You have abilities that most people couldn't begin to imagine. Sit."

I lowered myself down, cringing at the dew on the grass. "I don't want superpowers," I said. "I want control."

"You'll get it, trust me." Quentin took the spot in front of me, the guru before his disciple. I had to admit it wasn't a bad look on him.

"Do you remember when we first laid eyes on each other?" he asked.

I nodded. "You were just about where we are now."

"And *you* were all the way over *there*," he said, pointing over my shoulder far down the park. "You were more than three hundred feet away from me, Genie. You threw your bag farther than an entire American football field."

"That's impossible. I could see you right nearby, plain as day. And there's no way I'm that strong."

"Your sight works beyond human limits," he countered. "Your strength is enough to challenge the gods. And, as you've clearly seen, your true reach knows no bounds."

I looked at my hands and clenched my fingers. That time when I blocked Maxine into next week. Had I accidentally stretched myself without anyone noticing?

"Close your eyes," Quentin said. He shut his own and rolled his shoulders a few times.

"Are we meditating?"

"Yes. Close your eyes."

"Is this the single step that the journey of a thousand miles begins with?"

"*Close your eyes.*"

I did as he told. And then I cheated. I kept one lid open a crack so I could watch Quentin breathe deeply in and out. Watch him settle his mind. I was only doing it so I could crib his technique.

But damn it if he wasn't beautiful right then.

This was a completely different side to him. I mean, Monkey King or not, most times he acted like the worst kind of bro. But here, I was looking at a master of the universe. He radiated calm and tranquility, becoming so still that the Earth seemed to rotate behind him like a time-lapse video.

"Truth and spells, revealing all," Quentin chanted, his voice echoing off I'm not sure what.

"They come from vapor, essence, and spirit.

Stored in the body, never to be revealed

A radiant moon shining on a tower of quicksilver

The snake and the tortoise are twisted together

Then life will bear golden lotuses

Turn the Five Elements upside down

And you may become a Buddha or an Immortal."

■   ■   ■

Quentin opened his eyes and smiled serenely at me.

"What the hell was that?" I asked.

"Huh?"

"That made no sense. You just zoned out and spouted a bunch of gibberish. What do snakes and turtles have to do with anything?"

He made an expression like I'd hocked a loogie on the *Mona Lisa*. "Did you not experience the Way of Heaven and Earth ensorcelling you just now?"

I scratched my head. " . . . Sort of? I think I felt something. The air around us got a little warm and fuzzy."

Quentin buried his face in his palms. "Those were the first words of true wisdom Master Subodai ever expounded to me, and all you have to say is that they make you warm and fuzzy, *sort of?*"

"Look," I said. "I don't learn well with vague instructions. Can't you lay out all the steps from start to finish, so I can see what I'm supposed to be working toward?"

"Lay out!? These aren't differential equations we're talking about!"

"Well if they were, I'd pick them up faster! That's how I do things! I arrange my curriculum into manageable chunks and then I destroy them piece by piece. You told me I had abilities far beyond those of mortal men. Now, what are they?"

Quentin jumped to his feet and paced around, swearing up and down. I sat there unyielding as he glanced at me, which set him off into a fresh round of expletives each time. He couldn't *believe* me right now.

Finally he threw in the towel and plopped back down, abandoning a proper cross-legged position for a don't-give-a-crap-anymore slouch. The guru image had popped like a soap bubble.

"You have the ability to keep up with me as I perform my Seventy-Two Earthly Transformations," he said, staring up at the sky.

"That sounds lame."

"Says the girl who doesn't want superpowers. Don't you realize what that implies? You can split into as many copies as I can. Each one as strong as the original, and capable of acting independently."

I thought about that for a bit. Having extra mes to go around would be useful in the extreme. One copy for school, one doing extra plyos in the gym, one racking up more volunteer work in the city. Assuming that recombining let you keep all of the good you did.

"Okay, okay." I was starting to get vaguely excited. "What else?"

"You can grow as tall as a mountain. You can be like a Pillar of Heaven. As I change, you change."

Yeah, less interested in that one. The view from my current altitude already wasn't kind. Stomping around downtown like a '50s sci-fi monster was far from an appealing prospect.

"What else?" I asked. "Something good."

"You weigh a whole lot," Quentin said.

"Excuse me?"

"You're supernaturally heavy," he explained. "It's what makes you such a fearsome weapon."

In his defense, he wasn't trying to needle me. In his mind he was rattling off a fact. Obliviously.

"Your true weight is seventeen thousand five hundred American pounds," he said, not noticing that my cheeks were turning red hot. "You can hit like a ten-ton truck because you weigh nearly ten tons. It's demonic, how much you weigh—*OOF!*"

I tested out the truth of his claims. On his chest. With my fist.

Just checking to see which one of us was denser.

13

"YOU NEED TO CONTROL YOUR TEMPER," QUENTIN SAID. HE winced as he rubbed the spot where I'd clocked him.

We'd hit a roadblock in my training earlier than expected. Meditating wasn't optional for this project, it was required. And I absolutely sucked at it.

The two of us had spent the entire morning in the park trying to get me to relax and focus. I had no idea why I wasn't catching on. Discipline, self-governance—those were supposed to be my strong points. Failure got me more and more annoyed until finally Quentin insisted we take a break at a nearby bubble tea shop.

I *hate* bubble tea. So now I was cranky about two things.

I kicked a rhythm into the steel wire table we were sitting at. The feet of my chair scraped the sidewalk concrete inch by inch. It sounded as if I was abusing a metal songbird that chirped in pain with each impact.

"Get in line," I muttered. "People have been calling me a hot-head my whole life."

Quentin slurped his pearls. "I didn't mean it like there's something wrong with you, I mean you only need to reach the point of tranquility where you can absorb my teachings. After that I don't care what you do with your emotions."

"That doesn't make sense. I thought achieving gongfu requires maintaining a calm, virtuous character?"

"It does, but only while you're still learning. Think of it this way. At one point you had no volleyball skills at all, right? So you were probably open-minded and humble toward your coaches and seniors. Otherwise it would have been impossible for them to teach you. But now that you have a certain amount of gongfu, there's nothing preventing you from getting pissed off at an inferior opponent and running up the score in a display of poor sportsmanship. You're not going to suddenly lose the ability to play volleyball just from that."

"But I'm not actually that good yet. Jenny and Coach Daniels keep telling me that I'm relying too much on my height and not enough on technique."

"And yet you don't seem to be upset about that," Quentin said. "You have room to develop. Just like you have room to develop as the Ruyi Jingu Bang."

He swirled the ice around his cup. "If you want another example, most of the enemies I fought on my journeys were animals or demons who trained their bodies and minds in the exact same way that holy men did. They cultivated their conduct and performed austerities. If they can do it, you can do it."

"Evil beings can also become stronger by being disciplined and working out? They're not barred from the wizard club? Chinese magic is jacked up."

"The Way is there for anyone to grasp," Quentin clarified. "If an evil person trains harder than you, they will be stronger than you, and that's that. Spiritual power isn't just or merciful. It's *fair*. That's what makes it so dangerous."

Hearing him say that actually cheered me up a bit. If learning special abilities required a kind heart or a pure soul, I'd be screwed. This system was like climbing the corporate ladder. Or getting tenure.

"I mean, look at me," Quentin said. "I achieved spiritual mastery and immortality. And *then* I made war on Heaven."

"Which basically makes you Chinese Satan."

He drained the last of his drink. "Two sides to every story."

I watched him for a bit. There was nothing about Quentin that betrayed any sort of legendary origin. In the short time I'd known him, his behavior had smoothed out into that of a regular teenager. Albeit the cockiest one I'd ever seen.

"If you're not from these parts, how did you acclimate so fast? Clothes aside, you picked up modern culture pretty fast. You even ordered the small boba without anyone telling you."

"I only need to pick up the tiniest part of something in order to understand the whole," he said. "I simply watched your classmates until I absorbed how to act. Same thing with our schoolwork. It's all pretty easy stuff; I don't know why you spend so much time on academics."

Overpowered bastard. "Is that how you got into my school? You dazzled them with your standardized test scores?"

"No, I just used a harmless spell. All the adults think I go there, but there's no Quentin Sun Wukong in the records."

"So then where do you go after school? When you're not with me?"

He grinned. "I interact with other people. I explore the area. Not everything is about *you*, you know."

"Oh, bite me. You were the one who was all, '*waaah you were my dearest companion, waaah.'* If the Ruyi Jingu Bang was so important to you, how did you lose it in the first place?"

He pretended not to hear me. I never let anyone pull that move on me if I could help it.

"It would have had to die in order to reincarnate," I said. "So what gives? Did a demon break it? Did you try to crack a magic Walnut of Invincibility?"

"I don't want to talk about it!"

I was going to tell him that given he'd insinuated himself into my life on the basis that we were once a demon-slaying tag-team in the distant past, I had a goddamn right to know how the partnership broke up to begin with. But my words exploded into a coughing fit.

I turned around in my chair.

"Excuse me," I said to the man smoking a cigarette at the table behind me. "You're not supposed to do that so close to the shop entrance."

He said nothing. And blew another deliberate plume of smoke into the air.

The metal of Quentin's chair screeched as he stood up. "The lady is asking you to put it out."

Ugh. There wasn't a need to escalate like that. But the man got up, too.

Friggin' dudes and their pissing matches. Fine. I got to my feet as well. *Ace card played, buddy, tallest person right here.*

The man turned around and looked up at me. I nearly jumped backward onto the table.

"Something on my face?" he said with a grin.

He looked to be a middle-aged construction worker, judging by how much blue denim he was wearing. There were tons of guys like him in the surrounding towns, tearing down and putting up houses at the behest of newly minted tech families.

But that was only from the neck down. His face was a Halloween mask, a really good one. Black-ringed eyes, a long muzzle, and facial hair that went all the way round like a mane. A big cat straight out of the savannah.

The bipedal lion exhaled more smoke, and suddenly his face fritzed back to a human's. His entire appearance was a broken TV unable to decide which channel to land on.

Quentin obviously wasn't seeing what I was seeing or else he would have immediately flipped out into rage mode. But he could tell something was wrong.

"Genie," he said, his voice full of suspicion. "Does that guy look normal to you?"

"Probably not," the man answered for me. "Given that I'm a demon."

16

"SO," THE MAN SAID TO QUENTIN IN A CATCHY-UPPY TONE. "How have you been?"

I wanted to smack myself for being so stupid. Quentin and I had spent the entire morning cozying up over which member of the X-Men I wanted to be, when what really mattered was the two of us had killed a monster only three days ago. I should have pressed him about whether the Demon King of Confusion was some kind of onetime incident or not.

Because the answer was most decidedly *not.*

From the look of it, though, Quentin was as much on his back foot as I was. He frowned like he was at a party where he didn't know anyone.

"Something wrong with your eyes?" the man asked. He pointed to himself. "Huangshijing? No?"

The name finally rang a bell for Quentin. "Tawny Lion," he said. "I didn't recognize you without your trash brothers around."

"That's rude of you. Especially since they're right here."

Six more men filed around the corner to back up the first. They had human faces, but they were dressed identically to the smoker, down to the last stitch. The costume department somewhere had gotten lazy.

They made a semicircle around us, hemming us in against the building. I'd always thought the shots of the criminal gang pouring in to attack the hero in martial arts films were silly. But in real life, from the hero's perspective, being outnumbered? It was actually rather terrifying.

Quentin tensed up for another knock-down, drag-out fight. His muscles snapped into readiness hard enough to be audible. My stomach lurched at the prospect of more bloodshed and violence on the level of our previous encounter.

"Oh come on," said the leader of the gang. "Have you no decorum?"

A young couple pushed their baby stroller right by us. The street was filling up. Whatever we did outside was sure to be noticed.

The man tossed his cigarette butt aside and motioned to the inside of the tea shop. "Let's talk. The girl, too. I wouldn't want to be rude to your guest."

Possibly as a show of good faith, he went in first. His brothers began to trickle in after him.

"When you said you sensed a demonic presence in my town, did that include *these guys*?" I hissed at Quentin under my breath.

"No! These assholes are supposed to be dead!"

"According to you, a lot of assholes are supposed to be dead, and yet we keep running into them!"

Only one member of the gang remained outside. This was our last chance to book it. None of this demon business, dead or undead, had anything to do with me.

As if he knew what I was thinking, Quentin tapped the back of his hand against the back of mine.

"Stay," he said.

"Because it'll be safer?"

"Because I might need your help if this gets ugly."

It was jarring how gravely serious he sounded. I could tell he really was at a disadvantage here. But somehow *I* leveled the playing field?

The last man held the door and whipped his hand in a circle, telling us to get a move on.

Following Quentin inside was less of a struggle than I expected. My better instincts were failing me.

■ ■ ■

The shop was empty except for one person. "Something else I can get you folks?" asked the piercing-riddled college student who was working the register.

"*Sleep,*" Quentin told her.

I knew Quentin had mentioned it, but I never would have believed he could bewitch people with a single command. Not without seeing it here. The girl's eyes fluttered shut and she sank to the floor, disappearing behind the ice cream counter.

"*Conceal,*" said Tawny Lion, gesturing at the front of the store.

The glass windows and doors turned into a hazy amber. People moved about outside, but they were vague shadows. Not one tried to enter the shop.

The six men, the ones who'd arrived later, settled in around the biggest table toward the back. The way they watched like attentive students made it clear their leader was to do all the talking. Tawny Lion remained in the three-way standoff with Quentin and me.

"First things first," he said. "You should apologize for calling my brothers trash. One of the very first things we do with our newfound freedom from Hell is to seek you out so we can make amends, and you insult us? You haven't changed a bit."

"A pack of thieves like you *is* trash, and you should still be rotting in the pits!" Quentin snapped. "Did the Jade Emperor install a revolving door since last I checked?"

"Hmmm, I suppose I could tell you how we got out," Tawny Lion said, tapping at his bottom lip with his finger. "But then again, the first rule you learn in prison is 'no snitching.' "

Quentin looked ready to break the cease-fire and give him stitches anyway. I motioned for him to calm down. The situation was still negotiable.

"He's only miffed because we pulled off the same feat he did, breaking free from Diyu," Tawny Lion said to me, tilting his head at Quentin. "He's also the one who sent us there in the first place, which makes it even more embarrassing for him."

If the demon was going to speak to me like a familiar fellow conspirator, then maybe I could play along.

"Well," I said nervously. "You sure showed his dumb ass."

Quentin stared at me like I'd laid an egg right there on the floor, but Tawny Lion beamed.

"It's really impressive that you've managed to escape Hell itself," I said, remembering how satisfied the Demon King of Confusion was with himself for the feat. "The mystery makes it all the more mysterious. I mean intriguing. Fascinating."

The demon pointed both hands at me, palms up. "See?" he said to Quentin happily. "Someone gets it. This is a feat that only you accomplished before. In many ways this makes me your equal."

"Yes!" I said before Quentin could protest at being compared to the demon. "But now that you two have made your peace, I'm sure you'll be on your way. Back to your home, wherever it is. Probably some place far from here."

LEAVE this mortal realm! I wanted to shout. I would have sounded like a reality-show medium dealing with an invisible poltergeist in the rafters.

The very solid, tangible demon in front of me laughed.

"On the contrary," Tawny Lion said. "Confronting the specters of our past is only the first item on our to-do list. If we want to make any headway toward the rest of our goals, we're going to have to settle in right here on Earth."

Dammit. So much for the "weaseling out of small talk" strategy.

"What, uh, are your goals exactly?" I felt like a Super Bowl sideline reporter forced to interview her least-favorite team. "Because maybe you don't have to be here to accomplish them."

"Eh, you know, a bit of this, a bit of that," Tawny Lion said to me. "Mostly they revolve around becoming stronger. You may not believe it, but for a yaoguai, self-improvement is the greatest goal imaginable. To have ultimate control over your body and mind is to move closer to enlightenment. All demons want to attain the Way."

He winked at me. "And the wealth of powers that come along with it aren't so bad."

I yielded to his explanation with a slight nod-shrug. Quentin had only just been saying that a lot of his enemies trained themselves to level up as much as possible. And from what I'd read so far in the book of Sun Wukong's journeys, the bulk of the demons attacked the party because they wanted Xuanzang's flesh as a spiritual steroid boost.

"Earth is like one big nature retreat, ideal for discovering your inner strength," Tawny Lion said. "Slim chance of getting anything done in Hell with so many distractions. Now that we're alive again, my brothers and I are going to continue our personal development and pick up where we left off back in the days of Xuanzang."

Quentin did not like the name of his old master crossing the demon's lips. "You mean you're going to cheat your way to power by eating any human being that suits your needs!"

"Whaaat? Nooo," Tawny Lion said, teasing. "That's not our plan at all. Maybe that's what the other yaoguai are going to do once they get here, but not us."

. . .

The bottom had just dropped out of this conversation. Not that it was a sparkler to begin with, but now it was fully pear-shaped.

"*Other* yaoguai?" Quentin said slowly. "*What* other yaoguai? You mean the Demon King of Confusion?"

"That weakling? I guess he's around somewhere, too, but I meant the other yaoguai coming to Earth," Tawny Lion said, as if it were common knowledge. "I'm talking about your old friends from your little road trip."

The look on Quentin's face told me I could start freaking out any time now. I was way ahead of him. The sinking feeling that had been in my stomach since the beginning of this encounter was now the size of an iceberg.

"Oh dear," Tawny Lion said. "I thought you knew. Because there are some real bad characters in that bunch. I wouldn't want to be a human caught in their path. Can you say *bloodbath*?" The demon chuckled at the thought.

"Quentin?" I said, unsure of what to do.

He didn't answer. He was lost in thought, moving his lips silently over a number of possible futures, all of which appeared to be very, very bad.

"See, that's what I'm talking about," Tawny Lion said to me. "Check out the monkey's face! That's how you can tell I'm an okay guy. Most other demons take shortcuts on the path to power by eating anyone they think will give them the slightest leg up.

"I've got a different strategy," he went on, obviously fishing for the follow-up question.

I fell for the bait. "Which is?"

Tawny Lion smiled. "*My* shortcut is that I'm going to steal the Ruyi Jingu Bang."

■ ■ ■

He made a quick signal, and the six men in the back pounced on Quentin.

"*Barrier,*" Tawny Lion said, spreading his hands out.

The shop snapped in two. Not physically. But I could feel a wall slam down, separating me and Tawny Lion from Quentin and the others. I could still see them, but the sound of their scuffle was muted by half.

"*Bind,*" Tawny Lion added.

My legs and arms jerked together, and I stood up so straight it hurt, a fresh recruit ordered to attention by a drill sergeant. I couldn't move.

"Genie!" Quentin shouted. The other men weren't brawling with him; they were focusing solely on containment. Three of them were grappling him physically, and the others were standing back to channel a similar binding spell, muttering the command over and over to hold him down. Between all six, they were succeeding.

The invisible constriction around me tightened, and I cried out in pain.

"Don't be so dramatic," Tawny Lion said. "I know who you are, and that's not even close to causing you harm."

He leaned in, secretive. "I didn't track down the monkey's aura, you know. I followed yours. The original feud between me and Sun Wukong started because I tried to take the Ruyi Jingu Bang once before. Why do you think he hates me beyond all proportion?"

I strained against the bindings, hoping to find more room to breathe. "I thought—it was because—you're a pompous piece of trash."

Tawny Lion laughed. "Well get used to it. This pompous piece of trash is going to be your new master now. Whoever controls the staff of the Monkey King controls enough power to take Heaven by force. Once I figure out a way to strip that pesky human form from you, I'll have the gods kissing my feet."

The demon's attention turned away from me to someone I'd forgotten about the whole time.

"You know what?" Tawny Lion said. He walked over to the counter and bent down behind it. "Given how much I have to celebrate, I think I'm going to cheat on my diet a little."

He reappeared holding the girl who had been working the register. She dangled limply in his arms. Her bandana had fallen off and tresses of wavy red hair covered her face.

I expended the last of my air. "But you said you didn't eat—"

"I lied. I'm a lion, you fool. Did you think I was a frugivore?"

Tawny Lion cha-cha'ed with the girl's unconscious body out to the center of the room, swaying his hips to the radio song trickling through the barrier's muting effect. He dipped her toward me and her head lolled back, her pupils dilated and unseeing.

"Ah," he said, "This one has a surprising amount of spiritual energy. I'd bet she has excellent gongfu. A talented artist, maybe? She looks like the type."

He sniffed her exposed neck. "Great bouquet, too. Xuanzang-esque, you might say."

I thrashed back and forth, desperately hoping that I could wriggle free by sheer oscillating force.

Come on! I shrieked inwardly at myself, wishing more than anything that I hadn't treated Quentin's catalog of powers so lightly before. *Strength, magic, kick in! PLEASE!*

The demon grasped the girl by her shoulders. He opened his jaws wide, exposing a pink, ridged throat and rows of pointed carnivore's teeth. His mouth kept impossibly distending, reaching an angle so obtuse he resembled a lamprey more than a cat. He drew her head into his bite radius, working his lips forward as if he meant to crunch the top half of her skull off in one try, like a child impatient to get at the bubblegum in the center of a lollipop.

．　．　．

"Da ge!" shouted one of the men in the back. "The monkey!"

Quentin had slipped free. He hurled himself at the invisible wall between us. A loud *whump* rattled the store as his shoulder made contact—a hockey player crashing into the Plexiglas.

The barrier held, but Tawny Lion stumbled. I felt the constriction around me loosen.

The demon quickly drew his mouth away, unraveling his jaws from the girl's head with the insulted air of someone whose phone had rung during dinner. He threw her into the nearest chair, where she sprawled out, unharmed for the moment. I squeezed my elbows outward with all my might and felt the magic give.

"One thing, you idiots!" he yelled, his words distorted and jowly from speaking before his mouth shrunk fully back to normal. "I ask for just one thing!"

He took a stance and raised his hands like he was going to recast the spell that was keeping Quentin away. But right now he had something bigger than the Monkey King to worry about.

Me.

17

I'D TRIED GYMNASTICS AS A CHILD. THIS WAS WHEN I STILL HAD a chance of fitting between the uneven bars, so that tells you how long ago it was.

The coach explained to us that when you weren't used to doing a sudden move like a handspring or flip, it was common to lose your vision for a second or two in the middle of it. Your eyes wouldn't be able to process the motion without practice, so you could be watching your own limbs the whole time without really seeing them.

That's what happened to me. I couldn't visualize my surroundings clearly.

But I was doing *something*.

And then suddenly, there I was. Out of breath. Panting and sweating in the middle of the room with no one around.

The men who'd been fighting with Quentin now littered the corners of the café, crumpled and discarded like straw wrappers. They hadn't been beaten. They'd been caved in, wrecked to the point where they weren't even twitching.

The remnants of a broken chair lay at my feet instead of theirs, and there were splinters in my hair. If I didn't know any better, I would think someone had smashed the heavy piece of furniture over my head. But I didn't feel a thing. No lumps, no bruises.

Given the demons' identical dress, it took me a second to locate Tawny Lion. I used deduction to find him—seeing who'd gotten the worst of it. There he was.

The leader of the demons had been hammered face-first into the wall so hard he was partially embedded like a nail. It would have been comical—Sunday morning–cartoonish—if not for the blood leaking out of the cracks. I watched it drip to the floors, wondering when I would start to feel sick or scared or anything but hugely satisfied with the carnage.

I heard a whistle. "Damn," said Quentin. "Remind me never to piss you off."

"I did this? It wasn't you?"

"Nope. I just got out of your way. I was afraid you wouldn't be able to tell us apart."

An awkward silence passed. It probably should have been filled with me vigorously denying everything. *There was no way I could have done any of this! I'm not that strong! I'm not that violent!*

But instead, nothing.

Ah dang it. I kept forgetting the girl in the shop. I ran over to her and laid her on the ground. She was breathing, deep and slow enough to give me pause, but breathing nonetheless.

"You saved her life," Quentin said. "I didn't get through the barrier in time. She'd be dead if it weren't for you."

It had been such a close call that a drop of blood trickled down her forehead from where one of Tawny Lion's fangs had pricked the skin. I dabbed it away with my sleeve, a brief motherly instinct overtaking me even though I was younger than her.

"I thought from reading the book of your stories that consuming spiritual power might be like a ritual, or a vague kind of energy vampirism," I said.

"Nope. Straight-up chewing and swallowing."

The sound of tapping on glass startled me out of my reverie. I looked over to see the opaque shield that Tawny Lion had put up over the front of the store beginning to fade. There were people outside, some of whom looked like they wanted in.

Oh god.

What was I *doing*? There were bodies in this store. Dead ones, maybe. We couldn't be caught like this.

Oh god oh god.

I ran over to the door and locked it before anyone could come in, but once the veil disappeared completely we'd still be visible to bystanders. "Quentin!" I shouted. "What the hell are we going to do about this?"

"About what?"

I waved my arms around. "This!"

"Oh!" he said. "Right. Wow. This is not good for you, is it? Not a thing that happens to people these days. Hrm."

He began pacing about like we had all the time in the world for him to think. I wanted to scream.

"Can't you hide them with magic?" I pleaded.

"I could, but the next people to walk in here might, oh, I don't know, notice tripping over invisible bodies? You know this would have been a lot easier if you had killed them."

"What!?"

"Yaoguai disappear back to Hell once they're dead. These guys are still alive, even Tawny Lion. You want me to, uh . . ." He made a clicking noise with his teeth and a twisting motion with his hands.

"No!" Fighting was one thing, but straight-up killing a downed enemy was a line I couldn't cross yet.

Quentin rolled his eyes at me like I was being the unreasonable one.

"Then the only other option is to have a member of the celestial pantheon come and take them into custody," he said. "But Tawny Lion and his brothers were never associated with any gods. There's no one who'd be willing to pay bail. Except for maybe—"

"No maybes! Get help now or else the two of us will be seeking enlightenment from the inside of a juvenile detention facility!"

He scrunched his nose. Whoever it was I was making him call upon, he really didn't want to owe them one. He sat down in the middle of the floor and pulled his legs underneath him.

"What the hell are you doing?"

"Praying." He took a deep breath, inhaling for what seemed an eternity, and lowered his head.

A vibration like a brewing storm emanated from his throat. It hardened into syllables. He was chanting, not like a monk but like a whole choir of monks in an echoing stone abbey that doubled and redoubled their voices. The air tingled with a sense of urgency.

"*Na mo guan shi yin pu sa,*" Quentin droned.

"Namoguanshiyinpusanamoguanshiyinpusa*Namoguanshiyinpusa.*"

I could have sworn the ground was shaking under our feet. Quentin grew louder and louder until it seemed like all the glass inside the shop would crack.

"Na mo guan shi yin pu sa," Quentin continued. *"Salutations to the most compassionate and merciful Bodhisattva."*

A burst of light came from the window, startling the bejeezus out of me. Quentin, however, appeared to be expecting it. He got up, opened the door, and motioned for me to come outside with him.

I was so worried at what I might see that I shielded my eyes, a bomb shelter refugee stepping out of the hatch. But the scene in the street was fairly normal. Sunshine, people, cars.

Everything was just frozen in time, was all.

Pedestrians had stopped mid-stride. Anyone who had been talking had their mouths open. A driver checked her mirror for a turn that had been paused indefinitely. The entirety of Johnson Square, as far as the eye could see, had been turned into a snow-globe without any white flakes.

There was no sound anywhere. I snapped my fingers to see if my ears still worked. Thankfully they did.

"Did you do this?" I asked Quentin.

He shook his head. "I'm not that powerful."

I tried not to touch anything. I'd read enough sci-fi to be unsure of what time manipulation rules applied here. Maybe I could have posed everyone's bodies in amusing positions, or maybe any contact with them would have triggered a quantum wave collapse or something.

Quentin led me to one person who turned out not to be frozen, just standing still across the street. I probably should have noticed her earlier. She was only the most gorgeous woman I had ever seen in my whole life.

She was as tall as I was. But she wore her height with such grace and poise that it made me feel unworthy to share that trait with her. Her elegant face was the kind that needed to be painted and housed in a museum, just to be fair to everyone born in the next century. She smiled at Quentin, and then at me.

"Genie Lo," Quentin said. "This is the Bodhisattva Guanyin,

the Goddess of Mercy, She Who Hears the Cries of the World. Benefactor to Xuanzang and my friend from the old days."

"Hey girl!" Guanyin threw her arms around me in a fierce hug.

Huh. I thought the deified personification of kindness and compassion would have touched down on Earth in flowing robes and a crown of jewels. Not jeans and a pixie cut.

"Nice to meet you," I said, my chin stuck on her shoulder. "Who's that guy?"

There was another person who was free to move about. He was dressed like a cross between a Secret Service agent and a *GQ* model. He was as handsome as Guanyin was pretty, his facial features sharper than his five-figure suit. But his air of cold disdain made it clear he wasn't in the business of handing out hugs. Quentin tensed up when he saw him.

"Erlang Shen," he hissed with more vitriol than he spent on the Demon King of Confusion. "What the hell are you doing here?"

Erlang Shen pulled off his sunglasses and scanned the block with an imperial, unblinking gaze.

"Escorting the Lady Guanyin," he said while completely overlooking Quentin. "Aren't you going to introduce me as well, Keeper of the Horses?"

That had to have been some kind of insult, because Quentin looked as if he'd rather Erlang Shen's face get acquainted with his fist. All I knew of the other god was that he was the only person who'd ever bested Sun Wukong in a fight. The grudge must have run deep.

"Of course not," said Erlang Shen. He smirked as if getting under Quentin's skin was the sport of kings. Then he turned to me and bowed slightly.

"You're . . . the nephew of the Jade Emperor, right?" I asked.

"Among other things. I prefer to be known for mastering the torrents and bringing life to the fields."

"He's basically a glorified ditch-digger," Quentin said.

"Be nice," said Guanyin. "I heard you two needed some help."

"Yes!" I chimed in. "We do. We need to get rid of some demons, quickly."

Erlang Shen made a move like the bodyguard he resembled, stepping forward and reaching inside his jacket, but Guanyin held him off. "Where are they?" she asked.

"Inside the shop. We need someone to take them away, or else I'm going to be in trouble. A lot of trouble."

"Okay, sure." Guanyin wiggled her fingers vaguely in that direction. "Done. Bibbity bobbity boo."

"What?" I said. "Just like that?"

She smiled. "Sometimes it's just like that."

The door to the shop swung open and lions filed out. Not men in lion masks, like what had briefly appeared to me before. Full-on lions with lion bodies, walking on all fours. I had to do a double take to make sure it wasn't a group of oversize housecats or possums or any other more plausible animal. But no, seven lions limping meekly on parade.

They picked their way through the forest of frozen humans and went up to Guanyin, pushing me aside. The wounded beasts flocked around her and nuzzled at her outstretched hands. She looked like a Disney princess befriending the local wildlife, her munificence taming even the most vicious of creatures.

One of them was in way worse shape than the others. That must have been Tawny Lion. It cringed when I looked at it and tried to keep to the opposite side of Guanyin.

It was a lot harder not to feel bad when they were in this form. I wasn't big on animal cruelty.

He nearly killed someone, I reminded myself. *He's lucky he's not a rug by now.*

Guanyin stepped back and made a face of slight concentration. The pride of lions began to quiver. Not like they were afraid or cold, but like they couldn't decide whether they wanted to exist or not. In a final small flash of light, only the strength of a disposable camera maybe, they were gone.

I stared at the space where they'd been, trying to wrap my head around the last ten minutes.

"I'm having a hard time believing what I'm seeing," I said. "The lions, the people in the street, all of it."

"Do not doubt the Lady Guanyin's abilities," said Erlang Shen. "She once pacified Hell itself by giving away her own good karma. There was so much overflowing from her that Yanluo, King of Death, had to beg her to leave before her virtuous aura quenched the fires of suffering and allowed the guilty demons to escape their sentences."

"I'll . . . take your word for it?" I said.

Guanyin turned to me. "That's that. I put them in one of my divine sanctuaries, where they can do penance for their crimes. It's not as harsh as sending them to Hell, but at least you won't have any trouble from Tawny Lion again. I took care of that poor girl, too; she'll be fine. Won't remember a thing."

"Thank you," I said. "Is there, uh, anything I can do for you? Light some joss? Recommend a restaurant?"

"You could give me the pleasure of your company for a while," Guanyin said. "We really need to talk."

She raised her hand as if to cast another spell. "Let's do it somewhere more private. Your place, if you don't mind?"

I flinched. "You're not going to zap us there, are you?"

Guanyin smiled. She swirled her finger and suddenly the street came back to life. People resumed what they were doing, unaware that anything had happened.

"Actually, it's such a nice day that I was thinking we could walk."

18

I'D NEVER POURED TEA FOR A GOD BEFORE. AND NOW THERE were two of them in my house. Mom was missing out on the biggest guests of her life.

The composition of the scene in my kitchen was disjointed in a way that was hard to describe. Guanyin and Erlang Shen didn't quite fit in the frame. They were larger than life. Or a lot better looking than it, anyhow. To have them casually and patiently wait for me while I played host was like those moments where your favorite celebrities proved how down-to-earth they were on camera.

Quentin ruined the divine triptych by refusing to sit at the same table as Erlang Shen. He skulked off to the side, pacing back and forth.

I brought the tray over and poured for everyone. I was glad that we had jasmine instead of oolong. I didn't want Guanyin thinking I was being cute, serving her a drink named after her.

She took a sip to be polite and set her cup aside.

"So you're her," Guanyin said with a warm smile. "I never would have guessed. You look a little like Xuanzang."

I knew I looked like that drawing of him, but hearing someone else compare me to a guy made me hitch a little. "Xuanzang was prettier than the Four Great Beauties," Guanyin said, sensing my discomfort. "It's a compliment."

"Thanks, I guess? You know who I am?"

"We know you're the Ruyi Jingu Bang," Erlang Shen said, eyeing me side-to-side like a vase that he would have been upset to find any cracks in. "Any spiritual being who has been in the As-You-Will Cudgel's aura would recognize it if they got near enough. The Lady Guanyin and I have both seen your original form many times."

It was unsettling to hear the two of them talk like that. Like meeting a distant aunt and uncle who only remembered you in diapers. "The two of you are really gods?"

"Yes," said Guanyin. "We're members of the celestial pantheon of immortal spirits, over which the Jade Emperor presides."

Oookay. "And you're from . . . Heaven?"

She nodded. "A different plane of existence than the one that contains Earth, if that helps you think about it."

It really didn't. My skeptical side was taking an absolute beating right now. *But science!* I wanted to shout. *Empirical thought! Magnets!*

"I know you might be a bit confused," Guanyin went on. "But by and large, there's no need to be. Earth is still Earth. Your universe is still your universe. It's just that sometimes there's bleed-over from other spiritual dimensions. Like today, for instance."

I wasn't sure what other kind of explanation would have kept my head from spinning, so I decided I'd have to roll with this one. Gods in Heaven. Check.

"To preserve order and stability, we retain dominion over the mortal realm in many areas," Erlang Shen said, interjecting in case I'd gotten the wrong idea about the power balance. "Such as those involving yaoguai."

Quentin slapped the nearest wall at the end of his lap around my kitchen. "Yes!" he said, his not-great patience already running thin. "Can we talk about that for a moment? Why a bunch of demons I personally dispatched a long time ago suddenly show up out of the blue?"

I cared more about the broader issue than the particulars of whom Quentin killed or didn't kill once upon a time. "Why are there *any* demons walking around my town in the first place?" I asked, raising my voice above his. "These aren't ye olden days of legend!"

"And why did Tawny Lion claim that more are coming!?" Quentin shouted, topping me with one last demand.

Erlang Shen met our agitation with stoicism. He picked up his tea, quaffed it, and set his cup down before speaking.

"The answer to all of your questions is that there's been a jailbreak," he replied.

Quentin couldn't believe what he was hearing. "A jailbreak? From Diyu?"

"Yes. A number of yaoguai have escaped the plane of Hell, and we have good reason to believe they're headed to Earth, if they're not here already."

Quentin didn't respond, either a minor miracle in itself or a sign of impending disaster. He rubbed his face up and down.

"You would have learned about this had you not run off to Earth, itching for a fight, at the first sign of demonic presence," Guanyin said to him gently.

"Hold up," I said. "That doesn't explain why a bunch of these escaped demons showed up in my hometown. There's nothing special about Santa Firenza."

"Of course there is," Erlang Shen said. "You."

It was my turn to go mute.

Erlang Shen saw that he needed to elaborate. He took the lid off the teapot and pushed it to the center of the table. This explanation needed props, apparently.

"Imagine the tea leaves are yaoguai," he said.

"Okay," I said. I had chosen the glass set, so I could see the loose tea scattered across the bottom of the broad, round pot.

Erlang Shen held up his index finger. "And this is you. The Ruyi Jingu Bang, former axis of the Milky Way."

He dipped his finger into the vessel. The pale green liquid began swirling around it in a miniature vortex. The tea leaves were whisked along by the flow, rising and falling in a tightening loop, faster and faster until Erlang Shen ceased the water's motion. Once everything had settled, there was a tight pile of tea debris gathered right under the spot he was pointing at.

He withdrew his finger and flicked the moisture away.

"Every otherworldly being has its own spiritual gravity," he said. "That's why they aggregate in the same general locations instead of dispersing to the four corners of the Earth. They're drawn to existing supernatural masses like moons around a planet. *You* are what's pulling them to this location."

I looked at Quentin. He looked at me.

"Technically, the Monkey King also being here makes it even worse," Erlang Shen said. "It's not fate or destiny that has you running into your old enemies. Sun Wukong and the Ruyi Jingu Bang are each the equivalent of a black hole. Any yaoguai that come to Earth are going to get sucked into your orbits, without fail. It's just a matter of how close and how fast."

"Oh my god," I said. "You're telling me a horde of demons is going to show up on my doorstep?"

"If only," Erlang Shen said, insensitive to how that sounded. "Then it would be a lot easier to track them down. I'd say they could show up anywhere within a couple hundred miles around your physical location, give or take."

That wasn't a whole lot better. I mean, it was, but still not great.

"Please tell me you're going to do something about this," I said. "You can't let demons from Hell wander freely over the entire Bay Area."

"Heaven has a plan to deal with the situation." Erlang Shen stretched in his chair with the litheness of a panther, hinting at a wiry martial artist's build under his suit. "My uncle the Jade Emperor has decreed that the fugitive yaoguai will be apprehended by a pair of champions who are well-tailored to facing this particular menace."

"Okay then." I breathed a little easier. "I'm glad you and Guanyin are on the job."

The god returned to his normal posture and fixed me with a pointed stare. "I wasn't talking about us."

I didn't get it. Were there other divine beings nearby I didn't know about?

Quentin coughed and kicked the back of my seat.

Oh.

Ohhh.

Oh *fu—*

19

I DON'T THINK I COULD BE BLAMED FOR BEING SLOW ON THE uptake. It isn't like one gets conscripted as a demon hunter on the reg.

"Whoa," I said. "Whoa, whoa, whoa. That is a bad idea. A very bad idea."

"I wish I could say that the circumstances were different, and that the two of us could take charge," Guanyin said. "But for better or worse, the Jade Emperor's policies adhere strictly to the philosophy of *wu wei*."

"*Without action?*" I asked, translating the words directly.

"Yes. The belief that doing nothing is the best, most natural way to behave. That everything will play out as it should, as long as you don't interfere. This is why he's ordered the rest of the pantheon to stand by as Sun Wukong and the Ruyi Jingu Bang take care of the problem. The two of you are not true gods, so you don't represent a commitment of Heavenly resources."

I glanced at Quentin. His face said, *I told you so*. This must have been why he was so reluctant to call upon divine help in the first place. The favor they'd done for us today was snowballing out of control.

"It is the Way of Heaven to act on Earth through lesser

intermediaries," Erlang Shen said. "This is how it's been through the centuries, from the first dynastic kings to Xuanzang to now."

"But I'm not the intermediary you want doing this!" I said. "I don't know anything about monsters and magic. You want some kind of sorcerer with a cage full of gremlins. Or a wushu master who's been training his whole life for this sort of thing."

"Did you not just wipe the floor with several yaoguai at once today?" Erlang Shen asked.

"I don't . . . I can't do that on command."

"Then I suggest you learn how. And quickly."

"What happens if I say no?"

"Look, I don't think you understand," he said. "You don't have any choice in the matter."

"What do you mean? Xuanzang chose to go on his journey to get the sutras. The gods didn't make him."

"That was different. Xuanzang had a say because he was a human. You, however, are not."

Clank.

My fist hitting the table sloshed the contents of the cup in front of me over the sides. Tepid water dripped on the floor but I made no motion to clean it up. Quentin shifted uncomfortably. He'd gotten pretty good at telling when I was primed to go off.

"Would you like to say that again? I don't think I heard you right."

Erlang Shen was unfazed by how long I'd dragged out the sentence through my teeth.

"Yes, you have a human form," he said. "Yes, you're mortal. But humans don't have the essence of a celestial body inside them. Humans aren't walking weapons so powerful they're strategic assets in their own right. My uncle's stance is that you're still the lost property of Heaven and thus beholden to his will."

I flexed my fingers open and closed a few times.

"From what little I understand of reincarnation," I enunciated very carefully, "any person, spirit, or whatever can become human. So long as they work hard enough at it in their past life. I thought those were the rules. That everyone gets their chance to spin the Wheel of Life and Rebirth in the hopes of bettering themselves."

"I'm sorry, Genie," Guanyin said. "But there aren't rules for what's happened to you. A weapon reincarnating is completely unprecedented. Not in the history of gods and men has this ever happened. When you were the Ruyi Jingu Bang, no one even guessed you had a soul."

Welp. Nothing like having your personhood denied in the morning to start the day off right.

I finally understood the piercing, migraine-y anger that shot through my core the first time Quentin had called me the Ruyi Jingu Bang. If there was any of my past self in me right now, it hated being thought of as an object. It hated not being acknowledged for what it accomplished by turning human. It valued Genie.

Even if no one else did.

"What a pile of crap," said Quentin.

I turned to find him giving me a hard stare.

Most people probably would have thought from his facial expression that he was agreeing with the Jade Emperor. After all, he was the one who'd lost his most valuable possession as a result of my very existence.

Except that he glanced at the gods, and then back at me. I had a sense of what he was thinking.

"You come here to Earth to tell us how it's going to be," Quentin said to Erlang Shen. "Let me tell *you* how it's going to be. If Genie refused, the Jade Emperor would be up the creek without a paddle. Your uncle has made the biggest gaffe of his career, letting these demons escape, and he's so afraid of losing face over it that he needs to beg for her help without appearing to do so. Meanwhile you're too much of a kiss-ass to go against his orders and pitch in the effort, you *goutuizi*."

Erlang Shen didn't change expressions, but I could have sworn the room got several degrees colder and draftier as he bristled at Quentin. A duel might have broken out in my kitchen right then and there, but Guanyin put her hand on the rain god's forearm.

"Enough," she commanded.

The thunderclouds slowly rolled back. Erlang Shen calmed himself under her grasp, but Quentin eyed the contact between him and Guanyin, not liking it one bit. Interesting.

Guanyin faced me with a wince of sadness and right then I knew I was in trouble. She wasn't throwing in the towel with her long-suffering air. She was powering up.

"Genie, I know none of this seems fair," she said. "But if demons are returning to the mortal world, this no longer becomes solely about you."

I knew that. And I'm sure she knew I knew that. But we were going down this road anyway.

"These particular fugitives—they're ambitious," Guanyin said. "They'll stop at nothing to gain more power. And their go-to strategy is to consume humans with strong spirits.

"It doesn't have to be a holy man like Xuanzang. There are plenty of laypeople in this day and age who have the essence they're looking for, like that girl in the shop. Once the demons arrive, they'll begin hunting, picking off innocents from the shadows."

Guanyin motioned at Quentin. "Tell her. Am I exaggerating?"

Quentin let out a deep sigh.

"She's right, Genie," he said. "If this is the bunch that I'm thinking of, then the common folk are in trouble. Obtaining human energies was an obsession for some of these demons. A madness. They won't stop, not even in the face of death."

I squeezed my nose between my palms. Partly out of frustration and partly to keep the stench of the Demon King of Confusion from flooding back into my nostrils. Closing my eyes only brought the image of Tawny Lion's gaping, distended jaws back to the forefront of my mind. Monsters like these couldn't be left alone.

Guanyin sensed her victory was near. "I can tell deep down that you want to help," she said. "You're the type of person who takes matters into her own hands. You're like me in that regard."

I remembered some of Guanyin's legend. The story went that she was once a mortal girl who was so pure, kind, and enlightened that she easily attained Buddhahood in her youth. Just like that, in a relative snap, she accomplished what some holy men couldn't in lifetimes of training.

But as she was about to leave the planes of Heaven and Earth entirely for the ultimate nirvana, she looked back and heard the cries of the suffering and downtrodden. Her compassion led her to stay behind as a Bodhisattva, a lesser divine being, so that she could do her best to relieve the pain of humanity and guide it to its own enlightenment. She was a figure of self-sacrifice and humility. I couldn't see how we compared.

This sucked.

This sucked so goddamn much.

"Fine," I said, in a grouchy harrumph that was very un-Bodhisattva-like. "I'll do what I can."

20

GUANYIN'S EYES SPARKLED AT ME. IT WAS TOO PRETTY TO look at, and I wanted to sneeze.

The sunbeams of her countenance traveled around my kitchen until they found Quentin, still the only one of us who hadn't taken a seat at my table.

"What about you, dear?" she asked.

"Sure," he replied with a shrug. "I have my reputation to think about. Sun Wukong doesn't shy away from a fight."

Maybe I was reading into it too much, but that was a pretty weaksauce reason to go along with everything, even for someone as prideful as Quentin. Which meant he was taking up this burden to protect the little people, like in the old stories. Or he was doing it simply to have my back.

It was a nice feeling either way. The cockles of my heart and such.

"So do you have names?" Quentin asked. "Or do we have to wait until every yaoguai shakes our hands and reintroduces themselves?"

"Baigujing," Erlang Shen answered. "The Immortals of Tiger, Deer, and Goat. Linggandaiwang. The Hundred-Eyed Demon Lord. Huangpaogui. General Yin. The Wolf of the Twentieth Mansion . . ."

He went on. And on.

And on.

Quentin's frown grew more and more profound with each successive name until finally he threw his hands into the air.

"Tamade!" he shouted, interrupting the roll call. "What's the point of having a Hell in the first place if you're going to let every asshole walk free?"

"What's the total count of escapees?" I said. "Or do you not know how many?"

"We know how many." Erlang Shen squared his shoulders like an accountant about to report to his boss that the whole company was insolvent. "It's one hundred and eight."

"A HUNDRED AND EIGHT?"

"Well a hundred now, after today's events," Erlang Shen said. "If it gives you any reassurance, I can almost guarantee you won't have to fight them all at once."

I could certainly guarantee him that it did not. A wedding guest list's worth of demons. A Roman centuria. Enough demons to create a half a professional soccer league, without substitutions.

While my fretting brain coped by forming worse and worse analogies, Quentin laughed bitterly.

"A hundred and eight," he said, shaking his head. "A hundred and eight! If it had been a handful of the small fry slipping through the cracks, I could have chalked this up to your uncle's usual negligence! You want to tell me how every demon from Chang'an to Vulture Peak managed to parade through the gate?"

"We think Red Boy broke them out," Guanyin said.

Quentin immediately went silent. He stood where he was for a brief second, and then stormed over to her. He grabbed her arm.

Erlang Shen and I both started to say something about him being too rough, but Guanyin didn't pull away. Quentin shoved her unseasonably long sleeve up to her elbow, exposing her wrist and forearm. It was covered in burns.

The wounds had healed, but they'd been bad. Really bad. The vicious, blood-colored splotches shone under the ceiling light. Against the rest of Guanyin's beautiful skin the injuries looked like an act of vandalism.

Without a word Quentin led Guanyin out of the kitchen, never letting go of her hand. The goddess followed him into the hallway, where she gestured over their heads. I could feel something come down around them, similar to Tawny Lion's spell of concealment, only the two of them were still visible.

Quentin's wild-eyed screaming, however, was completely muted. He and Guanyin began noiselessly going at each other.

"So, uh, what's going on?" I asked Erlang Shen.

"During his journey with Xuanzang to recover the sutras, the monkey faced an exceptionally powerful demon named Red Boy," Erlang Shen said. He watched the proceedings with an unreadable look on his face. "Red Boy had the ability to breathe True Samadhi Fire, which no substance, mortal or divine, could resist. The monkey tried to defeat him several times but could not."

I didn't know there was anyone Sun Wukong flat-out couldn't beat in a fight. I'd assumed even Erlang Shen was a coin flip.

"He asked the Lady Guanyin for assistance. With her magic, she captured Red Boy and bound his limbs. The monkey wanted to slay him, but Guanyin pushed for mercy."

"Well that sort of makes sense, given she's the Goddess of—"

"Three times," Erlang Shen interrupted. "Three times Guanyin released Red Boy after he swore to give up fighting. Three times he went back on his word and attacked her."

"Wait, he attacked *her*? After she took his side?"

"Yes." Erlang Shen's mask of dispassion slipped a little, and I could see how upset he was underneath. "Guanyin finally subdued Red Boy for good. In order to receive the clemency he'd thrown away so carelessly before, he promised to become her disciple. Instead of being thrown into Hell, he was given an acolyte's position on a small island shrine in the middle of a Heavenly ocean—isolated from other spirits, but still a paradise compared to what he deserved.

"Over the years he served faithfully. He appeared to have reformed. But the last time Guanyin was with him, he attacked her yet again and fled. That was when she suffered those wounds."

No wonder they were screaming up a storm. Nothing to light a fire under an argument like an "*I told you so.*"

"Red Boy wants revenge against everyone that he believes wronged him," Erlang Shen said. "Springing the other demons from Hell is his return stroke against Guanyin and Sun Wukong. A personal message. All the events that have transpired so far are his doing, ultimately."

"You're certain of this?"

Erlang Shen nodded. "There aren't that many ways out of Hell before your sentence is up. You can either get out on borrowed karma from someone like Guanyin, or you can make an escape route if you're powerful enough. Red Boy is that powerful."

"But if that's the case, why'd he wait until now to make his move?"

"He must have caught word that the Ruyi Jingu Bang was no

longer the fearsome weapon of the Monkey King," he said, making a valiant attempt to keep the irony levels in his voice from reaching critical mass. "The fighting power of his enemies has been reduced immeasurably. Now is the perfect time for him to exact his vengeance."

Erlang Shen didn't go so far as to say this whole deal was my fault. Which was good, because if he had I would have blown my stack from here all the way to Canada. The god seemed to be learning where to toe the line with me much faster than Quentin had.

"How strong is he exactly?" I asked. I had a tough time placing supernatural beings on a relative power scale. "Like if the Demon King of Confusion is a 'one' then Red Boy—"

"Red Boy once burned a country to the ground," Erlang Shen said curtly, without a trace of exaggeration.

I hesitated. "Wouldn't that have been noticed in history somewhere?"

Erlang Shen shook his head. "He *really* burned it to the ground."

"Holy crap. You know, this is the kind of news you should lead with. Seems a little important not to mention right away."

His response was to gesture at Guanyin and Quentin tearing each other apart. "If I had, there would have been no chance whatsoever of a reasonable conversation afterward."

Touché, I guess.

Quentin and Guanyin must have reached a tipping point in their monumental argument, because the goddess left the zone of silence and came back to the kitchen. On the way she ran her hand over my backpack, which had been lying on the countertop.

"Mind if I borrow these?" she asked. I didn't know what she was referring to until she opened her hands. My earrings rested in her palm.

"Those are actually kind of important to me," I said.

"This won't work unless they are." Without waiting for my permission she went over to Quentin, who was fuming in the corner. Before he could resume shouting, she leaned over and pulled him into a kiss.

Quentin was so surprised that he went completely rigid as her hands caressed the back of his neck. Erlang Shen grunted in protest. But I was at the right angle to see that it was a total fakeout. She stopped just short of his lips, needing only for him to hold still while her fingers brushed his ears like a pickpocket.

Guanyin straightened up and waved the silencing spell away. My souvenirs from the Happiest Place on Earth were now fastened to Quentin's earlobes. He realized he was involuntarily wearing jewelry and began pawing helplessly at the clasps. They were probably stuck on there with magic, but it could also have been that he was a boy and didn't know how to undo them.

"What was that?" I asked her.

"A bit of forbidden help," she said. "Those earrings will let the wearer know every time a demon gets too close to a human."

"Okay," I said. "How close are we talking about? Like restraining order distance or county lines distance?"

She gave me a look that said I was examining her gift horse in the mouth. "Far enough away that you should be able to react accordingly. The magic in them will provide a general sense of what direction the demon is in, but beyond that you'll have to do the searching yourselves. Once you receive the alarm, you must strike as soon as you can, Genie. A yaoguai that has fed will be exponentially more dangerous."

The human tragedy inherent in that statement was probably implied. "But what about Red Boy?"

A shade of agony passed over Guanyin's face. "For now we have no choice but to wait until he shows himself. There will undoubtedly be a confrontation with Red Boy at some point, but until then you have to minimize the damage caused by the other demons."

She gestured behind her at Quentin. "The earrings will also help if he gets out of control. Just say the magic words. You know which ones."

She swept past Erlang Shen and motioned for him to follow, in no mood for any departing pleasantries. The mighty nephew of the Jade Emperor got up without a peep. He nodded to me before closing the door.

Another flash of light streamed through the windows and then faded. I didn't feel the need to go outside and check that they were gone. Guanyin really did not screw around when it came to making an exit.

I turned to Quentin. "How much of a dick do you have to be to upset the Goddess of Compassion into leaving without saying goodbye?"

He glowered at me, hands still on his ears.

"I'm joking," I said. "I understand how you feel, honestly. It's maddening to see those you care about get hurt, even if it's their own fault."

"It was my fault," said Quentin. "If I had could have defeated Red Boy on my own she never would have come near that son of a bitch. I shouldn't have gotten her involved."

I took a closer look at the side of his head. "What did she do to you?"

"I'm assuming she put the Band-Tightening Spell back on, only with a different focus item. It'll trigger if you say the chant that kept me imprisoned under the Five Elements Mountain."

"What, you mean, Om Mani Padme Om?"

The words left my mouth before I realized what I'd done.

. . .

Quentin's back snapped into a crescent. His scream of pain was shut off by the closure of his airways. He toppled over to the ground, hitting his head hard on the floor.

"No!" I shouted. "Stop! I didn't mean it!"

He was having a seizure. I raced to his side and put my hand under the back of his skull as it slammed into the floor over and over. I had to hug him to my body to keep him from smashing into the base of the counter.

I could feel Quentin wail into my shoulder, his teeth caught in the weave of my shirt. "I'm sorry!" I cried, even though he was in no condition to hear me. "I'm sorry! Please stop!"

The spell must have been on a timer. After a few more eternal seconds, Quentin's body slowed to a halt. I realized I was smothering him and sat up so he could breathe.

His skin was burning up like a fever that hadn't broken. When his eyelids fluttered open they were mostly whites.

" . . . hot," he mumbled.

I let his head down as gently as I could before grabbing a towel and wetting it under the cold tap. I slid my lap back under him and patted his face and neck until he shivered and relaxed.

Quentin opened his mouth to speak. I wiped my eyes and nose so I wouldn't drip on him when I leaned in to hear.

"So anyway . . ." he whispered. "That's what that spell does."

I could have killed him for joking after what just happened. Instead I held him while he laid his head back and rested.

• ■ •

The microwave clock said that ten minutes had passed. It was getting late in the day, the shadows in my house growing longer across the kitchen floor where we lay. My mother would be home at some point.

"Genie," Quentin said, his voice back to its normal strength. "I think I'm okay now. Thank you—*urk*!"

I shook him by the neck. "*That's* the Band-Tightening Spell? That's what happened to you every time Xuanzang said those words?"

Quentin was either nodding or his head was just flopping back and forth. "Pretty much."

"Jesus Christ!" I shouted. "How was that okay with anyone? That's screwed up! What kind of holy man just tortures another person? What kind of human being?"

I tried to pry the earrings off Quentin without success. "If I ever meet Xuanzang I'm going to knock his teeth down his throat," I said, my fingernails jamming against the clasps. "And I'm not too happy with Guanyin either, right now."

"Genie, stop! Ow! You're pulling my earlobes off!"

He tried to fend me off but I didn't let him. We struggled against each other, using our hips for leverage. He flipped over on top of me and managed to pin my wrists to the floor before we realized what we were doing.

Quentin picked up on the sudden flush in my cheeks and slowly pulled his hands away as if I might be upset by any sudden moves. But he didn't unlock his eyes from mine.

"I should go," he said, sitting back on his heels. "Before your mom finds us like this."

"Wait."

I reached up and buttoned the top of his shirt. I'd undone it part of the way when I was toweling him off. The damp fabric clung to his skin. I could see his muscles twitch like live wires as I slowly popped each button through its hole.

"Thanks." He let me fix and smooth his collar before we finally got up. Benefits of having a long reach.

I walked him to the door and he lingered on the steps. "So I'll see you at school then," he said, giving me a drawn-out, hungry look.

"I guess so."

"Or if you want to meet elsewhere, I have a phone now. It could be any time, any place."

My breathing picked up at the hint.

"That's good," I said. "You should have one."

I could feel where this was leading. And as glorious and satisfying as it would be to dive headlong into it, to drink deeply from the river, I wasn't quite ready yet.

"Thanks for introducing me to your ex," I said.

Quentin's face went scandalized, a rarity that was particularly delicious. "The Lady of Mercy is above any sordid entanglement!" he said. "Her virtue is unquestioned! How could you even imply such blasphemy?"

"Way to put your ex on a pedestal."

"God, I hate you," he muttered.

That was more like it. The moment successfully ruined, I laughed and shut the door in his face.

21

"OH MY GOD," SAID YUNIE. "I KNEW THERE WAS A DIRTY GIRL waiting to come out of that shell of yours."

"What are you talking about?"

"You *marked* him," she said, pointing at Quentin, who sat across the library reading by himself. "That is the hottest thing I've ever seen happen at this school."

Aw, hell. I should have remembered that Yunie, sharp-eyed as ever, would recognize my earrings on Quentin. They weren't exactly small. They weren't exactly meant for anyone but a ten-year-old girl, either.

"Is he like your toy now? Does he have to obey your every command?"

I racked my brain for a feasible explanation and couldn't.

"Just . . . just don't tell anyone they're mine, okay?"

Yunie grinned so wide I thought her face might split. "Sure," she said. "I'll keep your twisted little game a secret. Oh wait, look."

Rachel Li had sauntered up to Quentin. I couldn't hear what she was saying, but the way she nearly brushed his hair with her fingers, it was obvious she was asking about his ears.

Quentin was completely oblivious to her flirting. He said

something and pointed at me. Rachel frowned and glared daggers in my direction before stomping away.

"Oops," Yunie giggled. I slammed my forehead into my open textbook.

As if on cue, a note fell out of the pages and fluttered to the floor. I picked it up and held it to the light. It was in Chinese, a messy cursive written with as much forcefulness as lack of convention.

Meet me after your practice is over. Where I first showed you my true self.

He must have meant the park again. I looked up to see Quentin giving me an intense stare. He really couldn't do anything with subtlety.

Over my shoulder, Yunie squealed with glee as she read the overdramatic note.

Crap. I forgot she understood traditional characters as well as I did, if not better. I wadded up the paper and shoved it as far down as I could in my backpack.

. . .

I cornered Quentin in the hallway the very next break.

"I thought we were meeting after school," he said. "Didn't you get my note?"

"You can just come over and talk to me, you dingus. Instead of skulking around like Batman."

"It's not safe to have our conversations out in the open."

"I think we could tell if there were demons lurking around the corners of our school," I said. "We have those earrings, remember? You're being paranoid."

Quentin grimaced. "You don't understand. Tawny Lion got the drop on me. In the old days he wouldn't have been able to come within a dozen miles without me spotting him."

"What about the Demon King of Confusion? I thought you came to Earth because you sensed his presence."

"I did, but I should have been able to pick him out immediately instead of bumbling across him like an idiot. The fact that he and Tawny Lion got so near means that something is incredibly wrong with my senses, earrings or no."

He glanced around uncomfortably, as if the admission were a sign of weakness the hall monitors would just pounce on. "My true sight hasn't worked since I came to Earth," he said. "In fact, I think when you left my side to become human, you took a lot of my power with you."

"So you're weaker than you were in the stories?"

"Shh!" he hissed. "Do you know how many people would kill to know that?"

I pinched the bridge of my nose. "Okay, so what does this mean for us?"

"It means you have to develop your abilities, and fast. Especially your vision. Or else we'll be running around picking fights with random mailmen and lawyers and skateboarders who turn out not to be yaoguai."

"Oh my god. That's what happened the first day we met, wasn't it? You weren't being mugged. You just got aggro with a bunch of strangers thinking they were demons in disguise."

"Yes, and I could have killed them by accident. We need another training date. Soon."

"I'm busy this weekend."

Quentin shook his head like he couldn't hear me. "You're busy?"

"I have plans on Saturday. We could meet on Sunday. Given how crappy our last session went, we're not going to lose out on a ton of progress if we postpone a single day."

"You can't postpone the secrets of the universe!" he seethed. "Cancel whatever you're doing. It's not important now."

"Don't tell me what is and isn't important! I told you when I was free, and if you don't like it you can take a hike!"

I turned around and nearly bumped into Androu.

"Is there a problem here?" he asked, peering over me at Quentin.

Quentin was right—we did need to be more discreet in our conversations. The whole hallway could have heard me deliver that last line.

"No problem," I said to Androu. "We were just talking about . . ."

Quentin didn't help me fill in the blanks. He left me swinging in the breeze. I bared my teeth at him and then turned it into a smile for Androu.

"Dinner," I said. "I had his parents over for dinner and they want to return the favor at their house."

Androu was still standing very close, so I patted him on the chest reassuringly. "You should come over for dinner someday, too. My house, I mean. Not Quentin's. Not that his parents don't want you in his house. They just never met you. That would be sort of weird."

"Yeeeah," Androu replied. "Genie, can we talk for a minute?"

He pulled me around the corner and behind a locker.

■　■　■

Now, I had fantasized about this moment—sneaking off somewhere private with Androu—a bunch of times before. So in theory

I should have known how to play it smooth, from the flirting to the intensifying conversation, all the way up to the halting but tender first kiss.

But the gesture was less exciting than I'd imagined. Turns out I didn't like being dragged by the arm.

Androu checked to see that we weren't followed.

"Hey, so, what's up with you and Quentin these days?" he asked. "I thought you two didn't get along."

"We've . . . come to an understanding," I said. "Why do you ask?"

"You seem different lately."

"Different how?" I got ready to panic in case he said "stretchier."

"I can't put my finger on it, but it's like ever since Quentin came to this school you've been . . . I don't know. Distracted. You've always been such a focused person, but not around him."

This was a big letdown. I hadn't seriously been expecting a romantic conversation, but I thought at the very least Androu would want to talk about me and him in some regard. Not me and Quentin.

"That's what you wanted to ask about? There's nothing else you wanted to say?"

He shook his head. "Just concerned about you. I'm your friend, you know."

Aaand down went the Hindenburg. Blown up by a heat-seeking F-bomb. I held back a sigh.

"Quentin and I are working on an extra-credit project," I said. "Actually, it's more like we got stuck with one against our will. That's all there is to it. Work."

Androu opened his mouth to say something, but I cut him off. "Also, I appreciate you looking out for me, but honestly, what he and I do together is kind of our business, you know?"

I knew that wasn't what you were supposed to say to a guy to assure him you were still available, but that was the truth. I didn't owe anyone a reason for spending time with Quentin, regardless of what we were doing.

Androu seemed ambivalent about my response, but if there was one signal I did know how to give off, it was *I don't want to talk anymore*. He smiled and clapped me on the shoulder.

"As long as it's strictly professional," he said. "I'm always here if you need me, in case things get weird."

Well, too late for that. If things got weirder than they already were, I would need a lot more than the support of a platonic *friend* to cope.

After Androu left, I went back to Quentin. He was waiting patiently, leaning against the wall. He was also giving me god-level side eye.

"Really?" he said. "You and Mr. Straightlaces?"

"Oh shut up."

"Hey, you can do whatever you want. Though you might as well go out with Erlang Shen if that's your type."

"Maybe I should," I snapped. "Erlang Shen's as good-looking as you and he's a better dresser to boot."

Quentin waved his fists rudely at me and walked away down the hall.

"He probably wouldn't show up for a date in our school uniform!" I called out.

22

SATURDAY MORNING, THE LADY OF THE CASTLE AWAITED HER chariot to the ball.

Only her castle was a parking lot so barren that not even fast-food franchises wanted to risk planting a flag nearby. The only building at this train station was a little barnlike wooden depot with padlocked doors and a dark, shadowed interior. I had been coming to this place my entire life and had never once been inside or seen the lights on.

Santa Firenza in a nutshell, folks.

I sweated under the sun, my exposed arms browning in the heat. Because of my general hawkishness on time, I ended up with a lot of moments like this, where I had nothing to do but wait for the rest of the world to catch up.

After about fifteen minutes or so, the clang of bells and an air horn announced that I was done. The northbound train was here, ready to whisk me away. A magical journey redolent with the odors of bicycle grease and blue porta-potty liquid.

Sometimes the cars could be full of rowdy pregamers rocking orange and black, gripping paper-bagged tallboys and woo-ing at each other. Today it was less crowded. I watched a man who was much shorter than me splay his legs into the aisle, putting his feet up on an opposing strut even though he could have fit perfectly well into his chair.

We stopped at every station along the way, letting me take in the landscape as it became stripmalls, then regular malls, and then stripmalls again. I could tell I was getting closer as freestanding offices bearing signage for various unicorn startups began appearing.

It took an hour and a half for the train to reach the end of the line in the city. I stepped out onto the platform and shivered. I untied my spare jacket from my waist and put it on properly. This was a different climate system entirely. Different rules.

I looked around, orienting myself under the gray sky of the city. If I strayed to the south I would be in the SoMa district, which if I understood correctly was composed entirely of loft condos and coworking offices. Following the avenues too far to the east would take me to the water's edge, where I might find the Ferry Building disgorging tourists out of its maw.

There were too many buses heading in the same direction, and I never remembered the numbered routes. Eventually I gave in and did what I always did. Follow the old Chinese people. I hopped on the line that had the most passengers carrying plastic bags and settled in for more waiting.

Public transportation among my kind is its own special hell. No bus has ever moved so slowly as it does through a Chinatown. I was pretty sure that if you needed to decelerate a photon for a physics experiment, all you had to do was throw some cardboard boxes full of dark leafy greens in the laser beam's path and let nature take over.

Eventually, the bus I was on burst through the stasis field of budget realtors, dry goods stores, and oddly terrible dim sum shops.

Upon reaching a petite, bright-green park, we swung a westward turn, both literally and figuratively.

Instead of bubble tea shops, you now had cafés that served lattes in a bowl so you could dunk your Viennoiseries easier. You had eyewear galleries that displayed three, four different frames, tops. Tiny dogs. Double strollers. "Hallelujah" (the song—the new one).

Most of all you had space. Personal space, breathing room, everywhere. On the sidewalks and in the two-bedroom apartments and in the career tracks. I didn't know if I needed that much space, but I was damn sure I'd work my ass off for it first, and then decide.

Speaking of which, my stop. I got off the bus at a plush little walkup, the brass plate reading SILVERLINE ADMISSIONS COUNSELING.

Inside the second-floor lobby I sat waiting in a pod chair surrounded by pots of bamboo. The furniture was eggshell white. The walls were eggshell white. I tried to ignore the tasteful indie rock and R&B, played low and targeted at my generation more precisely than a payload from a stealth bomber.

The door opened and it wasn't Anna who stepped out. It was a girl my age—another client.

I could tell immediately she was more put together than me. I didn't mean my appearance, though that, too. It was the way she carried herself with enough confidence and quirk and receptiveness that it could have been a sign plastered over her head: I AM WHO EVERYONE WANTS.

Her session had run to the end and might have gone over had someone not graciously noticed the clock. That's how much raw material Anna had to work with. My sessions were always punctuated by five minutes of awkward chitchat.

"Hi," the girl offered, blushing cutely. She swung her backpack over her shoulder, revealing patches from both Habitat for Humanity and Amnesty International. I was severely outclassed. What kind of scrub game had I been playing?

"Man, talking with Anna's fun but terrifying," she said, trying to start a conversation. She didn't even have the decency to be catty with me. I just wanted her to tuck her charmingly wispy curls under her beret and go, before I had to get out of my chair.

"Genie," Anna said as she bustled into the room. "So sorry, dear. Come in, come in, we're not late yet."

I sighed and stood up. The decor in the room always made me look more like a skyscraper than usual. I glanced down at the other girl. She made a cowed squeak, waved politely to Anna, and then scurried away.

■　■　■

Anna Barinov had never reacted that way to me, not even the first day we met. She was a certain kind of unflappable, a scion of old money who had forged a successful small business of her own. Insured against disaster at either end of the economic spectrum. I envied that.

I chose her from the kajillions of admissions consultants in the area because out of the ones I could afford, she had the best background. Lengthy stints as an admissions officer for several top-tier universities decorated her resume. She knew better than anyone what colleges looked for in applicants, because she had done the looking herself. Anna would provide valuable feedback as to how I could present myself as a better candidate.

That's what my Western sensibilities believed. The Chinese running through my veins said *come on*. COME ONNNN.

All those years working for the Ivy League had to have meant she'd stockpiled a nuclear arsenal of inside connections. Friends back in Cambridge and New Haven. People she could drop hints to over lunch about this one really impressive young lady she'd crossed paths with.

If that idea sounded corrupt, it was. It was *guanxi*—exerting social influence to get the outcome you needed. The grease in the gears of Asian culture. The need for networking was why so many overseas students crashed like waves against the doors of American universities in the first place—so they could make powerful, long-lasting connections.

Granted, I had little reason to believe Anna operated in this manner. But she had the power to. I told myself that maybe once I impressed her enough, she'd pull out a big red phone that went straight to Princeton.

Anna settled into her chair behind her desk, and then settled again like a falcon adjusting its wings.

"Practice essays," she said. "I believe we were looking at first revisions."

"Right," I said. I fumbled with my bag trying to get at the papers I should have already been holding. I handed them over with only a few extra creases.

Anna began scanning the first of my essays, and already I was starting to get uncomfortable with how fast her eyes were moving. Was she even reading the sentences? Couldn't she at least *pretend* not to skim?

And then she was done. A month's worth of work consumed in

thirty seconds. Maybe that was what the supposed time difference between Heaven and Earth felt like.

"Well, given that your initial draft was you listing your statistical performance at various activities, I'd be lying if I said this version wasn't an improvement."

"But it's still not good enough," I said.

"Genie, we talked about this. You only have one chance to tell the admissions board who you really are."

"I didn't do that? I thought I did that."

"What you've done is address the prompts directly, word for word," she said. "But there has to be an underlying current of your personality. A cohesive story of who you are."

These conversations always left me frustrated. I didn't know how to do this kind of doublespeak in real life, and I sure as hell didn't understand how to do it in six hundred fifty words or fewer.

It didn't help that this portion of the application infuriated me on a fundamental level. The message that I got from these drills was that I wasn't a real person. Not by default. My humanity had to be proved with a vague test where "getting it" meant everything and hard work meant nothing. It was the Way, and I couldn't see past the tortoises and snakes to grasp it.

"I could write about the time I fought a demon," I said out of sheer frustration.

"A personal demon?" said Anna.

"No, a Chinese demon. An actual monster. Yaoguai, they call them."

Anna pursed her lips. "I didn't know those still existed."

"They do, and they're back in a big way. The first one I saw was this big ugly SOB who tried to eat me alive. I kicked his ass pretty bad."

"Hmmm. There could be some traction there."

This was the first hint of excitement I'd gotten out of Anna. I leaned back in my chair and put my feet up on her desk, buoyed by my newfound confidence.

"I've fought other demons, too," I boasted. "Just recently I beat up a bunch of shape-shifting lions. It was easy once I started using my magic powers."

Anna was so pleased with me she began grinning like a maniac. "Well, there's your angle. In fact, I'm pretty sure Brown offers a guaranteed full scholarship for their new demon-slaying track."

"*Pfft.* We can do better than Brown." I picked a tropical umbrella drink off her bar cart and sipped it through the crazy straw. "That's like the caboose of the Ivy train."

"You're right, Genie. What you deserve is some kind of joint program along with some merit fellowship grant money to do with as you please. All the grant money in fact. You deserve it all."

"Aw, let's leave a few bucks on the table for the other meritorious fellows."

"You're so kind, Genie. Genie? Genie?"

■ ■ ■

"Genie?" Anna said. "Are you okay?"

I blinked. Someone calling me kind was too much to believe, even for a daydream.

"The story of me," I parroted.

"Try this exercise," Anna said. "Completely ignore the essay prompts and word limits for now. Write about yourself however you can, with your thoughts, your feelings, some personal anecdotes. Get something down on paper first, and then we'll refine it from there.

"*Who is Genie Lo?*" she said, wiggling her fingers. "That's what the admissions board wants to know."

There is no Genie Lo, I wanted to shout. Not the kind that lived prettily in air-quotes. There was a sixteen-year-old girl from the Bay who answered to that name, but there wasn't some sparkling magic nugget underneath that I could dig up, polish, and put on display.

I swallowed my pride and smiled.

"I think I get it," I said. "I'll have a better draft next time."

■ ■ ■

I left Anna's completely fried, but that wasn't anything new. I bought two coffees from the café next door that was too fancy to sell a "large" and chugged one immediately. The other I took into the cab with me.

The taxi was a waste of money, but in my current state I couldn't handle getting back on a bus. The driver took a different route downtown through the financial district, which was mostly empty on the weekend. We pulled up to a building that only looked like a bank. The second half of today's trip.

I opened the door to the gym and was immediately greeted by the latest remix of the latest EDM hit. The girl behind the counter who tagged members' badges with a bar code reader smiled and waved me on by.

It wasn't crowded, not on a weekend afternoon. The gym was

gigantic—an orchard of pulleys and benches—but I found him in the corner wiping chalk off the barbell grips. I tapped him on the shoulder and he turned.

"Hi, Dad."

My father beamed and gave me a big hug.

Then, without so much as a word, he held up his hands. I grabbed them and we began trying to twist each other's arms off, laughing the whole time.

I don't know when playing Mercy became our standard greeting, but I did know that he hadn't won in a very long time. Dad wasn't much bigger than Mom.

As soon as I'd bent his wrists beyond ninety degrees, he squawked, "I give, I give!" I let go and he shook his hands out. "I don't remember you being that strong last month."

"Coach Daniels has us doing grip training now," I said. "We squeeze tennis balls."

"They've got a class here like that for the rock climbers. You should see the new wall they're planning. *Shhoop.* Goes all the way to the top."

I listened to him enthusiastically describe the various improvements going on at the gym as if he were an owner and not part of the cleaning staff. Business must have surged again recently, the energy rubbing off on him. It was good to see him like this.

My father was born the same year as my mother, but you wouldn't have known it from looking at him. He was the portrait of Dorian Gray that took all the slings and arrows of Time bouncing off Mom's youthful skin. Only his still-dark hair kept his weathered face from looking painfully old for his age.

Dad was a specimen that not many people saw out in the open, or at least admitted to seeing. He was a failure. An abysmal, no-bones-about-it failure. One of the worst things you could be in this era.

My family used to be slightly more prosperous. That's not saying much, but it was a meaningful difference, a trip to Disneyland's worth, perhaps. Dad used to work at an insurance company when I was very little. He had a modest, nondescript career, but a career nonetheless.

Until one day, to hear Mom tell the story, he decided he was too good to work for someone else. He quit his job, took out a loan, and opened a furniture store, like an idiot.

In Dad's version it was a calculated risk, an attempt to get the better life that his wife had always passive-aggressively demanded. He'd carry cheap inventory in parts and assemble it with the help of cheap employees and sell it to cheap customers. A foolproof plan.

I have memories of the store. The desks that smelled like dust no matter how much they'd been spritzed with lemon. A whole series of glass coffee tables that only came in octagons. I used to run between the aisles of the showroom, before I learned not to by way of a splinter the size of a toothpick buried in my cheek.

There's nothing worse than just enough success. The store was a slow death that took years to metastasize, sucking in more and more of Dad's money and soul. He tried everything, including going upscale in a brief, costly branding experiment. All he learned was that reinventing yourself was not something people allowed you to do very often.

Once the writing was on the wall, Mom refused to work the

register anymore. She had to get a job somewhere else to make ends meet, or so she said. Dad thought it was a betrayal. They grew heated and icy with each other in ways that didn't cancel out.

After the store was liquidated at great loss—after we were thoroughly ruined—he left the house. Or was kicked out. It didn't matter. His ability to interact with other people in a professional environment had deteriorated to the point where it was even worse than Mom's. He wasn't getting any kind of old job back.

Especially given that he had no higher education. My father had never gone to college.

■　■　■

When Mom told me he was living in the city on his own, I'd imagined the worst. A squalid apartment in a bad neighborhood. Unable to make ends meet. Drinking.

When I finally saw him after the split, he told me that I'd been spot-on. But only for the first few months or so of his exile.

At his lowest point, after he'd given up all hope for his continued existence, he'd taken a walk that brought him past this gym. The door had been open, blaring *untz-untz* beats into the sidewalk. He'd peered inside, confused by the sculpted bodies and clanging iron.

The one thing he understood was the Now Hiring sign. On impulse he asked about it. Perhaps also on impulse, the young things on duty at the time took him onboard as the newest member of the CleanUp PowerDown Crew.

It probably saved his life. He was a middle-aged person doing an entry-level job, sure, but no one asked questions, no one wondered how it came to this for him. Perhaps that was due to condescension, everyone assuming that a minority sweeping up was the natural state of affairs.

But the trainers and therapists treated him with kindness, and he found he'd missed that very much. He had a wage and people to talk to. The elements of sanity.

And thus it was, up to this day. I liked visiting him here, where he was happy. And truthfully, he looked better each time. The employees had a good health plan and were allowed to use the equipment during off hours. He'd put on a little muscle for his age.

"How's Mom?" he asked.

"Same." I couldn't think of a whole lot of news. About her, at least. "She entertained for some school friends. Got really into it, too."

"Good. No better medicine when it comes to your mother."

That reminded me that I had to have Quentin and his "parents" over again sometime. For Mom's sake. I could stomach the embarrassment to see her cheered again.

"And how about you?" he asked.

"Honestly? Not good. I feel very . . . put upon these days. You ever get people telling you to do things you don't want to do? Ordering you around?"

I realized that was a dumb question right after I asked it. I'd forgotten where we were, and thought I'd set him up to complain about the downsides of his current job. But he surprised me.

"I remember back at the insurance company I had a chain of

bosses who were pretty awful," Dad said. "They wouldn't give you a reason for their decisions, and everything that went wrong was your fault, not theirs. It's hard to work for those kinds of folks.

"I know you're capable of handling anything life throws at you," he went on. "But you shouldn't feel forced into a situation. Nothing good will come of it."

He didn't press me on who or what was bothering me, which was exactly what I was counting on.

I never had to get into specifics with Dad. He and I could have whole conversations without proper nouns. I mean, sure, his disregard for details probably contributed heavily to the shattering of our household, but for the moment I was grateful to not have to go deeper than I needed about gods. Or college.

"In this case, I should probably go along with it," I said. "It's actually pretty important that I do."

"Then it's an easy decision, right?" Dad said. "You have to pick and choose your battles. Fight too much and you'll wear yourself out."

Dad smiled at me. "You take everything so seriously. You're still young, you know? I feel like I have to remind you every so often or you'd forget. Your future's not going to be set in stone because of what happens today."

His certainty, the same certainty that had gotten him into so much trouble, flowed out to me like a balm. He couldn't conceive of my failure, of my unhappiness. All my faults lay buried deep within his mile-wide blind spots, where I could pretend they didn't exist.

I didn't love my dad more than my mom. But it was hard not to think of him as my favorite person in the world sometimes.

"Is that who I think it is?" said a booming voice behind us.

I turned to see two of the gym's trainers—Brian and K-Song—quickstep over.

"Miss Loooo!" Brian hooted. "Whaddup whaddup?"

I traded high fives with the two bros like we were three bros. They knew me from previous visits.

"Hot damn, girl, you're even taller than I remember!" K-Song said.

"She's a beanpole!" Brian roared. "We got to get you in the cage! Strong is the new skinny! A lady with your length could be putting up two plates!"

I laughed. Brian always said the same thing every time I visited. He was a great proponent of women lifting heavy, but he had a hard time convincing the clientele. His biker beard and tattooed cannonball shoulders probably scared them off. Sleek, hairless K-Song was more trusted by the ladies.

These two random coworkers of my dad's were oddly the only people I didn't get pissed at for commenting on my body. They were meatheads, sure, but they were the most well-meaning, least snarky meatheads I knew. They thought of my flesh purely in terms of its output and potential.

"I got your pops pulling one-thirty," K-Song bragged. He slapped Dad on the shoulder. "New PR."

"*Pfft.* One-thirty *sumo*," Brian said, rolling his eyes.

"IPF legal, dickbag!" K-Song shouted back. "Get with the times!"

The two started arguing viciously about the merits of different deadlift techniques. It would be resolved around the same time as the heat death of the universe.

I turned to my dad. "I'm gonna go."

"Give my best to Mom," he said, his eyes shining at me.

I rushed forward and gave my father one last hug. I would see him again soon. In the meantime, it would be back to trying my hardest not to turn out anything like him.

23

I LEFT THE GYM AND WENT AROUND THE CORNER TO WHERE Quentin was waiting. It wasn't him stalking me—in a moment of weakness, I'd called him during the cab ride after leaving Anna's and he promised he could meet me soon, regardless of the distance. Better to think about demons than my future.

I laughed as I walked up to him. He'd taken some of my advice to heart. He was still wearing his school uniform, but with a gigantic chunky candy-cane-striped scarf around his neck and shoulders.

"What?" he said. "It was cold."

The look actually worked, in a Tokyo-street-fashion sort of way. Another instance of beautiful people looking beautiful, no matter what.

"I was waiting at Viscount and Second," Quentin groused. "You told me the wrong address."

"This is *New* Viscount and Second, and no I didn't. Anyway, I've been thinking. I have a theory about you and where you come from."

"Which is?"

"Scientists say once it becomes possible to create computer simulations of reality, simulated universes will vastly outnumber real ones," I said. "Heaven and Earth are both virtual realities. Beings like you and Guanyin use different number values for things like gravity and light, so when you're inserted into the Earth simulation, you bring your own laws of physics into localized surroundings. That's how you do magic."

Quentin raised an eyebrow.

"It explains everything," I argued. "Earth time passes faster because our clock speed is faster. Reincarnation is when the source code for a person is pasted into a different era."

"That is the nerdiest thing I have ever heard," Quentin said. "Even coming from you."

I shrugged. He wasn't wrong.

"I have a theory about you, too." He brought his hands out from behind his back. In one he held a cup of bubble tea he'd already finished drinking, and in the other was a coffee.

"Thanks, but I've already had some."

"Have more. I want your heart racing."

I took the still-hot cup from him and sniffed it gingerly. It smelled divine. "This is for your theory?"

"Yes. I may have taken the wrong approach with your training by asking you to attain stillness."

The coffee tasted like rainy mountains and toasted honey. I'd have to ask him where he got it.

"Yours is a power born of battle," Quentin said as I drank. "Rage. Bloodlust."

"Way to make me sound like a monster."

"You're as much of a monster as I am. The only times your power has manifested so far have been when you were absolutely furious. We shouldn't run away from that. We should embrace it."

"That is the complete opposite of everything you've told me, and everything I've read about gongfu."

"That's because most teachers and disciples are focused on the aspects of soft power. Wavy, flowing soft power that redirects instead of confronts. There's hard power, too. The kind that moves in straight lines and overcomes instead of giving way. It's just as valid and just as essential.

"In my hands you were the living embodiment of hard power," Quentin continued. He looked nostalgic. "We'll double down on that instead of trying to suppress it."

"Won't that throw my *yin* and *yang* energies off balance? I thought balance was an important concept."

"Screw balance," he said. "What are you, old?"

I grinned and banked our empty cups into a nearby recycling can. No I was not.

Quentin motioned me into the alleyway where no one could see us. He held out his arms.

"Hop on."

"What?"

"I'm going to hold you for a moment, as an exercise. Carry you."

I shook my head. He was acting like he wanted me draped across his arms bridal-style but wasn't considering our relative proportions. I would have dangled all the way down past his knees.

"Will you stop fighting me on every single little thing and get in my arms?" he hissed. "I have to lift you up completely for this to work! Just trust me for once!"

Well fine, if he was going to be pouty about it. I spun him around, ignoring his protests, and made him lean over so I could get on top of him piggyback.

This wasn't much better. I had to straighten my legs out to the side and hold them there or else my soles would've touched the ground. I felt like I was riding a child's tricycle downhill.

Quentin shifted me around for a better grip as easily as if I were a sack of feathers. Unfortunately his hands landed where they weren't supposed to.

"Hey!" I yelped. "You're grabbing my aaaaAAAAAAAAHHHH!"

Then we disappeared into the sky.

24

"AAAAAAAAAHAHAHAHAHA!"

The ground shot away from Quentin's feet. It looked like that footage from NASA launches where the camera's mounted at the top, pointed downward, and you can see the coils of fire and thrust pushing you higher and higher. Only this was a million times faster, and there was no smoke to obscure the view of the rapidly shrinking Earth.

Street, block, district, peninsula. I screamed as each gave way to the next. The wind stung the tears right out of my eyes. I probably should have died of fright right there on his back. It would have served him right if I voided myself on top of him.

But somewhere, probably right around the time I recognized we were passing over Fisherman's Wharf, the terror turned to joy. The first plunge of the roller coaster wasn't going to kill me, and I was free to whoop and holler to my heart's content.

We were doing a slow turn as we traveled. The world gradually flipped upside down and then right side up in an astronaut's sunrise. Quentin was doing one big somersault.

That meant we were going to descend now. I clutched him tighter as a thrill went through my body. Maybe we would die after all, smashed against the Earth so hard there wouldn't be anything left. We were about to find out.

I thought Quentin was going for some kind of water landing before the rusty red towers of the bridge came into view. I braced for impact, but he did not.

His feet slammed into the painted iron and stuck without moving an inch, a perfect 10.0 landing. The sudden stop should have liquefied my internal organs. The impact should have sent a bell-like clang throughout the platform. But neither happened.

Localized laws of physics, I told myself.

"We're here," said Quentin.

I didn't get off him. Instead I clapped his chest excitedly.

"Again!" I shouted. "Again! Let's go to Wine Country!"

He dumped me on my feet. "This isn't a joyride. We're here to train."

"Nerd." I flicked his ear, making a little clack against what used to be my jewelry.

We were alone high up in the gray sky. I knew they let people go to the top of the bridge on occasion, so the platform wasn't without the trappings of safety. But I was still heady from the way we'd arrived, making the red tower feel like uncharted alien territory. Olympus Mons.

"Look around and tell me what you see," he said.

"I see the city. The Bay."

"Good. Now open your eyes and tell me again."

I did as told before realizing the incongruity.

■　■　■

The landscape suddenly became a painting, full of bright brush-strokes and swirling pigments. I could see the details of the world in thick outlines of color and black. My sense of scale was limitless, unconfined. The daubed-on windows of the smallest building were as visible to me as the tallest spires of the city.

"Oh wow," I murmured.

Cars in motion danced across the bridge like flipbook animations. I could see inside to the passengers, their faces zoetroping between emotions. That man was hungry. That woman was bored. That child held a secret.

I felt as if I could touch things on the far side of the Bay. Farther. I was hemmed in only by the Sierra Nevada and the western horizon.

I glanced at Quentin, and then stared. He blazed like a golden bonfire.

Energy poured off him in licking waves, an act of inefficient combustion that leaked so much power into the air I could hear the atmosphere whine and sizzle. There was a scorching heat at his core, and I was immune to it.

Around his shoulders was the faintest palimpsest overlay of another form. Skin as hard as diamonds. Fur as soft as velvet. A face of becalmed savagery. He was magnificent. Godlike. A Buddha victorious in battle.

"Well," he said in two voices, one his normal classroom baritone and the other a bass that could crack the sky. "Do you have anything to say?"

"Yeah. Did you put something in my coffee?"

Quentin laughed, and I could have sworn they heard him in New York.

"No. The only magic there is that it was expensive. You have true sight now, Genie. Technically you have *my* true sight. I used to be able to see the world like you can right now, but that's mostly gone. My guess is that our powers had become so intertwined in the old days that when you became human, you ripped this one from me like dirt clinging to a stump."

"I am genuinely sorry then," I said. It would have felt like a tragedy if I had to give this experience up to someone else, and I'd only had it for seconds.

"Try the lie detection," Quentin said. "It's pretty neat."

"Well, you have to tell me a lie then."

He blanked for a bit, one of those understandable moments where you have too many options to choose from.

"I hate you," he finally settled on.

As Quentin said it a dark, metallic bubble popped out from his lips, like he'd blown it from mercury. It pulsed in the air, a tiny opaque jellyfish, before floating away and dissipating.

"That's freaky," I said. "I don't think I'd want to know all the time if people were lying to me."

"It'll come in handy at some point, trust me."

I went back to drinking in the view. It was moving artwork, zooming and flattening where I wanted it to for my inspection. I watched a container ship full of almonds and canned tomatoes steam away into the distant Pacific. One of the crew members was bluffing his ass off in a poker game, holding nothing but unsuited low cards.

I turned toward land, drawn by a column of smoke. The wildfires in the scrubby hills north of the city were no closer to being put out than when I'd first heard about them on the news. The black whorls looked more like a series of opaque screens than vapor, blocking out anything behind them.

"You should try looking at yourself," Quentin said.

My eyes were starting to get tired, but I held my hands up in front of my face. As I wiggled my fingers, rippling lines of pressure played out in the air, almost like a topographical map or an artist's rendition of sound waves.

"That's how I recognized you," Quentin said. "Guanyin and Erlang Shen, too. Out of the billions of humans that have come and gone since the old days, only you have an aura as steady and unshakable as that. Just like the Ruyi Jingu Bang."

I watched one of the bigger pulses travel from my skin across the distance until it made contact with Quentin's erratic inner fire. Rather than clashing, the two energy signatures meshed with each other to become brighter. Stronger. On some fundamental level, Quentin and I harmonized.

Then the waves vanished. My vision reverted back to normal.

"Ow," I said, fighting back the ache in my corneas. "Is there a time limit on this thing?"

"Sort of. It's extremely difficult to sustain if you're not used to it. You'll have to build up your endurance through practice."

"Oh my god, everything is always practice, practice, practice with you Asians."

Quentin laughed, and then suddenly hiccuped. His whole body began shaking like a phone on vibrate. He dropped to one knee and clamped his hands to the platform we were standing on in order to steady himself.

"Jeez, it wasn't that funny," I said. "Is there something wrong?"

Quentin wriggled his shoulders back and forth to clear the spasms. "The magic in the earrings is going off. There must be a yaoguai within striking distance of a human."

"Where?"

He pointed to the south. "Somewhere over there. The feeling is stronger on that side of my body."

"That's as much resolution as you get from those things? That's barely better than a grandpa saying it'll rain because his trick knee's gone all a-tingly."

"Well, Guanyin said they're meant to be an early warning signal, not a map with GPS."

I leaned on top of Quentin, using him like a tripod over his protests. Turning true sight back on was surprisingly easy, merely a matter of knowing there was an extra level of vision available to me and then concentrating until I got there. I didn't know how I was supposed to pick out a demon from the rest of the visual noise, but once I started looking in the direction Quentin was pointing, the answer made itself pretty clear.

A blip appeared that was both brighter and darker than anything else around it—a smear of white ash on top of black soot. I was able to zoom in farther by instinctively squinting.

The flare was coming from inside an industrial building. What industry I didn't know; something that involved large gray tanks and a jungle of pipes next to a broad warehouse. Judging from its state of disrepair and the long weeds growing around the entrance, the facility should have been completely abandoned. But the eerie, colorless light moved from room to room in the pattern of something alive.

I realized why I was having such a hard time making out the source's silhouette. It didn't have one. It was a translucent skeleton, completely fleshless. My eyes kept passing through the spaces between its ribs.

"Quentin," I said, thoroughly weirded out by the apparition.

"Do you have any friends who are skeletons?"

"Skeletons? Is that what you're seeing?"

"I see one skeleton," I said. "Kind of floating around, pacing back and forth. It's giving off light like you do, except without any color or brightness. Am I even making sense?"

Quentin's grim expression alone told me yes, unfortunately I was. "Baigujing. The White Bone Demon. Don't let her out of your sight."

Watching the yaoguai waltz to and fro unnerved me beyond the fact that its appearance was firmly lodged at the bottom of the uncanny valley. I felt like a vulnerable Peeping Tom. In horror movies, the person trying to watch the monster through a telescope is usually moments away from biting it.

"What do we do now?" I asked. "Do we . . . do we go get her?"

"*Hell* no. We sit our asses down and think of a plan."

I was so surprised at his tone, I nearly looked away from Baigujing, but he reached up and propped my chin back into place.

"I'm serious," he said. "She's bad news—extremely bad. I don't think we're ready for her yet. Find whatever human she's lurking too close to and then we can make sure their paths don't cross."

I looked around the edges of the factory for a night watchman or a delinquent tagger sneaking onto the property. Nothing. The demon didn't look like she was hunting down any intruders.

Wait.

She wasn't pacing back and forth. She was walking around in a circle, her eyeless gaze fixed on a small shape on the center of the floor.

A little girl of five, looking too scared to cry.

. . .

"Damn it!" I screamed. "Damn it damn it damn it! There's a kid with her! Like *with* her!"

"What?" Quentin sprang to his feet and nearly clocked me in the jaw with his skull. "How did she get her hands on a human so fast?"

"I don't know, but we have to get there now!"

"I don't know where 'there' is!" You're the only one who can see her from this distance!"

I grabbed Quentin's shoulders and pointed him toward the derelict building. "I'll guide you! Just start jumping!"

Quentin made a handhold for me to climb on his back. "You have to give me some indication of where I'm trying to land!"

"About half the distance to my house, but in this direction! Go, damn it!"

Quentin and I took to the sky. The natural curve of his leap made it easy to fixate on our target while we sped through the air. The skeleton had stopped wandering and was now crouching directly in front of the catatonic child, contemplating. Any number of thoughts bounced inside its empty, polished skull.

"Hurry up!" I shouted into Quentin's ear.

"We're not flying! I can't change direction or speed in midair!"

I cursed, and then cursed again even louder as we overshot. "That factory we just passed!" I yelled. "Second floor, the biggest room!"

"I saw it," Quentin grunted. "Hold on."

We came down in an empty municipal baseball diamond that might have been in the same town as the factory. Quentin took the landing much harder than on the bridge. We slammed into the ground, gouging up fountains of dirt and grass. Before the debris even settled, Quentin had us back in the air, on a smaller arc in the opposite direction.

This leg of our journey took much less time. As the building loomed near, Quentin stuck out an arm to act as a battering ram. I buried my face in his shoulder as we made impact with one of the huge glass windows.

I heard us burst through and land on the other side as easily as if it were a pane of sugar. Quentin held my head down while shards tinkled around us, to make sure I didn't catch an eyeful.

Once it was safe he patted my knee. I got up and took a measure of our surroundings.

The hall we were in had been stripped of equipment a long time ago. Exposed I-beams buttressed walls of cinderblock that had never been painted. The dust under our feet was thick enough to pass for light snowfall.

I found the child in the center of the open space. She looked scared out of her wits, but whole.

Standing over her in a flowing evening gown was a beautiful, shapely woman. With no lips. They were simply missing. Her teeth, otherwise perfect, lay bare to the world, giving her the same insouciant smirk as a poison bottle.

She reached out and brushed a nail down the little girl's cheek. A razor line of blood followed it, and the girl cried out in pain.

"Get away from her!" I shrieked.

"Or what?" said the demon. "I'm not afraid of either of you."

Her voice was like nothing so much as a pepper grinder. She compensated for her liplessness by rolling her tongue to make certain sounds, the same way a ventriloquist did.

"Now or never," Quentin said to me.

"Now."

I ran straight at Baigujing. Whatever magical toughness had protected me from being cut to ribbons by a plate-glass window would have to do. Quentin got clever and flickered off to the side, rounding the demon to hit her in the flank.

Unfortunately for us, I got there first. My wild, untrained punch met Baigujing right in the center of her chest, but she went limp and weightless the split second before, offering no resistance. She and I tumbled together a few steps before disentangling.

Quentin had the wherewithal to change his target. He scooped up the kid and wrapped her in his scarf. Then he leapt out of the window.

"Looks like you've been abandoned," Baigujing said.

I nearly smiled; Quentin had only done exactly what he should have. I just needed to stall until he got back from putting the child somewhere safe. I raised my hands like I knew how to fight, hoping that Big Joe's "don't mess with me" stance from the self-defense class was a good enough bluff.

This was it. I was facing off against a demon. For real this time, with no blind rage to act as a crutch. There was a clarity to every second that passed while I was guarding a life other than my own. I felt pure. Unassailable.

Not in the literal sense, though, because Baigujing advanced upon me steadily. She was either being unnecessarily wary or she was toying with me.

"We can wait until the monkey gets back," she said. "If you'd like."

"Sure." I jabbed at her eyes and missed. That must only work when they aren't expecting it.

The demon tutted. "You've got to put your weight behind it, or else there's no point. I've taken blows from you and the monkey at full strength."

"Here's another." Quentin reappeared and delivered a flying knee to the side of her head.

Baigujing's body rumpled and pinwheeled away. She righted herself, hardly any worse for wear.

"Displace," she intoned, making the motions for a spell.

"Oh no, you don't." Quentin lunged at her to interrupt it.

But he didn't succeed. In fact, he didn't even come close to Baigujing. He dove in the wrong direction by more than ninety degrees.

"What the hell?" Quentin was unable to believe the extent to which he'd whiffed. He flailed in the empty air and tried to lay hands on her again, but he ended up running in a new angle that was equally bonkers.

Baigujing hadn't moved at all, from my perspective. She must have screwed with Quentin's eyes. There was no telling what kind of illusion he was seeing at the moment.

"Can you hear me?" I asked him. "I can see her but I'm not sure if she's real or—"

The demon crossed the distance between us in one step and backhanded me all the way into the wall.

Okay, I thought through the smear of pain that was my spine hitting the bricks. *Guess she's real.*

I keeled over on my hands and knees, gasping for breath. I saw Baigujing's bare feet stop in front of me.

She nudged me in the chin with her toe. "Your turn," she said.

I planted myself, a sprinter in a starting block, and slugged her as hard as I could in the stomach. I could feel her flesh wrap around my fist without taking any of the punch. It was like trying to fight a plastic bag floating in the breeze.

Baigujing smiled at me. She had to use her eyes to do it. She grabbed me by the jaw and bent me backward, squeezing hard enough that I couldn't speak.

"You're not going to get anywhere like that," she said. "I met the monkey for the first time while disguised as a human. He knew I was up to no good, though, and struck me with the Ruyi Jingu Bang with all his might. I survived unharmed. Do you know how rare that is, to be able to shrug off direct hits from the Monkey King? I feel like I'm not appreciated enough for that."

I glanced over at Quentin, who was still chasing shadows.

"The funny thing is, after he struck me I left behind a body of flesh to make it look like he'd murdered an innocent girl," Baigujing giggled. "You should have seen how Xuanzang punished him for that one! The beast that threatened Heaven, rolling in the dust, clutching his head and pleading for mercy. I laughed for weeks!"

I didn't know how I had any nerves left to touch, but she found them. I took her by the hair with one hand. She merely grinned, figuring I was going to punch her with the other.

But instead I used my grip to swing my legs around and wrap up her neck and shoulders. My ankles found each other and I squeezed Baigujing with every ounce of strength I had left.

I was ripping a page from Quentin's playbook. Judging from the demon's howl, it was a good one.

She clawed frantically at my face but couldn't reach. My body was simply too long. I had her locked up with all the time in the world.

What did Quentin do next to the Demon King of Confusion? I wondered, my thoughts surprisingly cold-blooded. *Oh yeah. This.* I took hold of Baigujing's skull with impunity and began cranking her neck.

"Aaagh!" she hissed. "Ugly girl! Ugly, ugly girl!"

Really? We were going to do that now?

"Yeah, well . . . you're overdressed," I said. I squeezed tighter and heard something crack.

Through the cloud of adrenaline fogging my brain, an idea slipped through like a ray of light. I closed my eyes and reopened them with true sight on. Baigujing was a skeleton once more, her muscle and skin invisible under my X-ray vision.

"Where's Red Boy?" I bellowed. "Tell me, and I'll spare your life!" I didn't know if I was strong enough to dictate either way; but it sounded like the type of thing you said when you had a monster in a headlock.

Baigujing froze. But only for an instant. She began trembling in my grasp and making the most hideous noise. I almost let go out of fear before I realized she was simply laughing.

"I'll never tell you," she said. "Nothing you can do will ever make me tell you."

There were no lie bubbles. Either she didn't know or she really wasn't going to say. So much for my idea.

"Spare my life?" she sneered. "You don't have what it takes to end me. The instant you slip, I'll find that child and rip the meat from her *bones*!"

Still no bubbles. "Come again?" I said.

"I'll kill her and every other miserable human I get my hands on! I will turn this town into a sea of *corpses*! You will *swim* to me in dead flesh!"

The air was clear. If I let her go she'd do her best to make good on her threat.

"I can't be killed by the likes of you!" Baigujing roared. "Do you hear me? You can't kill me!"

Bubble.

"Don't tell me what I can't do," I said. I arched back and snapped her in two.

Unlike the Demon King of Confusion's slow melt, Baigujing burst into ink and nothingness like a popped balloon. I nearly hit my head on the floor as a result of her body's vanishing act. I flailed and spat away the black inky liquid that I thought would be covering me, only to find that it was already gone.

I closed my eyes and shook the true sight out of my head. With it went all the rush that had been keeping me afloat.

It felt as if I'd been run over by a dozen trucks. My body hurt where I'd been hit, sure, but I also seemed to have self-torn every muscle fiber I had.

One down, ninety-nine to go, I thought to myself. If the remaining bottles of beer on the wall were going to be similarly hard, then I did not like my chances of emerging unscathed from this mess.

I staggered over to Quentin, who was only now coming out of his daze.

"Way to be useful, chief," I deadpanned, slapping my hand on his shoulder. I kept it there for support, so I didn't topple over in the next breeze.

Quentin scrunched his eyes. "I could see you two, but you were always just out of reach."

He draped my arm over his neck and dragged me to the stairs. We took each step slowly.

"To think you beat her completely on your own," he said. "You were amazing."

"I was lucky. You have got to teach me wushu. I can't handle not knowing what to do in these situations."

"I keep telling you, I don't know any formal martial arts. If you want these fights to get any easier, we should work on shape-changing you back into a staff so I can wield you like I used to."

I smacked him on the chest with my load-bearing arm.

"That's gross," I said. "*Wield* me? No."

"We did it all the time back in the day! It would only be temporary."

"I'm not transforming into anything else. If everything you've told me is true, then I must have worked my ass off as the Ruyi Jingu Bang in order to get a human body. I'm not throwing it away just so you have a blunt object to beat on people with."

Quentin grumbled but gave up the argument. At least for the moment. He took me to the first floor, a much smaller room. The little girl sat in the corner on a pile of rubber hose, nervously chewing on his scarf.

She saw us and burst into tears. I kneeled in front of her and tried to pat her head soothingly. The cut on her cheek was clean and not too deep. Other than that she wasn't injured.

"*La llorona,*" the girl sobbed. "*La llorona.*"

Crud. "*Uh, todo bien,*" I said. "*Nosotros . . . ganamos? Todo bien, todo bien.*"

Quentin picked the girl up and hushed her, swinging gently back and forth. She calmed down immediately. I'd forgotten how much of a wizard he was with children.

"La mala mujer se ha ido," he murmured. *"Ella ha sido derro-tado. Vamos a traer a tu mama. Duerme ahora, preciosa."*

The girl nodded into his shoulder and fell asleep.

I gave Quentin a look. He shot one back.

"What?" he said. "I talk to non-Chinese people too, you know."

25

I DON'T REMEMBER HOW I GOT HOME AFTER WE SNUCK THE girl into the fire station. I don't remember how we did that without getting caught, either. Events were lost in a haze of exhaustion.

Mom usually gave me some wiggle room on when I returned from the city due to the vagaries of public transportation, but this evening was pushing it. I was only able to end her angry harangue by telling her I had run into Quentin on the walk back through town and stopped to chat. Her hypocrisy between me hanging out with "boys" as a vague concept versus an individual boy she knew and liked was astounding.

I ate a reheated dinner, showered any remaining demon residue off my skin, and collapsed in bed. I would never leave my mattress again.

But I couldn't sleep.

I slipped my hand out from the mound of covers and groped around for the replacement clamshell phone I'd been forced to use after Quentin crushed my real one. There was a message from my dad, just his usual ping about how glad he was to see me. There were status updates from Yunie trailing into a long, one-sided thread that made me laugh. She knew that I went into the city for these appointments and wasn't always online.

I scrolled past all of the messages and dialed Quentin while lying on my side. We were going full middle-school.

"What's up?" he said.

It was noisy on his end. "Why is it noisy on your end?"

"I'm at a casino off the highway."

"What?" I had to stop myself from speaking at full volume so as not to wake up Mom. "Why?"

"I'm earning money. I need cash to fit in and move around human society. Plus I don't need as much sleep as you do, and it's a decent way to kill time."

It shouldn't have been weird that he was blowing off steam by gambling; there were more ads for the local casinos written in Chinese than in English. But his teasing from before had been on point. It did feel strange, knowing that he did things without me.

"Did you just want to talk?" he asked.

I didn't have an answer. As cheesy as it was, maybe I simply wanted to know that I could hear him and that he could hear me, for a while.

"What's Heaven like?" I said to break the silence. "Is it nice?"

"It's very nice. Everything about Heaven is nice. There is nothing ugly, sick, or out of place in Heaven."

Whoops. From the shift in his voice I could tell we had started off heavy for a simple chitchat.

"Being allowed inside was everything I wanted for a very long time," he said. "When they let me through the door, I thought I would finally become content. At peace with myself. And then . . . well, you know what happened. Technically you were there, even if you don't remember it."

If the legend was true, then I'd been the instrument of the

Monkey King's wrath in Heaven after he realized he was nothing but a second-class citizen among the gods. The moral of the tale was probably supposed to be that patience and good manners were more important than power. But what I took from it was that the people in charge could withhold respect from you, and there wasn't a damn thing you could do about it.

"Can I see Heaven? Can you take me there?"

"Absolutely not," Quentin said sharply. "It's too dangerous for a normal person born of Earth. Your base humanity would be scorched away by the excess of *qi* energies, leaving only your spiritual essence behind. Genie Lo would be gone, and only the Ruyi Jingu Bang would remain. Forever."

"That's not what you would prefer? You'd get to fight with your stick like you used to, without any backtalk."

"Don't twist my words. Even if I took you to Heaven now, any powers you haven't recovered in your current human form would be lost forever. You've got strength and true sight, sure, but there are still a few tricks you haven't remembered yet."

"Well, if you didn't want your magic iron staff back immediately when we first met, what exactly were you hoping for when you came to my school?"

Quentin sighed and took a sip of some unknown drink, the ice cubes clinking against his glass.

"I was hoping you'd recognize an old friend," he said. "I assumed the memories would come rushing back and you'd be so happy to see me that you'd take my hand right there in class and I don't know . . . we'd run off and have an adventure or something. Go exploring, like back in the day."

"Ha! You wanted to sweep me off my feet. Dork."

I could practically hear him blush through the receiver.

"I'm going." His voice was adorably gruff. "You're distracting me. I'm down seven thousand bucks because of you."

I bolted upright. "You're fooling around with *that* kind of money?"

Quentin laughed in my ear and hung up on me.

■ ■ ■

School felt a little weird the next day. People stared at me like they knew something.

I wandered around from class to class until I caught up with Yunie at lunch. When she saw me she covered her mouth trying not to laugh.

"What is it?"

"Are you trying out a new look?" she asked.

The answer was no. I'd slept like the dead, and ended up having to run to make it on time without washing up. But half the school came in looking like slobs. I couldn't have been much worse.

Yunie pulled out her compact mirror and held it up. I peered into it until I found what didn't belong.

My irises were gold. Shimmering gold.

"You shouldn't leave those in overnight and forget," Yunie said. "It's bad for your eyes. But I like the color."

Shining, 24-karat eyes. Ten-year-old me would have been thrilled beyond belief.

Sixteen-year-old me had to go find Quentin.

■ ■ ■

"Well, of course," Quentin said. "My eyes turned gold when I gained true sight in Lao Tze's furnace. I'd be worried if yours *weren't* gold."

We were outside, near the away team's end of the soccer field. Quentin sat on a tree branch, eating a nectarine from a bag that was full of them. He really liked his drupes.

"People think I'm wearing contacts," I complained. "They're ridiculous."

He raised his hand solemnly. "One should never feel ashamed about their true self."

I picked up a rock and threw it at him. Yunie was still waiting for me back in the cafeteria.

"All right, all right." He hopped down to the ground and dusted himself off. Then he reached for my face.

I batted his hands away. "What are you doing?"

"Genie, you're asking me to conceal the mark of one of the greatest powers in the known universe, an ability that the gods themselves would envy. I need a little more contact with you than for a normal spell. This is going to take a moment."

Fine, whatever. I presented myself for a harsh grip as clinical as the Vulcan mind-meld.

But instead Quentin's touch was feather-soft. He grazed the back of his nails over my skin and brushed gently at my hair, tucking the loose strands behind my ears. I couldn't tell what he was whispering in his hushed tones, but it felt like poetry.

It was intensely soothing. Our faces drew closer as he chanted. The cadence of his voice seemed to be pulling me toward his lips.

God, he smelled good.

"There," Quentin said, suddenly stepping back. "They're brown again. Happy?"

No. Yes. Wait.

I collected the bits of myself I'd dropped on the ground and stacked them back in more or less the right order.

"You know you could have done that last night, before you left," I said.

He shrugged. "I forgot. Plus, I like the color. They're your real eyes, you know. The brown is just an illusion. I'll have to recast the spell every time you use true sight."

Great. I was permanently stuck as a Fae Princess from Emotionland.

"I don't get how 'spells' work," I said. "I've seen you and the demons perform them, but not Guanyin or Erlang Shen."

"A spell is just an application of a person's spiritual power to alter their surroundings," Quentin said. "The smaller and more generic the effect, the easier it is to do, which is why we normally stick to one-word commands. You need sufficient internal energies to power a spell, but you also need sufficiently refined technique.

"It's like throwing a punch," he went on. "You could throw a crisp jab that has no power behind it, or a wild haymaker that has no chance to connect. Spells are tools, not guarantees."

"Then what is Guanyin doing when she, you know, does her stuff?" I made jazz hands in a poor imitation of the goddess' awesome abilities.

"That's more of an innate thing. She's still using her spiritual power, but she has so much of it that an individual domain of reality is hers to control. She doesn't need to focus through words or hand motions."

"So I could learn spells too?"

Quentin scoffed. "You could if you weren't so ass at meditating.

We've been relying on your raw power to force your talents to the surface like a high-pressure boiler."

I glared at him but he simply shrugged. "Harsh truths. Red Boy's domain is fire. Erlang Shen's is water. *Your* domain is hitting stuff really hard."

I tried to come up with a different specialty that could have applied to me, but he pretty much had me in a corner.

"I've been thinking more about what happened with Baigujing, though," he said. "Did any of that seem strange to you?"

That was a dumb question. Besides the parts where we fought an evil skeleton and sent it back to Hell?

"She didn't say anything unusual," I offered. "For a demon trying to kill me."

"That's exactly what I'm talking about. She didn't say anything. She was just there, in the factory. It was all such a . . . set piece."

"Well, we could always deduce her motives by cross-checking police reports with eyewitness accounts of the security footage following the paper trail of blah blah-blah blah blah. Quentin, she was going to eat a baby."

"In an abandoned factory?"

"She probably took the kid back to her lair like a jaguar dragging its prey into a tree. People have eating habits. I've seen you bury your peach pits because you have some idea in your head that they'll magically grow into trees and you'll get a second helping of peaches. I hate to break it to you but the soil here probably isn't as fertile as the mystical mountain where you're from."

"I know that," he said with a scowl. "All I'm saying is that something doesn't add up."

"And I'm saying that if we waste time on recaps, we'll never get through this—this quest or geas, or whatever it is we agreed to. Quentin, that was *one* demon. One, and it nearly ended us! We have ninety-nine more to catch. Let's focus on them instead of fights we already won.

"We put the bad guy in the dirt and saved a baby," I concluded. "That's perfect math to me."

Quentin snorted. "Someone's taking to the demon slaying lifestyle rather comfortably."

26

YUNIE SLAMMED HER HAND DOWN IN THE MIDDLE OF THE textbook I was reading. She was the only person who could do that without pulling back a stump.

"*This* is the final round of the *concours*," she announced. "The last stage of the competition. The performance that counts."

I looked at the four concert tickets underneath her fingers, dated for a couple weeks out. One was for me.

I knew that two were for my parents. Both of them loved her like a second daughter. Mom had gotten all the "why-can't-you-be-more-like-Yunie" out of her system by fourth grade, and Dad was resigned to the fact that most of his family photos of me past a certain age also had Yunie in them.

It was unspoken that those two tickets were for me to decide a suitable arrangement. She wasn't *not* going to invite them to the most important event in her musical career to date. Nor would she ever show a favorite. But I could freely pick one or none or both of my parents to come, and feel guilty about whatever combination I chose in order to keep the peace.

It was the fourth ticket that confused me. "What's this for?"

"That one's for you to give to Androu as your plus one."

"Why would I take Androu and not Quentin?"

THE EPIC CRUSH OF GENIE LO

Yunie rolled her eyes at me like I was trying to play checkers at a chess match. "To make Quentin jealous. You really have to get with the program here, because your lack of game is disturbing."

She slid the ticket back and forth with her pinky. "And way to incriminate yourself. You didn't even hesitate there."

I prickled all the way up the back of my neck. My mind had only gone to Quentin because it'd be easier to explain his presence to my mother. And I'd talked to him most recently. And because demons.

"You didn't tell me the two of you were that far along," Yunie continued.

Anyone else would have thought she was teasing me. And she was. But my Yunie-sense, the only superpower that I truly believed in, indicated that she also sounded slightly hurt.

"We're not," I said. "I mean, we're not anywhere along. Of course I would tell you if we were anywhere. There's nothing to tell, really. Really."

I couldn't keep track of what I was embarrassed about at this point. I only wanted to make sure she knew that I wasn't trying to hide something as important as a relationship from her. While at the same time hiding a massive supernatural conspiracy that she could never know about.

"I'm sorry," she said. "I should lay off. I just like seeing you without that line of concentration running down your forehead all the time. Sometimes you get so stressed out from studying that you could hold a playing card between your eyebrows."

I looked at my friend. She was brimming with nervous energy, almost bouncing on her toes. Which meant for once she wasn't convinced she would win this competition. Yunie showed fear by turning even more radiant and pretty. Judging by the glow on her face, this one was for all the marbles.

I handed her back the fourth ticket.

"I won't need this," I said. "I'm going without distractions. You're the only person who matters."

She threw her arms around me and squeezed. "Well, yeah, duh."

■　■　■

"What's the need for secrecy?" I asked.

"Huh?"

Quentin and I were on the school roof again, giving meditation training another shot. I'd bought us this window of time by telling my mother that all team workouts had been changed to doubles, so I'd be home late every day. She wasn't happy about it, and I couldn't help imagining the gross liquid metal escaping my lips as I lied to her, but this was for the greater good.

The roof had become our own private spot, mostly because we could get there without tripping the stairwell alarms. The thrum of the ventilation units provided white noise that I had hoped would drown out my thoughts. That obviously hadn't worked, but at the very least I found this a relaxing way to cool down after practice.

"Every supernatural being I've met so far has been in disguise, or hiding," I said. "Or concerned to some degree with not being found out by a normal human. Why do they care whether people on Earth know about gods and demons?"

Quentin scowled at how quickly I'd given up trying to sit still, but he kept his eyes closed as if he could still salvage the session for himself. "In the case of yaoguai, the simple answer is because it's easier for them to hunt if no one knows about their existence."

"And the complex answer?"

He drew a deep breath. Either because his exercise required it or he was about to say something serious.

"At their core, every demon desperately wants to become human," he said. "Even if they're in denial about it."

"What? That doesn't make any sense."

"Are you sure? You are what you eat. There's a psychological drive behind a demon's hunger, besides the powers they might gain. The yaoguai who wanted to consume Xuanzang's flesh also wanted to become more like him, in a way."

I shuddered. That was the logic of cannibal serial killers.

"That's also why they wear disguises even if they can't really pull them off," said Quentin. "Back in the old days, the few demons who could successfully pass for human sometimes built entire lives inside monasteries and villages without being discovered. The really disciplined elite were able to manage it without eating anyone."

"Sounds like it would take a lot of willpower, fasting right next to your food source."

Quentin nodded. "Those demons tended to be either relatively decent beings, or the most dangerous monsters of all."

"Okay—but why would the gods bother with hiding? Why not reveal themselves in a big, glitzy display across the sky? The world would get pious in a hurry."

"More worshippers equals more work. More prayers to answer, more dynasties to support. The Jade Emperor got sick of it at some point and withdrew his direct influence from Earth. Now he can spout 'wu wei' as an excuse for not interfering with human matters, while laying back and enjoying the endless bounties of Heaven."

"Ugh, that's privileged BS if I ever heard it. 'Hey, I'm personally doing fine so let's not rock the boat, okay? You people who have nothing just need to wait and it'll all work out somehow.' "

Quentin's laugh petered out. "If you don't like it, you can wait a couple hundred eons until the Jade Emperor steps down and another god becomes Supreme Ruler of Heaven."

Huh. That got me thinking.

"Does that mean Guanyin could be in charge?" I asked. "I can't imagine she'd be so passive if she were the leader of the celestial pantheon."

Quentin frowned and opened his eyes at the mention of Guanyin.

"I asked her about it once," he said quietly. "She refused to think about leading the gods. She said it would keep her from tending to the suffering of ordinary humans."

"Too busy doing actual work." I replied with a sigh. Verily, on Earth as it was in Heaven with some people. I went back to my poor excuse for meditating and focused on my—

"Aaagh!"

Quentin suddenly leaned across the small gap between us and seized me by the shoulders. The shaking traveled from his body into mine, rattling my teeth. There was nothing I could do except hold him steady until the tremors passed.

"Sorry," he said once he'd settled down. "I didn't mean to grab you like that. The yaoguai alert doesn't hurt like the Band-Tightening Spell, but it hits me deep down in my body the same way."

I didn't mind. Mostly because his aftershocks resembled a dog twitching adorably from a vigorous petting session. I had the overwhelming urge to rub his belly and ask him who the good boy was.

But as enjoyable as that would be, it would have to wait. "All right," I said, getting to my feet. "We've got an hour and a half at most before I have to be home. Dial me in."

Quentin gave me a funny look, but if he thought I was being too cocky he didn't say so.

■   ■   ■

The two of us stood on the sidewalk, craning our necks upward to look at the grand stone residence framed by the evening sky. It was much smaller and older than the glass towers in the financial district of the city, but also much more elegant. The exterior was styled in fanciful Art Deco, as if to say, *Have fun in your liquefaction zones, losers—we're on bedrock.*

"Is he still there?" Quentin asked.

I touched my temple like a mutant with eyebeams; I'd found that the gesture helped me manage my newfound supernatural vision. The floors of the building dissolved away until only the penthouse remained. Sitting on a couch in the living room was a glowing green man with a face as blank and smooth as an eggshell. He had no eyes, no nose, no mouth. Nothing.

"He's still there," I said. "I think he's watching TV."

Despite not having any sensory orifices to speak of, the yaoguai was channel-surfing on a huge wall-mounted screen. Each time he clicked the remote, the surface of his face rippled like a pond with a pebble thrown into it. I had the distinct feeling that he was absorbing something from the experience, the way hit men in movies practiced different accents while looking into mirrors.

I couldn't see any signs of the apartment's original occupants. Maybe they were still at work. Maybe the demon had swallowed them whole. We had to move now.

"So the plan is we go in through the main entrance on the ground floor to cut off his escape," Quentin said. "I get us past any security on the way up, and we confront him once we're sure that no one's around to get caught in the cross fire."

A strange well of confidence filled my chest. "Let's do it."

We strode into the lobby like we owned the place. I approached the blazer-wearing man at the front desk and put on a cheery smile.

"Excuse me sir," I said, Quentin winding up for a spell behind me. "Can you tell me if the folks on the top floor have—"

The doorman leaped over the desk and clamped his jaws around my windpipe.

27

I LET OUT A SHRIEK OF SURPRISE. THE MAN'S TEETH SLID OFF my skin without drawing blood as I frantically pulled away. But the fury in his eyes was terrifying in its complete mindlessness. He would kill himself trying to kill me.

I reared back to clock him in the head.

"No!" Quentin snagged my arm from behind and brought me down, allowing the man to pummel me with impunity.

"What's wrong with you?" I screamed at him. My attacker was doing his best to cram more of my face into his mouth.

"He's a human!" Quentin said, pinned under us both. "You'll kill him if you hit him that hard!"

I was going to snap at Quentin for not giving me any options, but then I remembered how many I really had. The doorman was a massive, bulky guy, and only my head thought that I lacked the strength to throw him off. That wasn't the case anymore.

With a form that would have made Brian and K-Song proud, I grabbed the rabid human by the collar and belt and hoisted him bodily over my head. He continued to thrash and flail in the air, but he wasn't as frightening once I held him like an overgrown toddler.

"Okay, so what's his deal then?" I said to Quentin, craning my neck to avoid a frothy wad of spit dangling from the man's mouth.

"He's under some kind of frenzy spell. If you put him down he's liable to tear his own skin off."

"I can't hold him like this forever. We still have the yao-guai on the top floor to deal with. Do you think it noticed us by now?"

Ding!

All three elevators reached the lobby at the same time. The doors opened to reveal they were packed sardine-tight with people bubbling at the mouth with pure hatred for no one but Genie Lo and Quentin Sun. They barreled out the doors at us like horses at the Kentucky Derby.

"I would say yeah," Quentin called out before disappearing under a pile of rage zombies.

■ ■ ■

I got tackled to the floor and landed with my face in someone's armpit. As gently as I could under the circumstances, I shoved at the mass, hoping to get some breathing room. A few of the people went flying across the lobby hard enough to crack the full-length mirrors they landed on. Whoops.

"Cast Dispel Magic on them or something!" I shouted at Quentin.

"That's not a thing!" he said scornfully. "The effects have to wear off over time!"

A woman in hair curlers with a good left hook busted her knuckles wide open on my nose. "Then put them to sleep! For however long it takes!"

Quentin spun around, throwing attackers off his back with

centrifugal force. I acted as a human chain-link fence, keeping back anyone who would have interfered with his hand motions.

"*Sleep,*" he declared. "*Sleep!*"

"Why isn't it working?"

"This spell is really strong! Whoever cast it is nearly as good as I am!"

"Then you have to do one better! Now!"

Quentin inhaled so deeply that he could have snuffed out a campfire. "*SLEEP!*" he bellowed.

The shock wave of his voice expanded throughout the lobby, knocking people aside. The formerly berserking apartment-dwellers slumped against the walls and sank unconscious to the floor.

The room, littered with limply stirring bodies, looked like the aftermath of some devastating party. There wasn't time to deal with these people, though. We got in one of the elevators and slammed the button for the top floor.

The sudden acceleration pulled at my stomach, as if my own dread wasn't heavy enough. Each bell chime of the floors we passed was a countdown to a fight with a yaoguai that was smart enough and evil enough to use humans as expendable pawns. I'd known that demons were dangerous on an individual, starving-predator type of level, but this was different. Even Quentin was steeling himself, wringing the cricks out of his neck and knuckles.

The penthouse hallway only had one door. I didn't want to let my fear catch up to the rest of me, so I walked up to it straight away and kicked it off its hinges. Quentin and I filed in and took a position in sight of the yaoguai that stood in the living room,

F. C. YEE

his back turned to us as he gazed through the window over the landscape. Sunbeams filtered in through a large skylight over-head, casting dramatic shadows over our gathering.

"Okay asshole," I said. "Time to dance."

The demon turned to face us. *Face* being a relative term. The front of its skull had a slight taper to it, the way illustrators might draw a head by starting with an oval and a cross as a placeholder for the eyes. It looked at Quentin, rippled once, and then raised its hand into the air.

"Spell! Spell!" I shouted like a Secret Service agent spotting a gun.

Only it wasn't. The wiggling of the yaoguai's fingers didn't do anything. It was the toodle-oo gesture.

He set his feet and then jumped straight up through the sky-light. Glass shards rained down on us. It was like one of Quentin's takeoffs, only more destructive.

"Track him!" Quentin said.

I tried to keep my eye on him with true sight, but it was much harder than I thought—the equivalent of trying to watch a jet plane with a telescope. The yaoguai kept slipping out of my narrow field of view. It didn't help that right before I had a lock, I was hit in the back of the head with an upright vacuum cleaner, knocking me over.

I looked up to see Quentin with a rampaging cleaning lady wrapped up in a full nelson.

"Sorry," he said. "She was quicker than she looks."

I collapsed back to the floor and groaned.

■ ■ ■

Rearranging the hulking doorman back into his chair without making it look like he'd died mid-nap was an exercise in futility. I had to leave him slumped over, sleeping with the unnatural still-ness that came with Quentin's knockout spell.

I'd lost patience with the rest of the people in the lobby and stuffed them in the hallway of the first floor. They'd sort them-selves out once they woke up.

Quentin emerged from an unmarked room holding a bunch of tapes and computer equipment.

"We're lucky they had an old system," he said. "The newer secu-rity cameras upload recordings to the Internet automatically."

"How do you even know that?" I said. "Did you break into fancy apartment buildings all the time back in ancient China?"

He shrugged off the question and gave his armful of elec-tronics a squeeze over the nearest trash can. The broken bits filtered through his fingers, shades of my annihilated phone.

My self-imposed deadline had been blown, and my mother would be furious with me once I got home. But that wasn't what I was worried about right now.

"This is bad," I said, chewing my fingernails. "This is so bad. We effed up, Quentin. He got away. The demon got away. There's a hole in the roof of this building."

A middle-aged man in running shorts with a Yorkie on a leash entered the lobby as I was speaking.

"What hole in the building?" the man asked. He saw the door-man spread-eagled behind the desk. "What did you do to Lucius? Who are you two?"

"*Sleep.*" Quentin tossed the spell over his shoulder without looking. The man crumpled to the carpet. His dog began licking his passed-out face.

I rubbed my arms and paced back and forth, suddenly cold. This was the first time we tried to apprehend a demon with full knowledge and preparation of what we were doing, and we'd borked it.

"Look, I'm not gonna lie and call this the best demon hunt I've ever been on," Quentin said. "But look on the bright side. All of these people are . . . roughly okay. We scared off the yaoguai before it caused any real damage."

His words weren't much of a comfort. I kicked at the floor hard enough that it startled the dog into whimpering.

"We'll talk to Guanyin," Quentin said. "It'll be okay. You'll see."

28

"YOU LET HIM GET AWAY?"

It was the first weekend after our debacle with the faceless man, and our first debriefing with Guanyin and Erlang Shen. For our meeting spot we were in a dim sum restaurant near the train station two towns over from mine. The clanking, cackling, brunch-time chatter formed a cone of deafness around us as good as any silencing spell.

Which was good, because Quentin had severely misrepresented what Guanyin's reaction to our little escapade would be. The Goddess of Mercy was more upset than anyone I'd ever seen capable of, outside of me and my mother.

"You let him get away," she repeated incredulously.

"This one wasn't an eater," Quentin said. "I'm sure of it."

"And how do you know that?" Erlang Shen asked.

"He was too powerful. You can't reach that level of manipulation ability if you still crave human flesh. Also he had no mouth."

Guanyin looked at Quentin like his answer physically hurt her brain. "So it's okay that this particular yaoguai is running free, *because* he's strong enough to bewitch any human into doing his bidding. *Yau mou gaau cho ah . . .*"

I'd thought maybe being in public would have lessened our

gloom, but instead the restaurant mirrored it back on us tenfold. It might have been the sheen of grease on the floors, or the glass of the fish tanks lining the wall. Either way, it felt like a spotlight of unfestiveness was being aimed at us.

We ignored most of the carts that passed by. The two gods didn't bother with human food, and I couldn't muster an appetite in a situation like this. Even Quentin toned down his consumption to normal levels, having long finished his vegetable dumplings out of a sense of obligation rather than enjoyment.

"We searched the building after scaring him off, and we didn't find any remains," I said.

"Well that's nice," Guanyin said. "But that's not the only issue here. Having a ravenous yaoguai on the loose would have meant that the two of you were only on the hook for every missing person report until it was caught. Now that we know it likes controlling people against their will, you can also add every act of violence, depravity, and self-harm to your list as well."

Quentin shot to his feet. *"A word outside,"* he barked.

The goddess locked eyes with him for a long second, but eventually she stood and followed him out of the restaurant.

I could barely look up from the table. I felt like garbage.

I wasn't used to failing in ways that I couldn't make up for with sheer brute effort. I could usually cover my normal-world short-comings by hitting the books or the gym harder, but Guanyin was right. There was no way to spin this.

In the interim silence my phone vibrated, a period on the end of the sentence. Probably Yunie. I let it go until it stopped.

Erlang Shen took the moment to speak up.

"She takes her job very seriously," he explained. "When you first meet her she's all sweetness and favors. But if you ever disappoint her . . ."

"Yeah, she's got layers," I muttered.

"Don't take it too hard. In my opinion, you're holding up your end of the bargain as well as can be expected. The two of you have looked for this faceless man since then, right?"

"Yeah. For hours. And miles. But I couldn't find anything. I don't know if it's because my version of true sight is weaker than Quentin's, or what."

Erlang Shen looked gobsmacked at my admission. "*Your* version?"

Crap. "I . . . uh . . . yes. I'm the one who's got true sight now, not Quentin. Is that a problem?"

"No," he said. "Not at all. But it's a pretty big deal, the Ruyi Jingu Bang having that ability tacked on to the rest of its portfolio. You're more powerful than you ever were before."

"Even though I can't size change or make clones of myself yet?"

He waved dismissively. "Those are party tricks. They'll come to you eventually. But the strength of the Ruyi Jingu Bang combined with the all-seeing vision of the Monkey King? With those two powers alone you could conquer Heaven. I'm very impressed."

Flattery was nice. Especially when delivered with Erlang Shen's genuine, cloud-parting smile. But given my recent missteps, I would have preferred he lend me a hand instead of moral support.

"Are you sure you can't help?" I asked. "Being a warrior god and all?"

He seemed to appreciate that I'd remembered his stature, but he shook his head all the same. "Very sure. My hands are tied because of that idiotic *laotouzi*."

"What old man? You mean Quentin? I don't think he'd be so petty as to reject your help in this case."

"No," he said. "I meant my uncle. The Jade Dunderhead."

Whoa. I wasn't expecting that kind of talk from the god everyone understood to be the poster boy for filial piety. I nudged my chair away from him in case the ground cracked open and swallowed him whole.

"You look surprised. Did you think I liked my uncle's decisions? That I approved of his methods? That do-nothing is responsible for this world going to the dogs, in my opinion.

"Only the Goddess of Mercy stretches the limits of what we're allowed to do on Earth," he said. "If someone as active and strong as her were in charge, we would never have ended up in this scenario to begin with."

Huh. I approved of this outspoken version of Erlang Shen. We were aligned on a surprising number of levels. It was too bad I only got to see him while our counterparts were having it out.

"A word of wisdom, on both the demon-hunting front and on sharpening your powers," he said. "Don't let the setbacks mess with your overall progress. I know that Guanyin is going to hound you over every outcome, but what's done is done. Focus on becoming stronger, which you *can* control, over possible failures, which you can't always."

That was pretty decent advice. Anna-like, in a way. "Got any suggestions on getting into a good college?" I asked.

"Yeah. Bribe the hell out of everyone you can."

I laughed out loud. Erlang Shen pretended to look insulted, but he couldn't prevent his grin from peeking out.

"What?" he said. "It's the truest Way, if there ever was one."

∎ ∎ ∎

Quentin and Guanyin came back in and sat down, each wearing the sourest, most ex-boyfriend and ex-girlfriend-y faces I'd ever seen. Seriously, after that display nothing was going to convince me that they hadn't broken up with each other at least three times.

"You're doing well," Guanyin said. She was clearly not the Goddess of Lying to Make You Feel Better. "And I know that it seems unfair that I hold you to account for a perfect record like some overzealous schoolteacher. But a slipup like this, so early on in your endeavors, has consequences."

She waved at Erlang Shen. "Remember his thing with the tea, and the swirling, and the whatnot? If you don't, he can do it again."

Erlang Shen raised his eyebrows at her dismissive tone. "I remember," I said. "No need."

"Then if you'll recall, yaoguai are attracted to masses of spiritual energy," Guanyin said. "And that includes *other* yaoguai. Especially powerful ones. Previously it was just you and Sun Wukong involuntarily broadcasting your signals throughout the cosmos, but now this faceless man is doing it as well. The demons will be coming faster and in greater numbers now. You've made this job significantly harder on yourselves."

God.

Friggin'.

Damn it.

I *knew* there was going to be blowback. Erlang Shen and Quentin might have thought from their lofty, dude-tinted perspectives that everything was cool, but Guanyin's simple truth threw that idea right out the window.

"I don't let yaoguai get the best of me," Quentin said, falling back to platitudes. "We'll manage."

"I sincerely hope so," Guanyin said. "Once Red Boy makes his move, you two will need your undivided attention to stop him. If he comes to Earth while you're still chasing your tails, then there is no limit to the damage he could do."

She gave a brief, flat chuckle. "In fact, that's undoubtedly his plan, now that I say it out loud. To strike us at our lowest point, while we're distracted. It makes sense, don't you think?"

There was a long beat in the conversation.

"Come on now," Guanyin said. "I didn't mean to depress everyone. Sometimes I get worked up because, well . . ." She sucked in her lips as she searched for the right explanation.

"I think of us like a family right now," she said. "Strange as it is to say."

Huh. There were two other confused frowns besides mine on that one.

Guanyin reached out to either side of her, grabbing Quentin and Erlang Shen by the hand, hard enough to make them both wince. Since I was sitting across from her out of reach, I got the full force of her withering gaze.

"What's going on right now?" she went on. "It's like family business, when you look at it from a certain angle. Our little divine family is responsible for this awful mess, letting yaoguai run loose on Earth. But we're going to clean it up."

Now I knew where Guanyin was going with the metaphor. These weren't words of comfort. These were twists of the knife.

"And the reason why we're going to succeed is because we know what's important." She wagged Quentin and Erlang Shen's hands up and down for emphasis. "What's important is that we don't let anyone else get dragged into our family garbage. If someone who isn't family suffers because of our failings, then there isn't a word for the kind of shame we should feel. Does everyone get me?"

No one spoke. My phone started vibrating again, loud and insistent, until I finally yanked it out and put it on silent.

"I'm so glad you all understand," Guanyin said.

29

I LOOKED AT MYSELF IN THE MIRROR AND SMOOTHED DOWN the front of my dress. "I can do this," I said. "I can do this."

Mom poked her head into my room. "Do you remember when I last wore my pearls?" she asked.

"Huh? Why?"

She grunted at my inability to follow her logic with the precision of a mind reader. "Because if it was at Auntie Helen's gathering, then they're in a different jewelry box, not the normal one."

I was so confounded that I forgot what I had been preparing the last few minutes to tell her. "Then just check the other jewelry box!" I said instead.

"Don't raise your voice at me," she muttered before sweeping back down the hallway.

I couldn't really blame her for being scatterbrained at the moment. Yunie's competition performance tonight had her excited beyond measure. She reveled in any opportunity to show that her in-group was better than someone else's. And since volleyball was definitely not as prestigious as classical music on the Asian Parent Scale, I rarely scratched that itch for my mother in the right way.

She'd been looking forward to this night. It was too bad I'd have to ruin it for her.

■   ■   ■

I approached her in the kitchen as she was busy unwrapping hard candy so as not to make sounds during the performance if she needed a throat lozenge. She'd read that advice in an opera program once and had been fascinated with the idea ever since. Like it was the fanciest way possible to stifle a cough.

"Mom," I said. This was it. "I invited Dad."

She stopped what she was doing and looked up at me.

"He's got a seat at the opposite wing of the hall. I'm not trying to trick you into talking to each other or anything. It's just that it wouldn't be fair if only one of you got to come."

Somewhere in my head, the idea of telling her last minute so that she wouldn't back out had played out better than it was doing right now.

Because right now was the part of the action film where she dipped her finger in the wound I'd opened on her, tasted her own blood, and sneered disdainfully at me. The juggernaut had been unleashed. The human era had ended. The language of man could not begin to describe what would happen next.

The doorbell rang.

"That's not him," I said quickly. Then I ran, because whoever the hell it was, they'd given me the timeliest of outs.

I opened the door. It was Quentin.

"Is that also proper gear for outdoor exercise?" he said, eyebrow raised.

I didn't understand what he was referencing until I remembered that we normally snuck off to train at this hour. With everything that had been going on, I'd forgotten to cancel on him.

I closed the door behind me as silently as I could. "I can't tonight," I said. "I should have told you sooner. I'm sorry."

"I'm not." A roguish smirk spread over his face as he drank me in.

"Oh knock it off. Just because this is the first time I've worn something with bare shoulders around you doesn't mean you need to be all *'hurr, she cleans up real good.'* I know you think you're being nice, but it's condescending."

"Turn true sight on," Quentin said.

"What? Why?"

He shrugged. "Humor me."

I didn't know how much longer Mom was going to stay inside without bothering to check on me, so I did. Whatever would make him leave sooner.

"Are you looking at me?" he asked.

"Yes, and hurry up. It's like staring into a light bulb."

Quentin cleared his throat. "Genie Lo, you are definitely . . . NOT the most gorgeous human being I've ever laid eyes on."

A metal bubble bigger than our heads spewed out of his lips and rose into the air. It could have taken out a power line. It looked revolting.

How it felt was another matter entirely.

I couldn't keep an uncontrollable, dizzy grin off my face. And I started to get self-conscious about my neckline. I didn't need Quentin seeing how far down I blushed.

"That's messed up," I said. I reached out and poked him in the chest, but my touch lingered longer than it meant to. "Everyone keeps saying I look like your former master who used to torture you."

Quentin laced his fingers between mine and pulled me closer to him. "Maybe I have some issues I need to work through. You might be able to help with that."

I couldn't think straight. The look in his eyes was out of hand. This was first-day Quentin. Quentin standing on my desk, not caring who or what anyone else thought. A demigod who knew exactly what he wanted.

Whom he wanted.

The door opened behind me and I nearly tumbled backward into my mother.

"Pei-Yi, if you think for one minute you can—oh, hello dear," she said once she saw Quentin. "Are you coming to the concert too? Genie didn't tell me. Because *why would she tell me anything*?"

Quentin snapped back into propriety and raised his hands. "Just paying a visit. Sadly, I don't think I'm invited to whatever's going on tonight."

"Oh, such a pity," Mom said. Her voice was the tonal equivalent of a public assassination. "Who knows how she chooses which people to bring and who to exclude. I thought for certain that you'd be on the list."

I wheeled around. "I'm not the sole arbiter of who gets access to Vivaldi in the Bay Area!"

"Oh please! Don't pretend you don't know what I'm talking about!"

"I'd better go," Quentin said. "You ladies have fun. Try not to get into any trouble." He tucked his hands into his pockets and sauntered away, whistling into the evening air. The tune might have been the "Spring" concerto from *The Four Seasons*.

Mom let out a snort. "See? That's what happens when you act like that. You scare the good ones away."

■ ■ ■

It was not a pleasant car ride across the bridge and up the highway, but at least it was a silent one. The two of us knew that we needed not to show our asses this evening.

The performance was being held at the auditorium of a nearby state school. A good one too—one that would have been at the top of my list had I not been so desperate to gain some distance from Santa Firenza.

We pulled into a lot in front of the hall. It was a weird building, ugly concrete bones on the outside harboring a beautiful, creamy wood interior. People mingled throughout the upper and lower levels, mites inside a larger see-through organism.

"You should find him before the performance," Mom said softly. "You don't get the chance to talk to him much."

I tried to do what I should have done earlier and apologize, but she shushed me. "Go on," she said. "It'll take me a while to find a parking space. It's okay."

There was nothing I could do but get out of the car and go inside. I only prayed she wouldn't ditch the performance and drive off into the night.

The hallways of the auditorium were filled with older folks dressed to the nines, grim-lipped parents and grandparents readying themselves for battle by proxy. The stakes of this competition must have been even higher than I thought. The Tiger Mom Olympics.

Yunie and the other performers were in the back getting ready. I knew I wouldn't see her before she went on stage. Nor did I want to. The two of us never interrupted each other's warm-up routine before big events.

Instead I looked for Mr. and Mrs. Park and found them in the corner, avoiding the game of conversational one-upsmanship breaking out over the foyer. ("Oh, so your Guadagnini's a rental? How sensible of you.")

They looked relieved to see me. Yunie's parents were square, honest, open people, unsuited for this shark tank. Both were podiatrists who met each other at a podiatrists' convention. It was extremely difficult to figure out where Yunie got her sharper edges from, in both looks and attitude.

"Genie!" They got on their tiptoes to give me a barrage of kisses on the cheek. "We haven't seen you in so long. When was the last time you came over for dinner?"

"I'm sorry, I've been really busy lately." *With demons. And gods. I'm in over my head. Send help.*

Mrs. Park nodded solemnly. "It's a tough time for everyone in your grade. SATs are coming up, college apps are around the corner. I don't know how you kids these days handle so much pressure. It was easier for us when we were young."

Mr. Park clapped me on the shoulder. "We're just glad you could make it. And so is Yunie. She was getting really lonely without you."

I winced upon hearing that. Then I did a mental backtrack to confirm exactly how much time I had been spending with my best friend in recent weeks, and I winced much harder at the result.

Compared to how entwined we normally were, I'd basically cut her off. And she hadn't said a word. She'd picked up that I had something else going on and left me to it.

I was a terrible friend. Or at the very least, acting like one.

I'd make it up to her after the performance. Right now I had to focus on being a terrible daughter.

"My dad should be here somewhere," I said. "Have you seen him?"

Mr. Park arced his arm to mimic the curve of the hallway. "He's around the corner. I saw him talking to another student from your school."

I said goodbye to Yunie's parents with a big smile on my face that vanished instantly the moment I turned around. *Quentin*, I thought with murder on my mind. Whatever had passed between us on my doorstep didn't give him the right to sneak in here with magic. To introduce himself to my father without me being there. I stomped around the hallway to the other side of the auditorium and found Dad talking to . . .

Androu?

"Oh hey," he said.

I blinked a couple of times. "I didn't invite you," I blurted out.

Androu took my rudeness in stride—as if he had girls greeting him with insults all the time. "My cousin who lives in the city is performing tonight. He's a timpanist. Holds a beat like superglue."

"Androu here was filling me in on your volleyball season," Dad said. "He's a big fan of yours." Then he made the most obvious, over-the-top wink possible.

I stood there, catching flies with my mouth. The silence emanating from my throat was so thick that Androu coughed and excused himself to go to the bathroom.

Once he was gone, Dad turned to me with a twinkle in his eye. "I knew there was a boy," he said. "Given how mopey you were at the gym? There had to be a boy."

This . . . this wasn't so bad. Of all the misunderstandings.

"You should tell me about these things," Dad said. "You know I don't judge like your mother. I'm okay with you dating."

I could triage this. The patient was stable.

"We have to have 'the talk' though; I won't have you making irresponsible choices." He tried to say it sternly but couldn't hide his glee at getting to check off one of those American-style parenting milestones he'd read so much about in magazines. I wasn't sure if he fully understood what "the talk" entailed.

Androu came back. "We'll save it for later," Dad whispered.

"So yeah," Androu said, doing his best to ignore my father's blatant winking again. "I didn't know Yunie was performing tonight. Wild, huh? We should plan to go to more concerts together. It'd be fun."

Dad was about to joyously agree, but then he suddenly deflated, his high spirits gone with the wind. There was only one person who could make him go one-hundred-to-zero just like that. And she was right behind me.

My mother didn't say anything in greeting. She glanced at me. Then my father. Then up at Androu.

EKG flatline. Code Blue.

"I found a space," she announced.

She hadn't bumbled into us. She could have easily avoided this encounter. Every previous indication she'd given said that was her preference. And yet here she was, claiming this patch of land for Spain. I abandoned all hope of understanding this woman for what must have been the fiftieth time.

Mom craned her head forward. None of us knew what she was doing until the gesture stirred something deep and lost in my father. He pecked her on the cheek and then they both returned to their stations.

"Androu, this is Genie's mother," Dad said. He meant to gently prod my classmate forward, but the motion resembled a Spartan raising his shield against a hail of stones.

Androu gallantly bent at the waist to shake her hand. "Hello Mrs. Lo. It's a pleasure to finally meet you."

Mom was mildly placated in the sense that the new person she had to greet was at least polite and handsome. But then Androu, that sweet summer child, ruined all hope of a clean escape.

"I'd love to take you and Genie up on that offer for dinner at your place," he said. "I hear your cooking is legendary."

In his mind he was only continuing the last conversational thread we had. He had no idea what boundaries he was stepping over.

"Oh, so she's making invitations to people I've never met now," Mom said. She turned to me like a doll in a horror movie. "I suppose I can't decline, can I?"

Dad rushed in to try and douse the flames, but he was holding a jug of gasoline, not water. "Androu is Genie's very good friend," he said. With emphasis on the *very good*.

This did not compute with Mom. According to her programming, there was only ever supposed to be one boy at a time holding the Most Favored Nation spot. Preferably the same boy throughout my entire life.

"I thought Quentin was your *very good* friend," she said.

This was new. Tonight I got to discover the face Mom made when she thought I was being a hussy. Never mind the fact that her idea of promiscuity would be outdated in Victorian England.

"Quentin?" Dad said. "Who's Quentin?"

"I see now why you didn't want to invite him," Mom said. "It would expose the double life you've been leading."

Androu, still out of sync, postured up valiantly at the mention of Quentin's name. "Don't worry, Mr. and Mrs. Lo. If that guy's still bothering Genie at school, I'll put a stop to it. She can count on me. Right?" He nudged me with his elbow.

He was prodding a corpse. My soul had left my body a long time ago. It had flown to the top of Mount Can't Even, planted its flag, and dissipated into the stratosphere.

An usher came over and told us it was time for the performance to start. We all made shows of pulling out our tickets, as if they contained our queue spots for a kidney. Androu smiled and bumped my stub with his.

"Oh hey," he said. "I think we're sitting together!"

.　.　.

Androu and I went in first while Mom made her last-minute hellos to Yunie's parents. We picked our way through the narrow aisles like cranes in the mud until we found our seats.

The chair backs in front of us were too close, and they jammed our knees to the side. Tall people problems. He and I had that in common at least.

Androu chuckled to himself.

"What is it?" I asked.

"Oh, it's just—sorry if I'm being offensive, but that whole thing with your Mom and Dad out there. It felt like the stereotype was true. Asian parents not really showing a lot of affection in public."

I thought of the way Mr. and Mrs. Park clutched each other for comfort tonight, the way they loved to gross out Yunie whenever possible by cuddling and kissing in front of me when I visited.

I remembered a fleeting dream in a fairyland tale, where my dad had chased my mom around a fountain trying to put a mouse-eared hat on top of her head while I watched and laughed and laughed.

Maybe I had been subconsciously trying to *Parent Trap* them into speaking again. Who knew.

"Yeah," I mumbled, the vowels stuck in my throat. "You know what they say."

Mom came in and immediately made a disapproving click. There was no way for me and Androu to avoid our legs touching each other. We were leg-making-out right next to her. Had we no shame?

Androu tried to help her settle in. "Where's Mr. Lo—"

"Seating accident; not enough spaces together," she snapped.

We all suddenly found our programs very, very interesting. Luckily we didn't have to wait long for the curtain.

I tuned out the bespectacled, tweeded man explaining the history of the competition and how we could all get involved with the arts by making small donations. The pain was over for now. I could relax for as long as it took to determine who would emerge unscathed from musical thunderdome.

"Because they've already worked so hard to get here, we're going to do something a little different tonight," said the emcee. "Could our finalists please come on stage to take a bow? No matter who wins tonight, you all deserve a big hand."

The majority of the audience believed that was patently false. There could be only one. But we clapped anyway as the contestants lined up on stage.

I spotted Yunie. She looked like a star in the night sky. Mom,

Androu, and I mashed our hands together when she emerged, all prior conflicts forgotten.

And then someone flicked me in the back of my neck.

I turned around, ready to yell at the jerk who did it, but the little old grandmother behind me was busy trying to work up enough saliva to whistle for the brass section. It wasn't her.

The same flick hit me from the same direction. I peered down the aisle until I saw where it was coming from.

Quentin. Hovering in the shadows by the fire exit.

He raised his fist to his lips and blew. The little bullet of air that shot out from the tunnel formed by his fingers smacked me in the face. It would have been the most annoying sensation in the world under any circumstances. Right now I was livid beyond belief.

Quentin waved his hands once he saw that he had my attention.

I slid my finger across my throat at him.

He widened his eyes and tugged frantically on his own earlobes, hopping up and down to exaggerate the motion.

Oh god no. Not now.

I surreptitiously glanced at my phone, which had been on silent all evening. Forty-six notifications. Quentin had been trying to contact me for more than an hour.

More than an hour of a yaoguai doing whatever it wanted on Earth, with no one to stop it.

I tried to unwedge myself from the chair and kneed the man in front of me in the shoulder. He frowned at me but decided I wasn't worth it.

"Genie, what are you doing?" Mom hissed.

"I—I feel sick," I stuttered. "Light-headed. I . . . have to go outside."

"Now!?"

I was able to creep halfway down the aisle before I froze. On stage, Yunie was watching me. Watching me leave.

Of course I stuck out too much to make a clean getaway. Yunie's eyes followed my path and flickered at its end. She'd seen Quentin.

My universe was reduced to a handful of silent, screaming voices. The distress on my mother's face. The urgency of Quentin's. Androu's guileless concern.

And loudest of all was the confused heartbreak coming from my best friend on the biggest night of her life.

"I'm sorry," I whispered to anyone who would have it. I ran out the side door to where Quentin was waiting.

■ ■ ■

"We need to make up for lost time," he said in the bushes behind the auditorium. "What's the point of me having a phone if you're not going to answer my—"

"Quentin," I said, my voice as quiet as the eye of a hurricane. "I know what happened isn't your fault, but before this night is through, I *will* kill someone. I would rather that person not be you."

He shut up and pointed at where I should start searching. "There's barely any towns in that direction, thankfully. I don't think it'll be as close to the population as the other demons were."

I pressed the side of my head and swept over the landscape.

Quentin was right; the area around the dancing light was mostly empty grassland, dotted with sleeping bovines. Guanyin's alarm had given us a decent head start this time, for once.

"It's in a farm," I said.

. . .

Quentin plowed through the barn roof feet-first. I disembarked from his back and called out to the shadows.

"I'm not really in the mood," I said. "So I'd appreciate it if we made this quick."

A stream of sticky, gooey threads shot out of a dark corner with the volume of a garden hose. It methodically swept over Quentin and me, covering us in a thickening, hardening cocoon of webs. It didn't stop until we were encased from the neck down, our legs glued to the floor of the barn.

A man stepped into the moonlight in front of us and wiped his mouth. His face was bearded with fingers—human fingers. They sprouted from his skin and wriggled as he spoke.

"Ha!" the yaoguai cackled. "You've fallen into my trap! Vengeance is mine!"

"Who are you?" said Quentin.

"The Hundred-Eyed Demon Lord!" The fingers coating his face pointed in unison on certain words for emphasis. "Master of webs and venom!"

The yaoguai opened his jaws wide to flash a set of dripping fangs at us. "I've been distilling my poisons in the fires of Diyu for more than a thousand years, waiting for this moment! You cannot escape my bite, for the silk that imprisons you is stronger than the hardest steel—*bu hui ba, what are you doing!?*"

I tore my way out of the cocoon with a few thrashes of my arms. The strands of silk twanged like overtuned guitars as I snapped them. Looking down, I found that the one nice dress that I owned was completely ruined. There wasn't going to be a way back into the performance tonight.

Quentin shook his head, not bothering to try and free himself.

"Oh buddy," he said to the yaoguai with genuine sorrow for a fellow sentient being. "Oh, buddy, I couldn't do anything for you now, even if you begged me. This is the end of the line."

The Hundred-Eyed Demon Lord looked at my face. Whatever he saw there made him give off a high-pitched *skreee* in alarm. He fell to all fours and scuttled away from me like an insect. The yaoguai backed into the barn's wall and went straight up it, reaching as far as the rafters in his attempt to get some distance between us.

I didn't feel like chasing him. Looking around the floor, I found the nearest object I could, picked it up, and winged it hard at the demon with all my might.

The metal horseshoe zipped from my hand. It flew so fast I couldn't see its arc, but I did spot the hole it left behind in the roof after it punched straight through. The edges of the wood glowed red hot like a cigarette burn in a sheet of paper.

"Holy crap," Quentin blurted out.

"You—you missed!" the Hundred-Eyed Demon Lord said in nervous triumph.

"Good thing horses have four feet," I said, waving three more horseshoes in the air.

30

IT WAS THREE WEEKS AFTER THE NIGHT OF THE CONCERT WHEN finally I could take no more. We'd just finished a yaoguai hunt. A successful one, but somewhat of a Pyrrhic victory.

"Call them," I said to Quentin.

"Why?"

The demon had been aquatic. Hence the reason we were currently standing waist-deep in freezing ocean water, still in our school uniforms.

We'd cut class for the second time. A third strike would go on my permanent record and earn me an in-person parent-teacher conference. There was a piece of seaweed stuck in my ear.

"I feel the need to talk," I said. "Right now. Call them."

Quentin gazed over the coastline. This section of the beach was normally open for people to bring their dogs to play in the surf, but right now it was vacant. The picnickers up on the cliff who'd triggered the earring alarm hadn't seen our thrashing and flailing in the shallows on their behalf.

"In case you haven't noticed, I'm trying to keep our interactions with those two down to a minimum," he said. "They never end well."

"Quentin, we just spent the last hour beating up a fish. This can't go on. *Call them.*"

He closed his eyes, put his palms together, and grumbled under his breath for about a minute. It looked like he was throwing a tantrum instead of praying.

Nothing happened.

"Okay," I said. I waved my hands at the general lack of gods in the vicinity.

"What, you think they're going to plop down in the middle of the water? They're somewhere on shore. Go find them and talk to them."

I couldn't believe how much attitude he was giving me. "You're not coming?"

Quentin responded by leaning back and floating on top of the water, arms crossed behind his head like he was relaxing in a lounge chair. The tide began carrying him slowly out to sea.

"Fine!" I waded back to shore by myself. My clothes were soaked through and the wind made me shiver down to the bone. If I was magically resistant to cold, it was only to the point of not letting me collapse of hypothermia.

There were no gods on the beach, which meant I had to continue up the low cliff using a sandy ramp that gave way under my steps. Grit got into my shoes. Probably dog poop as well.

Once I got to the top, I saw a lone figure standing by the roadside. It was Erlang Shen, sans Guanyin. He eyed my wet, bedraggled state.

If he had said one smartass sentence, even something as innocuous as "Rough day, huh?" then I might have committed deicide on the spot. Instead he silently raised his hand and made a "come hither" gesture.

It wasn't me he was speaking to. It was the water. The dampness in my clothes wicked away, flying off my body and gathering into a sphere of liquid that hovered in the air before me. It grew and grew until I was completely dry. Not even the salt remained on my skin.

Erlang Shen flung the skinless water balloon back toward the ocean. Then he said the magic words that made me want to marry him right then and there.

"Let's get you some coffee."

■ ■ ■

"Hold on, hold on," he said, trying to keep his laughter contained. "You destroyed the Hundred-Eyed Demon Lord, the Guardian of Thousand Flowers Cave at Purple Clouds Mountain, by chucking horseshoes at him?"

"What can I say." I gulped from my cup of burnt water. Non-dairy creamer had never tasted so good. "I was out of lawn darts."

It would have been generous to call the shack we were sitting in a diner. The surly, rotund man behind the counter had a hot plate to cook on but nothing else. This particular eating establishment was more of a hedge maze made out of single-serving potato chip bags.

Our conversation, if anyone could even hear beyond the sports radio blaring the scores, probably sounded like we were talking about a video game.

"It sounds like you could have also grown to giant proportions and swatted him down," Erlang Shen said.

"I still haven't figured that one out. I must have some kind of mental block against it."

"Like I said before, it's nifty but not essential." Erlang Shen leaned back in his chair and gave me an appraising look up and down. "Is there something else you want to talk about? I don't need true sight to see that something's bothering you."

My fingers trembled around my paper cup.

"Yeah, there is actually," I said. "So we beat the Hundred-Eyed Demon Lord, right?"

"Yes. A while ago, if I followed your story correctly."

"You did. And since then we've also taken down the Yellow Brows Great King, Tuolong, the Pipa Scorpion, Jiutouchong, and some generic-looking guy with bells whose name I didn't catch. Today out there in the ocean was the King of Spiritual Touch. What kind of name is that for an aquatic fish-demon?"

"An unfortunate one."

If I wasn't so tired I would have laughed. "And then there's Baigujing. Also the two others from before you and I met. Eight if you count Tawny Lion's brothers."

Erlang Shen nodded. "You've been productive to say the least. I know the faceless man still hasn't been found, but other than that your success rate has been flawless. Heaven has no problem with the pace you've been keeping recently."

"Yeah but what if *I* do?"

I was a little louder then I meant to be. Another customer glanced over at us before tilting the rest of his corn chips into his mouth and walking out the door.

The last three weeks had taught me that I wasn't a machine, as much as I liked to pretend I was when it came to doing work. Trying to act like a heroic yaoguai-slayer of old had left me with my gears bruised and my fuel tank bleeding.

"This is hard," I said to Erlang Shen. "This is really hard. I know that's an idiotic thing to say, but it's hard in a way I wasn't expecting. The demons keep popping up here and there and everywhere. They don't stop coming. It's a giant game of whack-a-mole."

My carnival game analogy may have been a little bit off. The pace of the demon incursions reminded me more of wind sprints, where Coach D would have us run end-to-end on the volleyball court until she decided we were done. It was supposed to improve our cardio, but without knowing when the whole thing would be over, it felt like pointless punishment.

"I don't feel like we're making any progress," I said. "None of the other demons will give up Red Boy's whereabouts, even under pain of death. Stamping them out while we wait for him is like having a sword hanging over our heads while we rearrange deck chairs on the Titanic."

I was mixing my references but Erlang Shen appeared to follow well enough.

"We've only found sixteen so far, and already the grind is getting to me," I said. "I can hardly believe it. What has happened to me since meeting Quentin and you and Guanyin has been the wildest mindbender imaginable and yet it *still* somehow turned into a grind like every other part of my life. At the current rate we're pushing, I'm going to break down long before we catch the other eighty-two demons."

"Ninety-two," Erlang Shen corrected.

"See? I'm so burned out I can't do basic math in my head. If you knew me, that would be a really worrying sign."

I put my face in my hands. It stayed there long enough to trouble him.

"Genie?" he said tentatively.

"I haven't talked to my best friend in a long time."

It was the safety of my rabbit hollow that let me finally talk about what was truly wrong with this whole deal.

"I screwed things up with her really badly because of this demon business," I said. "And I can't even tell her why. She'll never know what I've been doing, running around without her."

Erlang Shen tiptoed around the cracks appearing in my voice, an arctic explorer suddenly finding himself on thin ice. "If she's your friend, she'll forgive you, no?"

"I don't *want* her to forgive me. I'd rather she be angry at me forever."

An outside observer would have assumed I was being illogical. And overdramatic. They'd tell me that Yunie and I could hash things out easily. Such a close friend would understand that I had good reasons for shutting her out recently and might even be okay with me not explaining them fully. She'd trust me when I told her I hadn't ditched her for a boy.

Of course that was the case. I didn't actually believe our eight-year relationship was completely over because of a single spate of neglectfulness on my part.

But that wasn't the point. The looming monster here was the future, bearing down and unstoppable. Yunie and I were destined for different colleges, her to a specialized music program and me to any snob-factory that would have me. We knew this even before we entered high school.

We didn't have much time left together. Our little routines were precious to me, and our big events even more so. The day when the two of us would have to buckle up and accept our inevitable drift apart was coming, and I didn't want it to happen prematurely.

Reckoning with Yunie would be pulling up the anchor just a little bit farther. That was probably why I'd put it off for so long.

Erlang Shen, perhaps using some magical water-detecting sense, pushed the stack of flimsy brown napkins on the table over to me. I snatched them up and wadded them against my nose and eyes so that he couldn't see my face.

Great, now I was blubbering in front of a god. Go me.

"I think of my family when things get rough," Erlang Shen said. "When my resolve wavers."

"The situation with them is even worse," I said, muffled by the scratchy paper. "My parents think I'm a hot mess right now."

"Not my point. What I'm trying to say is that the people we care about make the grind worthwhile. Even if the two never meet."

He stared out the window, his fingers playing lightly against the table.

"The Jade Emperor doesn't know about half of what I do in Heaven on his behalf," Erlang Shen said. "And yet I put up with his incompetence, his passivity, his constant rejection. Because one day he'll see me for my abilities. I want to show my uncle what I'm capable of more than anything else in the universe. Your friend. She means a lot to you?"

"I'd do anything for her."

I surprised myself how easily and without embarrassment I said those words. Heartfelt declarations weren't my strong suit.

"Then keep up the good fight, for her sake." Erlang Shen smiled at me. "You know, when I originally fought back the waters of the

Great Flood, I was trying to impress my uncle and the rest of the celestial pantheon. Not invent agriculture."

I laughed in spite of myself.

"Genie," Erlang Shen said. "I'll talk to the Jade Emperor and convince him to let me help you."

"I wasn't trying to guilt you into—"

"No." He shook his head. "I should have been right beside you from the start. It was a mistake not to be more hands-on."

The weight in my chest lifted significantly. Sure, none of my problems had gone away. But given how few people with the full story were actively assisting me, my support network had risen by fifty percent.

"Thank you," I said. "I really mean it. Thank you."

The god shrugged. "Don't worry about it. In the meantime, remember that Red Boy's plan to keep you distracted has a chance to backfire on him. Each time you catch a lesser demon, you're training your true sight muscle, not to mention your combat skills. Eventually you'll get to the point where he can't hide from you anymore, in this world or the next. When that happens, I'll be right there with you for the showdown."

"Red Boy wouldn't stand a chance with you in our corner," I said. "He's a fire-type, right? If you're the master of water, you can just put him out."

Erlang Shen laughed as he got up and pushed in his chair. "It doesn't work exactly like that." Then he cocked his head, pursing his lips. "It works a little like that?"

■　■　■

I let the divine being leave first and gave him a few minutes to do whatever it was he needed to do to get back to Heaven. It seemed polite, though I'd only made that rule up in my head.

When I stepped out of the shack, Quentin was there by the roadside, waiting for me.

"Have a nice chat?"

I knew his peevish tone was his usual allergic reaction to Erlang Shen, but for some reason I didn't field it well today.

"Yeah, we really connected on an emotional level," I snapped. "I promised to turn into a stick for him."

That was perhaps the weirdest, most hyper-targeted dig I'd ever leveled at someone, but boy did it work. Quentin looked like I'd broken him in half and left him on the curb for pickup. He was completely silent the entire trip back to civilization.

He didn't call or text me that night either. It had become a little ritual for us to debrief and unwind over the phone after every yao-guai hunt ever since Baigujing but instead, radio silence.

While I could have reached out first to tell him I was extremely sorry he was being such a baby about this particular subject, I figured I had time to do it when I saw him at school. So I went to bed and thought little of it.

But I was wrong. Quentin wasn't the type to stew in anger by his lonesome. He preferred action to waiting.

Which was likely why the very next day at school, I came upon him in the hallway making out with Rachel Li.

31

WELL, THIS CERTAINLY ESCALATED MORE THAN I WAS expecting.

"Sorry to interrupt," I said. He and Rachel pulled away from each other, but not very far.

"Is this important?" she asked, her lips still wet.

"It is, or I wouldn't be interrupting."

Once Rachel saw I wasn't going to back down, she peeled herself off Quentin and walked away, trailing her finger across his jaw all the way up to his earlobe as she left. He gazed at her wistfully before turning to me.

"What is it?" he asked, as if nothing different had happened.

"It's Friday. We were going to try high-altitude training this weekend." My voice came out like a text-to-speech simulator, devoid of human emotion and jaunty in all the wrong places. "You know, to see if that would unlock more of my powers. You never picked a mountaintop. You said the feng shui had to be just right."

"Oh. Yeah. Whatever's fine." He glanced around, as if searching for more interesting people to sidle up to at a party.

"All right then, I'll pick a spot," I said. Focusing on logistics, appointment-keeping, the squeezing of blood through my veins would keep my roiling guts on the inside. Or so I hoped. "When I text you, you'll be ready to go?"

"Sure."

"Is there something you want to talk about?" I asked, on the odd chance that he wanted to explain his behavior. But he was already shoving past me, done with this conversation.

"I'll text *you*," he said, waving me off with the back of his hand.

I nearly put my fist through a locker.

. . .

Quentin didn't make good on his promise to text me. Instead, he found me in the cafeteria at lunch.

His personality had changed from spacey to grumpy. He must have been suffering withdrawal symptoms from Rachel's saliva.

"I forgot that the lunar cycle's not right," he groused. "Mountaintop meditation's not going to be the best for this weekend. We have to shift our whole calendar around."

"So now you want to make a plan? I thought we were winging it."

Quentin tilted his head. "You . . . don't want to make a plan? That's weird. I've seen you write to-do lists with only one item on them. You even put a number one on them with nothing underneath."

"Well, maybe it's time to loosen up," I said. "Act differently for a change. Improvise."

Quentin reached over and put his hand on my forehead to check my temperature.

I smacked his arm away only to see Rachel watching us and

laughing. She obviously wasn't threatened by her new boyfriend flirting with someone else. She knew there was no comparison.

Quentin returned a fake smile and a wave to her. "I don't know how I feel about that girl," he said. "We've only been spending time together because I'm bored. But I think she's imagining something that doesn't exist."

Okay, so that irked me to the core. Rachel was annoying, but she was genuinely into Quentin. He could at least have the decency not to use her as a stress reliever.

"Congrats on completing your assimilation into modern life," I said. "You've become something that's unique to this era."

"What's that?"

"A douchebag." I got up with my tray. "When you figure out how to stop being one, you can come and talk to me. Otherwise don't bother."

■ ■ ■

"I'm going to kill him," Yunie said once she found me in the library at my usual spot. "I'm going to rip his balls off and shove them in his eye sockets."

Gossip about Quentin and Rachel's hookup had gotten sufficiently around. Anatomical impossibilities aside, Yunie's first words to me since the concert fiasco were bittersweet.

On one hand, we were speaking again. That was a victory I'd crawl through salt and broken glass for. On the other hand, I could see the narrative playing out in her head, and it hurt my soul.

I'd done the crazy threatening friend routine on one of Yunie's terrible exes in the past, and the reason she could have been itching so badly to return the favor was because it was a perfect way to erase the cloud between us. There was more hopefulness than violence in her anger toward Quentin—hope that with this show of force, I might forgive *her* for whatever part she played in our rift.

My friend thought she needed to earn her way back into my good graces, which utterly destroyed me. This was our version of fighting. We were incapable of getting truly angry with each other, so instead we tore our hearts out and handed them over on silver platters.

I swallowed all the things I desperately needed to tell her and responded the way I knew she wanted. Like nothing had ever happened.

"For the last time, Quentin and I are not together," I said. Each word was leaden in my mouth, for multiple reasons. "He can do what he feels like."

The flash of relief in Yunie's shoulders was palpable. Once it finished circulating through her veins, it was back to business for her. Getting to cut someone for me, purely for the fun of it now.

"Of course he can," she said airily, the last couple of weeks gone with the wind. "He just needs to accept the consequences. Which in this case is having to see through his own testicles."

Normally I would have moved on right alongside her. Cracked a few jokes about nuts. Pushed and pulled in our familiar pattern. But this time, the burning lump of coal remained stuck in my throat. It didn't go away.

Quentin entered the library to return a stack of books. Yunie locked on to him like a planet-destroying laser.

"The bastard didn't even take off your earrings," she hissed. "That's the last straw. I'm going to get them back."

"They don't open. We tried once but they're stuck."

She grinned at me.

"Yunie, wait!"

My best friend, drunk on righteous anger, marched across the library. In her head Quentin wasn't only a two-timer; he was also responsible for making me miss her concert. She went up and gave him a ringing slap across the face that could have knocked Baigujing's teeth loose.

"*Pbthbdth!* What the hell!?" Quentin shouted.

"You creep!" Yunie roared. "Take them off or I'm going to rip them off!"

She lunged at his face and he caught her by the wrists. It gave me enough time to wrap my arms around her waist and lift her away. The good cop/bad cop routine worked better when bad cop wasn't smaller than most freshmen.

Of course the room had to be packed today. Everyone was laughing at us. Even without the boost from our half-assed making up, this was the kind of drama that could power Yunie for weeks. She'd be queen of the school by the end of it.

I, on the other hand, needed to shut this down. I put down my friend, grabbed my whatever-Quentin-was, and hauled ass out the door.

"What the hell was that?" Quentin asked once we were safe from prying eyes. "Did you tell her to do that?"

"No," I said. "She's upset about you and Rachel."

Quentin furrowed his brow. "Why would she be upset about that?"

"I have no idea," I said. The benefit of time had given me the ability to speak to Quentin in monotone, rather than whatever bird language I was yelping this morning. "I'm certainly fine with it. All I ask is that you not carry on with her right in front of me."

He frowned again. "*Everywhere* is right in front of you, you know that?"

Ahem.

I knew Quentin was referring to my true sight. If I ever turned it on at school, I'd be able to see him no matter where he was. Deep down, way deep down, I knew that was what he meant. No question.

But.

There was also the slightest chance that he was either A) making a comment about my height like he'd never done before, in a "yo' momma sits AROUND the house" sort of joke, or B) accusing me of being clingy and a tagalong, which honestly felt a lot worse.

I didn't want to play interpreter in my current mood. I shut my eyes and walked past him.

■   ■   ■

With nothing going the way it was supposed to, I did what I always did. I threw myself under the mountain. Schoolwork.

That afternoon in study hall I was so deep in a paper that it took me a minute to notice the fire alarm ringing.

Someone shook me gently by the shoulders.

"Genie," Androu said. "We've got to get out of here."

I blinked and looked around the classroom. Everyone else had left.

I swatted off his attempt to take me by the hand and ran into the hallway to see what was going on.

The air was hazy, like someone had smeared Vaseline on a camera lens. I got that there was a fire in the building somewhere, but this was too much smoke, too fast. SF Prep wasn't made out of dried pine needles.

Red Boy, I thought to myself in a panic. We spoke the devil's name too many times and now he was here. I turned on true sight.

And instantly regretted it. The irritating smoke became full-blown acid. It felt like I'd just scrubbed my pupils with sandpaper. I couldn't keep the vision going for more than a second before doubling over in tears.

But it was enough to catch a quick glimpse of blue-black light. A yaoguai, in my school.

I started pushing in that direction.

"Genie!" Androu shouted. "You're going the wrong way!"

I hadn't made it much closer to the source of the demonic energy when I noticed a teacher slumped over in his classroom, passed out. My first thought was that someone had cast sleep on him, but it could have also been a regular old fainting spell. Mr. Yates wasn't exactly a spring chicken.

Androu came running up behind me.

"I don't know how you saw him, but thank god you did." He scrambled past the student chairs and wrapped his arms around our AP calculus teacher's sandbagging weight, hoisting him away from his desk.

"He's still breathing," Androu grunted. "You should have stuck to that Paleo diet, Mr. Yates."

I bit my lip. I could help him carry the body out. But in that time the yaoguai . . . there was no way to tell how many people the demon had its hands on right now. I made the same choice as I did when I bailed on Yunie and my family at the auditorium.

"I saw someone else who needs help," I lied.

"Go," Androu said. "I'll be fine."

I left the classroom and ran down the hallway at a speed that would have made him or any other witnesses do a spit-take. The smoke tore and stripped at my face until I had to slow down.

Right when I thought I'd have to crawl on my hands and knees to get any farther, I heard a violent crash in one of the classrooms. I pressed myself against the wall outside and tilted my head around the door to take a peek.

There were two people fighting in the back, rolling around behind the lab tables. The air in the classroom was soupy with grit. There was no way normal people could have exerted themselves in it.

"Quentin!" I shouted. Just the one word made me want to hack up a lung.

"Genie! Stay back!"

The brawl spilled over the table into view. Quentin had his opponent in a headlock. The struggling figure in his grasp was . . . also Quentin.

There were two Monkey Kings.

"It's the Six-Eared Macaque!" said the one who was getting his trachea squeezed. "He's a shape shifter! He copied my form to infiltrate the school!"

"You're the fake, you bastard!" said the other. "You set this fire so she wouldn't be able to see through your disguise!"

A wave of anger washed over me. I'd been expecting the king of all monsters and instead I got two clowns playing grab-ass with each other.

I ran into the room, gathering all my frustration into my fist, and punched the one on top in the face. He went sprawling back over the table.

"Thanks," the other Quentin said. He rubbed his throat. "I knew you could tell the real—"

I kicked that one in the stomach. He curled up and gasped on the floor.

I backed away to block the exit and tried true sight again. Not a good idea. The smoke in the room flat-out blinded me. By the time I recovered so had the two Quentins, and we were now in a three-way standoff.

"He knows everything I know when he copies my form," said the one on the left. "Secret questions won't work."

"Then how did you beat him last time, back in the old days?" I said.

"The Buddha intervened," said the one on the right.

The Buddha. Oy vey. I dug the heels of my hands into my eyeballs.

Wait a sec, I thought. The Buddha could help me after all. I raised my head and put on my best ultra-pissed-off face, which wasn't too hard given the circumstances.

"OM MANI PADME!" I shouted, leaving off the last syllable.

The two Quentins were identical down to the last hair. And they were both wearing my earrings. But only one of them involuntarily cringed in fear for a split second like a whipped dog, his body flooding with whatever the monkey god version of cortisol and stress hormones were. Knowing of great pain was not the same thing as having actually suffered great pain.

I turned to the other Quentin. The Six-Eared Macaque, whatever the hell kind of yaoguai that was, realized his mistake in the face of my aborted spell. It threw him off to the point where his disguise briefly slipped, Quentin's eyes and mouth rippling away into a smooth, featureless surface.

"Psych," I said to the faceless man.

■　■　■

Quentin and I crawled outside the building and flopped onto the grass. I was bleeding from a gash across my forehead that he promised would seal itself and disappear within minutes, as long as I didn't die first. With the way I felt, we'd have to wait and see.

Quentin grabbed his own fingers and pulled, relocating his joints. The popping noise made me want to vomit.

"Dear god," I croaked. "How did . . . why was that . . . so hard?"

"He was an identical copy of me," Quentin said. He spat a bloody tooth out to the side. "What were you expecting, a pushover?"

I watched his blood sink into the ground and sprout a little daisy with perfect white petals. Whatever. I was beyond surprise when it came to Quentin at this point.

"He seemed so eager to get away from us before that I thought he'd be weaker," I said. "But he fought like a prison inmate from Krypton. He nearly killed the both of us just now!"

"You know we would have had a bigger edge if you ever let me use you as a weapon."

The bad atmosphere between Quentin and me must have also passed if he was bringing up this topic again. Hooray for a return to normalcy. "I told you no already."

Quentin pouted. "Think of it as a deeper, more intimate form of teamwork," he said. "There's no shame in it. If anything, you're the dominant one when we couple ourselves like that."

"Okay, so part of why I will never fight with you as a staff is your inability to describe the process without sounding like a total pervert," I said. "Besides, I can't imagine a worse opponent than your evil doppelganger. As long as you don't get your ass copied like a brand-name handbag again, we'll be fine in the future."

"I don't know," Quentin said. "There's Red Boy . . ."

"When I saw the fire I thought this *was* Red Boy."

He winced. "If it had been Red Boy, there wouldn't be any school left."

We lay on the lawn for a good while, gulping the clean air and prodding our bruises for deeper breaks.

"I need to apologize," I said.

"For what?"

"Making you think I was ever going to say that spell."

Quentin smiled. "I'm sorry, too. For believing that you actually might."

I hesitated.

"Where were you after Third Period?" I said. "Before we saw each other at lunch?" I felt pretty stupid asking; there were more important things to talk about.

"In the computer lab with Rutsuo," he said. "Why?"

That was all the way on the other side of the school from where I saw him playing tonsil hockey. "Really? You weren't with Rachel?"

Guilt dawned over Quentin's face. He ran a hand through his hair.

"I'm sorry for what happened earlier," he said. "I know you don't like her much but I didn't realize helping her with her Spanish homework would upset you. I'll stop."

I thought about turning on true sight to verify his statements, but decided to simply trust him instead. "That's all the two of you do together?"

He looked genuinely confused. "Yeah. What else would I be doing with one of your classmates? I have to fit into this school if I want to be near you, and everyone just studies all the time. You're a bunch of gigantic nerds."

Well there was my answer. It was the Six-Eared Macaque that had gotten to first base with Rachel. I cringed on her behalf and felt supremely glad that I'd sent the asshole who'd duped her to Hell.

It was going to be pretty awkward for Quentin though, the next time they ran into each other. In a lingering fit of pettiness I declined to warn him, even though the real Quentin had done nothing wrong.

"You can hang out with whoever you want." I closed my eyes and leaned back against the nearest tree. "It's not like I own you or anything."

■   ■   ■

Once Quentin and I were able to make ourselves presentable enough, we circled around the building to join the rest of our class.

The trail of smoke leading into the sky only made it seem bluer and clearer by contrast. The grass under our feet was as crisp and green as money. Even the plain, redbrick façade of the school looked handsomer than most days. Good old SF Prep! Dinged up a bit by today's events, but still standing proud.

I could feel my wounds melting away like Quentin said they

would. The tingling sensation was mildly euphoric. But even better than the mutant healing factor was the sense of closure. We'd found the faceless man, sewn up the loose thread. We'd corrected our mistake and could close the book on this case.

We ran into Mrs. Nanda coming the other way around the building. She was wearing a bright-orange safety vest over her dress and carrying a walkie-talkie.

"Genie! Quentin! Where *were* you two?" she cried out, angry and relieved at the same time. "You know our class's rendezvous point is by the baseball diamond! I was worried sick!"

"I'm sorry, Mrs. Nanda," I said. "The, uh, smoke got too thick and we had to use the opposite exit. We're fine."

"Well get over there right now and stay put!" She pressed the button on her handset and it squawked to life. "I found Lo and Sun," she said. "Repeat. Lo and Sun are with me."

The walkie-talkie beeped back. "Affirmative. What about Park and Glaros?"

Quentin and I stopped walking at the mention of Yunie's and Androu's last names.

Mrs. Nanda's voice wavered as she spoke. "Still no sign."

"I don't understand," said the person on the other end. "We've done a full sweep. A bunch of the kids said they saw them before the alarm went off. Where'd they go?"

"I'll check back in the East wing again, including the locked areas," Mrs. Nanda said. "Maybe they got past the doors somehow. Do another head count just to be sure, and call their parents."

Our teacher hurried off, concern for her missing students quickening her pace.

■ ■ ■

The siren of a fire engine wailed louder. Approaching. Imminent. My words echoed in my head.

An evil copy of Quentin.

A copy of Quentin.

According to the book, Quentin could make copies of himself.

"What are the signs of spiritual power in a layperson?" I asked, swaying where I stood, a palm tree buffeted by a storm. "How do demons choose their prey?"

"If you're not a monk like Xuanzang, then the biggest indicators are . . ." Quentin's eyes widened. "Unyielding moral character. Or exceptional talent."

I began to tremble.

"Genie." Quentin gripped me by the arms. "Genie, breathe."

I couldn't feel his hands on me. I couldn't feel anything. I would never feel anything again.

Quentin guided me across the school lawn to a side street where no one would see us. It took a long time. I was deteriorating rapidly.

He set me gently down on the curb. I squeezed my knees to my chest. I wanted to be small, to shrink myself until I died.

"We won't find her," I choked out over the tightness in my throat. "If the earrings aren't going off then they're not working for some reason. I won't know where to look."

"Genie, don't give up."

Quentin was doing his best to be resolute, but even he couldn't keep the act going. I could tell he thought the odds of getting her back were slim to none.

He began walking in a circle. "Think," he said out loud to himself, rubbing his temples. "Think."

I had never seen him do this before. He must have been truly desperate.

"We don't know where he is," Quentin muttered. "We only defeated a copy of him before. But if he took two humans for whatever purpose, he would have done it himself."

I choked back a sob. Yunie and Androu didn't even have names anymore in Quentin's clinical triage.

"There's only so far they could have gone," he said. "The farthest away they could be is . . . as far as *I* could have taken them."

He stopped pacing. A glimmer of hope poked through in his voice. "The Macaque's not an ordinary demon. He's not setting off the demon alarm . . . because he's me. He's me, down to the last hair on my head. He has my looks, my smell, my aura. My aura that reacts to your aura."

Quentin kneeled down in front of me. "Genie," he said. "I might be able to find them using *you* as a signal. But you have to be in a state of complete disconnection for your aura to be strong enough. This is a long shot and I know it's never worked in the past, but I need you to calm yourself and—and—"

I knew what he was asking. He needed me to meditate.

"You can do it," he said. "Just empty your mind and think of nothing. Nothing at all."

I didn't protest. This would be easy.

I took one last look around. The street was still empty and silent, the din of the emergency vehicles having ended. The firemen were probably making their way through the halls of the school right now, searching for two students who fit Mrs. Nanda's description.

I closed my eyes and found only hollowness inside me. I didn't want to continue anymore. I wanted to sever myself from the Earth completely.

■　■　■

A deep chime erupted from my core.

It was as if someone had struck a giant iron bell with a sledge-hammer. Concentric rings of energy shot out from me in every direction. I could sightlessly feel them carry over the landscape, like I had joined the ranks of whales and bats and other creatures with echolocation.

"Stay here," I heard Quentin say. "I'll come back for you once I find them."

He ran away so fast that a small dust cloud blew into my face. I opened my eyes. They were blurry with tears, so I could have been seeing things, but it looked like there was a geometrically increasing number of Quentins speeding off into the distance, chasing the invisible sonar waves of my aura.

■　■　■

I had no idea how long I had been sitting there in the street when Quentin returned. Even the position of the sun failed to register for me.

He came in hot. I felt the impact of his landing, a small quake in the ground under my feet, and then he was by my side again. Like he'd never left.

"Get on!" he shouted in my ear. "Hurry!"

He wouldn't have motored like this if the situation were either irrevocably lost or saved. But I couldn't share in his hope. I was still numb.

I wasn't moving fast enough, so he swept me onto his back, and we were airborne.

■ ■ ■

We landed in the middle of a tree grove. We'd traveled all the way to the city in one leap, touching down in the forested park that drivers had to pass before crossing the landmark bridge where Quentin first taught me how to use true sight.

The eucalyptus trees reached to the sky, forming bar codes against the waning daylight. There was no beaten path anywhere near us. The woods were silent, strained free of man-made noise.

This was the site of a showdown. Handpicked for maximum effect. The director of the scene stepped out from behind a thick tree trunk, still wearing Quentin's face.

"You made good time," the Six-Eared Macaque said, using Quentin's voice but in a slightly higher register, as if he was doing me a favor to tell them apart.

"So are you a copy, too?" Quentin said.

The Macaque grinned. "Nope. You're looking at the head vampire right here."

He was telling the truth.

"If you're relieved that you only have to kill me one more time, I wouldn't be," the Macaque said. "After all, I have your friends. They're still alive, but they won't be unless you do exactly as I say."

He spread his hands out like he'd arranged a delicious feast. "Let's play a little game. One that requires you to use every power of the Ruyi—"

I was upon him before either of us knew how.

I pinned the demon to the ground by the neck with one hand and punched him with all of my might.

My knucklebones broke with the first impact, but so did part of his face. I punched him again, hard enough to indent the soil underneath his head.

The Macaque's expression was one of total shock. "But—"

But nothing. The worldly detachment, the meditative calmness that had allowed me to harness my aura, was gone. Pitch-black hatred poured into my fist. I punched the demon again, knocking the Quentin out of him. The blank eggshell of the faceless man rippled into being and somehow under the smooth surface, he looked scared.

He was supposed to look dead. I smashed him again, over and over, and found enough rhythm to speak.

"DON'T YOU! EVER! TOUCH HER! YOU SON OF A BITCH!" I screamed, hammering him with each word. *"I'LL KILL YOU! I'LL FOLLOW YOU TO HELL AND I'LL KILL YOU THERE!"*

On second thought, I was glad the Macaque was tough. I didn't want him to die easily. My blows struck growing cracks into his skull. I ignored the equivalent injuries to my hand.

The demon screamed and writhed in my grip. Like a threatened animal with camouflage, he changed color and shape, trying to find a form that would relieve the assault. His face cycled through random people, including the doorman and the maid from the apartment building we'd first found him in. He even tried switching to Yunie and Androu in turn, but by that point I'd done so much damage that only half of his face was capable of changing, ruining the illusion.

I didn't stop. I hit him even harder. I needed to hit him so hard that my message would be stamped across the bones of the universe. There needed to be more of me just to hit him forever, until the end of time.

Suddenly the Macaque lost his solidness, my fist embedding in the ground up to my elbow. I would have kept going into the cloud of ink that indicated he was finally no more, but Quentin tackled me.

"Genie, stop!"

I flung Quentin away and looked around for something else to hit. My eyes still weren't functioning properly, because all of a sudden there were Yunie and Androu, lying unconscious under a tree. I'd completely missed how they'd gotten here.

At the sight of my friend I fell to my hands and knees and dry heaved all over the ground underneath me.

"What is wrong with you?" Quentin said. "The Macaque had spells rigged up like a dead man's switch in case you attacked him! I almost couldn't save them in time! You put her in the most danger she's been in today!"

I sat back down and clutched my ribs until they stopped fighting me. Quentin's accusation wasn't the half of it.

The Six-Eared Macaque had the Monkey King's strength and knew how to neutralize my true sight. Which made him the perfect infiltrator. Someone had sent him to hurt me personally.

How could I have been so stupid as to think the demons would be content to wait in their lairs until I showed up to fight them? That they wouldn't go on the offensive, hunting down me and my loved ones in kind? Yunie had been in danger ever since I took on this role—the instant I'd accepted that I was the Ruyi Jingu Bang. My first and biggest mistake.

I looked up to see Quentin angling his fingers for a spell. He put his hands on Yunie's head.

"Wait!" I screamed.

A pulse of energy bounced between his palms, and Yunie's eyes rolled around under her lids like she was dreaming. The whole effect was too close to a person in an electric chair and I panicked, throwing myself between them.

"It's just a *forget* spell!" Quentin said as I shoved him away. "She saw too much! If I don't keep recasting it on her, she'll remember the Macaque taking her, me using magic, all of it!"

"Don't do that!" After everything that happened today, hexing Yunie was another intolerable violation. I was terrified by the notion that when she woke up, she wouldn't recognize me, or even worse, herself. "Undo it! Take it back!"

"Genie, we don't have time for this!" Quentin turned to Androu and scooped up the much larger boy with surprising tenderness. "He's dying from smoke inhalation! We have to get him to a hospital right now, or he's done for!"

32

I CAME HOME EARLY FROM SCHOOL FOR THE FIFTH DAY IN A row. But that would be it—volleyball practice was going to resume a normal schedule on Monday.

I tossed my bag on the counter. Mom stood over the stove. I'd been trying to talk to her more in general, and I could tell she liked having the few extra hours with me even if they ended up being filled with more of our usual squabbling.

"What's for dinner?" I asked.

She didn't answer.

"Are you mad about something?" I couldn't think of anything I'd done. I leaned over to look at her face.

It was perfectly still. The pinch of salt she was adding to the pot arced from her fingers, stuck in the air. The pot itself probably would've burned over hours before, but the bubbles hovered under the surface, never bursting, never moving.

"What the hell do you want?" I snapped. I turned around to see Guanyin sitting on the stairs.

"To talk."

I looked around the house to see how much space had been affected. "I don't want you doing this to my mother," I snapped. "Don't cast anything on her ever again."

"You know she's not being harmed in any way."

"I said don't screw with my mother!"

Guanyin frowned. "Then we should take a walk."

.   .   .

I could have pretended we were headed to the town library. This was the long way, the same path Quentin and I had been walking when the Demon King of Confusion had shown up. Reality was an infinite loop.

"Quentin says you won't speak to him," Guanyin said.

I stepped on fallen leaves that were drying in the heat. Crushing their delicate, fractal forms felt good. I was ruining configurations that would never exist again.

"Perhaps you've decided you'll cover more ground if you hunt separately. I don't advise that. The two of you have always made a good team."

I said nothing.

Guanyin closed her eyes, trusting that I wouldn't take her into a ditch. "I'm sorry about what happened to your friends."

"Yeah?" I stopped where I was. "Then maybe you should have led with that."

"Forgive me my preoccupation with the bigger picture," she said, a little testier than before. "I understood that Yunie was ultimately unharmed. And that Androu made a miraculous, complete recovery in the hospital. Which I may have had something to do with, by the way."

"Gee, thanks!" I shouted. "It was the least you could do after nearly killing them both!"

"Genie, I didn't consider that a yaoguai with the right skills could have copied Quentin so completely as to bypass detection. Are you angry at me for being fallible?"

"No, I'm angry at you for being a liar! You and Erlang Shen told me I was going to be hunting demons. But that wasn't true, was it? The Demon King of Confusion and Tawny Lion took Quentin and me completely by surprise. Baigujing and the Hundred-Eyed Demon Lord were laying traps. Red Boy is probably watching me right now, laughing!"

These were all clues I should have pieced together myself, but this is what I did when I was upset. Shift blame.

"I'm not the hunter here!" I said. "I never was. The demons are hunting *me*. And you *let* them!"

Guanyin didn't deny my accusation. She stood there with the practiced air of a punching bag, waiting for me to finish. I didn't have much left anyway.

"I'm out," I said. "I'm done. You know what the Macaque proved? That I'm an awful person who doesn't care about everyone equally. I have a hierarchy of people I care about, and random strangers who might end up as demon food don't make the cut. Not when my friends and family are at risk."

What I didn't say aloud was that I was even worse than that. My loved ones also had their own ranks. Throughout the whole encounter with the Macaque, beginning with the fire in my school, I hadn't given a single thought to Androu. If I had helped him carry our teacher, if I had given him just an ounce of consideration in the forest, he might not have come so close to dying.

I could claim distraction and panic over Yunie all I wanted as an excuse, but the fact of the matter was that I *chose*, even if it was by omission. I disgusted myself.

"I'm not like you," I said to Guanyin. My anger was a burned-out husk at this point, exhaustion seeping in to claim the void. "I can't be the world's protector. I can't even protect my hometown, let alone the entire friggin' Bay Area. You have to find a different champion. Maybe Xuanzang's reincarnation is hanging around somewhere, wondering why you haven't shown up."

Guanyin crossed her arms and went silent for a while, tapping her foot slowly. I watched her ruminate, a gentle worry creasing her brow. She looked all the more beautiful and heavenly for it, an angel wondering what she could do to shepherd her charge back onto the right path.

When she finally opened her mouth, I braced for the inevitable speech about how wrong I was, how only *I* could do this. A stronger, better rehash of the talk she used to convince me in the first place.

"Wow, Genie," she said. "I never realized you were such a pathetic coward."

Meanness did not suit the goddess's lovely voice. It made her words creaky and rough. A muscle she hadn't used in a long time.

"So you had a close call," she said. "Big deal. You know what you learn after a few centuries of bearing the world's suffering? They're *all* close calls. The only victories you get are by the skin of your teeth."

I couldn't believe what I was hearing.

"When things break their way, most people call themselves lucky and move on," Guanyin said. "Instead you wallow in self-pity. How dare you."

"Are you *serious*?" I shouted. "Do you know what could have happened that day!?"

"I hear the torment of billions of souls hammering on my ears every second of every day of every year. I know exactly what could have happened, in every permutation of death and suffering there is to know. I'm not impressed by your guilt, Genie. Or your love for your friends. I get that you want to peacock in front of me how much they mean to you. But I don't care. I simply don't."

"You know what this is to me?" she said. "A numbers game. Perhaps I should have been more up front about that from the beginning. This is about head count. Not feelings."

Guanyin stepped closer, and it was all I could do not to crumple into a ball from her presence.

"I sacrificed the chance to leave Heaven and Earth behind me," she said. "I gave up *Enlightenment*. Can you imagine? The greatest personal accomplishment one can possibly achieve in existence. And I gave it up because *one* is not a very big number, is it?"

She was nearly toe-to-toe with me at this point. "I keep going because there's a chance I can help a few more people out of the billions. But you! Getting spooked because it's finally sunk in for you that stoves are hot, scissors are sharp, and someone could get hurt! If I were as weak as you I wouldn't have lasted a minute as a Bodhisattva."

The goddess finally looked off to the side, too disgusted with me to make eye contact anymore. Her jaw flexed angrily like a heartbeat.

I wasn't prepared for this line of attack. I had thought that somewhere deep down, Guanyin would have given me the same consideration she gave her other supplicants. I thought it was her job to do that, to cradle my hopes and fears. Instead she'd done the math of human suffering and figured I was merely the end of the lever she could pull for maximum results.

It took me a few swallows to force the lumps down my throat. "You ever give Xuanzang this kind of pep talk?"

Guanyin scoffed. "I didn't have to. Xuanzang was an incompetent boob who had nothing better to do than go on a journey where he faced zero hard choices. He never had to make any real trade-offs in the first place."

She'd said it with the sureness and momentum of someone treading on familiar ground. If she hadn't spoken those words out loud before, she'd certainly thought them countless times before.

"Don't you dare try to compare yourself to Xuanzang," Guanyin pressed on. "People like Xuanzang and the Jade Emperor are free to do as they please. People like you and me are not."

"What do you mean?"

"I mean that Xuanzang was free to bumble across a continent and fail upward into sainthood. The Jade Emperor is free to sit on his ass and ignore the world screaming for his help. You and I are not free. You and I have a duty."

"As what?" I could only spot one glaring difference between figures like the Jade Emperor and Xuanzang in one hand, and me and Guanyin in the other. "You and I have duties as what?"

She raised her palms up, letting her generosity flow out. It was the posture she was worshipped in. It was also a shrug.

"As beings of great power," she said.

We stared at each other for what could either have been an eternity or a time freeze. Maybe the problem wasn't that Guanyin didn't understand. It could have been that she understood too well.

The goddess broke the silence first.

"In the off-chance that it gives you enough spine to resume the hunt, I've put your entire town under my direct protection," she said. "You have no idea what that act cost me among the other gods, and you never will. But at least that's one less concern for *you*."

I didn't let on how much of a relief it was to hear that. Instead I decided to ask a question that I'd been holding in my head for a while. It wasn't as if there was going to be a better moment.

"Did Red Boy actually break out those other demons? Or did you make a mistake giving out your karma again, to the point where they could leave Hell on their own?" It would have explained why she was so dead set on me finishing this quest. She might have needed me to right her wrong.

"Please," Guanyin said. "That's the first thing everyone in Heaven accused me of. I made one error long ago, thinking that a general amnesty for those sentenced to Hell might be a good experiment, and I'm still dealing with the fallout to this day."

"Well it is kind of your M.O."

"Any powerful being can give away their karma. Erlang Shen can do it. The Jade Emperor can do it. I happened to be the only one who was willing to take the risk."

The corner of her lip hiked upward in amusement.

"But you're right in that the rest of the celestial pantheon thinks this whole mess is my fault anyway," Guanyin said. "'That stupid woman was too soft on Red Boy! What was she thinking, putting a fearsome demon on a blessed island instead of sending him to Hell where he belonged?'"

"You were thinking that imprisoning Red Boy in Hell would be pointless if he could break in and out so easily," I answered for her. "You cared more about minimizing the harm he could do than making sure he was punished. You put him on an island in the middle of a Heavenly ocean because that's as good a jail as any for a fire demon. You took the burden of watching him upon yourself because everyone else was too afraid."

Guanyin smiled, proud that I'd figured it out. "There's my smart girl."

It seemed like our talk was coming to a close. I didn't want to let her get away completely unscathed.

"You know, you wouldn't have to put up with crap from the other gods if you took over from the Jade Emperor," I said. "If you were sitting on the Dragon Throne of Heaven."

She looked at me incredulously. I could tell I was speaking treason.

"But that's me saying crazy things," I went on. "After all, you know your place, don't you?"

Guanyin blinked, and then burst out into laughter. Surprisingly deep, side-clutching laughter. It was as rusty on her as her cruel voice was.

"Oh man," she said when she was finally done. "If you ever try to provoke me like that again, I'll slap the taste out of your mouth."

She wiped a tear from her eye and smiled, her face put back to its normal serenity.

"And then I'll turn you into a goddamn cricket."

33

I MAY HAVE ACTED TOUGH, STANDING UP TO GUANYIN, BUT IN reality I felt as if I'd barely escaped that conversation with my life. I could finally see why Quentin was so hesitant to get on her bad side.

In what I considered a massive reprieve, she didn't show up again for a while. I assumed the goddess was plotting her next move now that her best piece was proving wayward.

Despite what I'd told her, though, I hadn't left the game entirely. After what happened to Yunie and Androu, I'd simply switched my priorities to defense. Guanyin might have put wards of some kind around Santa Firenza, but like she said, she wasn't infallible. There were still more than ninety demons out there, and I'd be damned if I let one get too close again.

I used true sight preemptively at school until the brink of exhaustion, trying to act like an early warning radar for the entire building in case a yaoguai came back for more. Eventually I had to settle for only looking during class breaks, or I wouldn't have had the stamina to extend the search at night.

I stayed awake in my room until my eyes nearly fell out of my head, scanning as far and wide as I could. Without the height advantage that Quentin's leaping provided, it took a lot longer to get a decent area covered. I began to feel like a human lighthouse, casting high beams into the endless sea.

With nothing better to do in between sweeps, I worked on my college application essays. If guilt and fear weren't going to let me sleep, I could at least be productive.

I wrote in a pensive, dreamlike state in the wee hours of the night. Hopefully that introduced a touch of whatever magic was missing, because I sure as hell didn't know how to add it on purpose.

I made so many revisions I might have created a wormhole in space-time. On the advice of some admissions blog, I interviewed myself in my head, using posh Oxbridge voices reserved for world leaders. I even tried staring at the page with true sight, and I felt pretty dumb when all it did was show me the raccoons eating our garbage in the yard.

The sheer amount of effort I was putting into these essays had to add up to something. It would be a violation of thermodynamics if it didn't.

■　■　■

The end of the month arrived. I bounded down the stairs to make my pilgrimage to Anna's.

"Wait." Mom pounced as I passed her. "You're going to let her see you wearing those?"

I patted myself down, confused. My clothes should have been fine. She'd never objected to how I looked on any of my city trips before.

Then it hit me. I hadn't seen Quentin in a while, which meant the spell that kept my (ugh) golden eyes hidden was long expired.

I'd been going out every day "wearing contacts," often right in front of my mother.

"I'll, uh, take them out," I said. "Why didn't you say anything about them earlier?"

"You're at that age." She made a face of intense bitterness where another woman might have been pleasantly wistful. "I can't stop you from doing everything. Even if you want to look like a cheap Internet girl."

I stared at my mother for a second, and then I wrapped her in a big hug.

"But if you dye your hair I swear I'll throw you out of this house," she muttered into my shoulder.

■   ■   ■

My knee was bouncing up and down so much, I was afraid Anna could feel it all the way through her thick, solid floors. I couldn't stop it. I was too nervous.

She had already blown past the amount of time she'd ever spent reading my essays before. A new PR. K-Song would have been proud.

Anna opened her mouth. I hitched in anticipation, fearing the worst.

Then she chuckled.

"Genie, this is a hoot," she said. "I had no idea you could be this funny."

Huh. My hope sprouted like the first daisy of spring. Ready to be obliterated by the slightest breeze, but present regardless.

"I, um, did what you said and focused on my own thoughts. I wasn't too familiar in my tone?"

"Not at all. I can't get enough of this bit about your parents. This is a major improvement in your writing, by leaps and bounds. Any reader would be happy to get this in their pile."

My god.

I'd done it. I'd gotten past the barrier of "If you have to ask, you'll never know." I was seeing the inside of their secret club, even if they'd only let me in through a case of mistaken identity.

I resisted the urge to run into the street and fist-bump the oncoming traffic in celebration. "Thank you," I said. "I guess once I get to Harvard I'll go out for the *Lampoon*."

My joke fell flat with Anna. She looked disappointed, like she wanted to stay in the happy place a little longer.

"We . . . should talk about that," she said, putting my papers to the side.

I didn't like how far she'd put them to the side. Had she kept them a little closer to her elbow, I could have pretended all was well.

"Genie, I played a little loose with the rules the other day. I called up a contact at . . . I won't say where exactly, but I talked to a relevant decision maker, let's put it."

Oh damn. She'd gone to bat for me. She'd gone. To bat. She really did have guanxi. And here I was thinking all I'd get from her was advice on how to articulate my inner nature.

"Now I didn't mention you or anyone else specifically," she said, "but I was able to talk about your scenario in a fair amount of detail because it applies to many applicants. And therein lies the problem. Based on how the conversation went, I think we need to adjust our expectations."

She was pulling a reality show host move. There would be

dramatic music leading to a commercial break, after which she would complete her sentence. *Higher!* she'd say brightly. *We need to be aiming even higher, with how strong you are! There's a secret exclusive university on the moon!*

"I—I don't understand. What problem are we talking about? My grades? I have perfect grades."

"You do," she said. "But so do a huge number of students, from great schools just like yours. Your writing is great, and so is theirs. This is the point I'm trying to make, Genie. The very reason why I could get away with talking about you anonymously is the fact that there are a lot of applicants with your exact candidacy profile."

I could feel the floor spinning away from me. I was being ensorcelled.

"Colleges care about geographic diversity as much as any other kind, and right now you're swimming in one of the biggest, most competitive pools," Anna said. "That's going to have a material effect on your application experience."

"I think I get it," I said. "Your contacts told you there's only so many Bay Area Chinese they're willing to take."

Anna looked pained. "Genie, that's not what I'm saying."

Yes it was, even if she didn't know it.

I didn't blame Anna. Hell, I didn't even blame the colleges. SF Prep was full of people like me. Grasping, thirsting, dying to get ahead. We were like roaches, and only multiplying by the day. I didn't want to be around my kind any more than the admissions boards did.

I had done everything I could to declare myself a real person. But it didn't matter. It still boiled down to a numbers game, and not one that tilted in my favor.

"I wish I had better news," Anna said. "I called my old office up because I can see how hungry you are. But my duty as your advisor is to help you make the right call in the long term, not just that one moment when you tear open the envelope. Your financial aid needs—they're not trivial. None of your top choices give athletic or merit-based scholarships. We have to consider what to do if they end up out of reach."

I closed my eyes.

"Out of reach," I said. "That's ironic, given that I've made my arms longer than this room."

"This room's not very big," she responded.

I stood up from my chair. "Colleges like well-traveled applicants, right? I'm well-traveled. I went from Chang'an to Vulture Peak to recover the sutras. It only took me a couple of years."

"That was a long time ago. A million tourists have completed the same trip since then. With selfies."

"Let's talk about volunteer work then!" I leaped onto Anna's desk and thumped my chest with my fists. "I've fought pure evil! Do you understand? Cannibalistic boogeymen! Nearly twenty and counting!"

Anna looked up at me and sucked in air through her teeth. "I'm sorry. The minimum requirement for a Van Helsing Grant is thirty demons."

■　■　■

It took me a while to come back. I opened my eyes.

Once I did, I was treated to the sight of Anna reaching across her desk and patting my hand in sympathy.

"I know it's hard to hear, but we should talk about what to do if we need to pivot. Consider local schools, maybe lean more on sports. There are plenty of colleges that could be a great fit. Many of them right here in the Bay."

Have a life just like the one I had right now. Stop all forward movement. Be pinned under the Milky Way.

"I could live at home instead of a dorm," I said, my voice cracking. "I'd save on boarding fees with my mother as my roommate."

Anna nearly said "that's the spirit" before she saw my eyes. She squeezed my hand. I couldn't believe how wrong I was about her before—how utterly kind she was underneath her imposing exterior.

"I think I should go for today," I said, suddenly short of breath. "Even if the session's not over. I have a . . . thing."

"Of course, hon. We'll prorate the time and I'll clear up an extra half-hour next month to make up for it."

I nodded and stumbled out her door.

Hon. That's how pathetic I was. I was a *hon.*

■　■　■

Quentin was outside Anna's office, waiting for me. I hadn't asked him to come, but here he was. People passed around us on the busy sidewalk like we were stones in a river.

"Back when I was storming Heaven," he said, as if it were the most normal thing in the world to start a sentence like that, "when you were in my hands, and together we were smashing the door to the throne room of the Thunder Palace—the most powerful barrier in the known universe, turning bit by bit to splinters and dust—a funny thought occurred to me then."

A funny thing happened on the way to the Dragon Throne. There was an epic punch line coming.

"Gatekeepers decide within a few seconds whether or not they're going to open the gate for you," he said. "And then once they decide to keep you out, you're out forever. All it takes is a few seconds."

"Once they make their snap judgment, they can't be swayed. They will *never* open the gate. You could be on fire and they could have water and they won't open the gate. They could be starving and you could be made of food, and they still won't open the gate."

Quentin scratched the back of his head, embarrassed to reveal he wasn't the insensate berserker the story made him out to be.

"I stopped swinging, one blow away from breaking through the doors to the other side and becoming King of Heaven," he said. "I sat down on the floor and waited for the Buddha to show up. I patiently waited for a very long time. Then once he arrived, I climbed into his hand, and he did his whole thing with the mountain."

It was a good story. But I wanted a different one right now.

"How did I die?" I said.

"Huh?"

"How did I die? When I was the Ruyi Jingu Bang?"

Quentin hadn't been willing to tell me before, but he knew better than to deny me now. He took a deep breath, as if he were the one who needed steadying.

"You didn't die," he said. "You moved on. I woke up one day and you were gone from my side. You'd taken all the karma you'd earned from hundreds of years of fighting evil and saving lives and expended it in one risky attempt to become human.

"I can't tell you how because I don't know. There was no guarantee it would work. You could have stepped into the Void and ended up in Hell, or worse. You could have disappeared entirely. But that's how badly you wanted to keep moving forward. That's how much you hated being told to stay in your place."

I felt my eyes burn in a way that they wouldn't for anyone else in the world. I'd let the old me down, more than I ever thought possible. After epic toil and hardship, the Ruyi Jingu Bang had erased herself from existence to become something new, and I'd failed her by hitting the wall within one lifetime.

"You should go back to Heaven," I said to Quentin.

"Why?"

"To sit there and wait eighty, ninety days."

"But if I did that you'd—"

"I know. If you did that, I would age out and die. For every day in Heaven, a year passes on Earth, right? So wait three months in Heaven. A fiscal quarter. After I pass away as a human being, maybe I'll come back as a stick.

"That should have been your plan all along," I continued. "You should never have come to Earth in the first place. The two of us are demon magnets, and being together makes it worse. Get out of here and let me run out my life span."

I knew exactly how much hurt would be in Quentin's eyes when I said it. So all the worse on me for letting him walk away without a word.

34

I WATCHED MY DAD FROM OUTSIDE THE GYM'S GLASS windows, whistling to himself as he sanitized the incline benches. He didn't know I was there. A few weeks ago I would have said he was the fish in the fishbowl, but now I knew that wasn't true.

He'd earned the right to a peaceful existence like this one. He'd taken the kind of risk that the extreme sportsmen he wiped up after would never understand. My father had given the finger to the system and sure, maybe that finger had been bitten off, but hey. The breaks. He understood thems.

And meanwhile his daughter, who'd gone to school on his meager dimes, and worn the clothes he'd put on her back, had thought she'd float into the sky and ascend gracefully into Heaven, buoyed by a cloud of rules followed and boxes checked.

I always faulted him for overconfidence. Thought I was better than him. But he'd at least put his blind faith in his own two fists instead of letting the fight go to the judges. I'd never been so brave.

For a moment, Dad looked up as if he'd sensed I was late. But a client entering the gym, a young banker type in Lycra knitwear, came over to say hi to him. The two of them, as different a pair of human beings as could possibly be, became engrossed in a conversation that involved pantomiming shoulder injuries.

I turned around and left.

■　■　■

I had a lot of time to kill after flaking on both Anna and Dad. I went to the park.

The weather was good, and it was packed sidewalk to sidewalk with sunbathing, wine-drinking yuppies. They formed a carpet of trim, attractive bodies over the grass that would occasionally bunch up as people rolled on their elbows to check each other out.

I sat against a tree in the back. The shade was cold and the knobs on the roots were hurting my thighs. I didn't deserve comfort.

I felt old. Older than everyone around me, even though that wasn't true. They came in different flavors of twentysomething. Unless they'd been trucked in from far away, they were uniformly well-to-do. Only people with large salaries could afford the rent nearby. Most of the accents I heard wafting on the breeze weren't local.

This, if I had to be honest, was exactly what I'd been fighting for. I was after a good school and a good job, wasn't I? Well, these people went to good schools and had good jobs. Chilling here on a sunny Saturday was what people who went to good schools and had good jobs did in these parts. Somewhere on one of these blankets was my spot. My eternal reward.

"None of you have ever fought what I've fought," I said out loud. "You can't see what I see."

I could have said the word *demons*. No one was listening, and even if they were, it didn't matter a lick.

My eye caught on a tall, starkly handsome man picking his way toward me through the crowd. He was wearing an athletic top and sandals like half the people lying on the grass, but he was in much better shape than all of them. When he got close enough he lowered his shades.

"I thought it was you," Erlang Shen said.

The last person I was expecting. "What are you doing here?"

He produced a can wrapped in a brown bag and wiggled it. "I'm getting drunk."

The last thing I was expecting him to say. He must have seen the confusion on my face because he laughed as he sat down next to me.

"There's a Peach Banquet going on in Heaven," he said. "Lots of wine flowing freely. But I can't stand celebrations, and I don't like indulging in front of the other gods. So in times like these I find various watering holes on Earth and drink human drinks. I was at a bar down the street but I felt your presence nearby."

"Do you need three hundred and sixty-five human cocktails to match one Heaven serving?"

"Actually the exchange rate for alcohol is a binary logarithm, so it's one thousand twenty-eight," he said. "Right now I'm on six hundred thirteen."

I snorted. He was as big of a dork as I was.

"By the way," he said, waving the can. "I have completely failed on every promise I gave you before."

"There was just the one promise. Your uncle won't let you help round up the remaining demons?"

"Nope. He refused to entertain the subject during the celebration and told me that bringing it up further would be a sign of disrespect. That I would be displaying to the other gods a lack of filial piety."

Erlang Shen raised his drink in a toast.

"Here's to the delicate sensibilities of our elders," he said. "The most important and fragile treasures in the universe. May we break our backs protecting them."

"Hear, hear."

We watched the newly minted adults frolic on the green. Most of them probably only called their parents once a month on average.

"I didn't ask what you were doing here," he said. "You don't live in this city. And when I first saw you, your face looked like death itself."

"Gee, thanks," I answered. "I was gazing into my future."

"What did you see?"

"That the only way to keep my loved ones safe forever is to self-immolate," I said. "I have it all planned out. I'm going to sit on top of Half Dome and send a golden light into the sky like I did when I was still in Ao Guang's treasure hoard. It'll be a beacon for every yaoguai to come and get it. A dinner bell.

"I'll fight them all in one big battle," I went on. "King-of-the-hill style. If I can't defeat them all, I'll take down as many as I can."

"It's not a bad plan. Do you know how to glow with Heavenly light?"

"Nope. I'll have to figure that out first. And I notice you're not trying to talk me out of it."

"There's nothing wrong with grand gestures sometimes. I will say this, though, if you're planning to go down in flames . . ."

He leaned back on his elbows. "I, as an immortal with infinite eternities to enjoy, advise you, a pathetic insect whose life span is but a candle flicker, to at least have some fun before you die."

I could only laugh at his brutal honesty.

"That's partly why I chose the nearest national park," I said. "I've never been."

"What else do you want to do?"

"It'd be cool to stop a crime in progress. Like a superhero. It'd have to be a regular, human crime. I don't know why, but yaoguai wouldn't count."

"Of course not. You'd need the change of pace. Anything else?"

"I want to destroy something."

He was taken aback at how quickly I said it. And perhaps at how much I meant it.

"I want to lose control and utterly wreck something," I said. "I don't know what. Probably not anything anyone cares about, like a building. But maybe a boulder. Although some people would be angry if certain landmark boulders were destroyed, so I can't do it in the park. I'd have to go to a quarry."

"You've . . . given this some thought, haven't you?"

"Yeah, that's not a Ruyi Jingu Bang desire. That one's pure Genie."

"You know where you could really go nuts with your powers?" he pitched. "Heaven."

"I'm sure that would go over well with the other gods, seeing as how I wrecked the place the last time I was there."

"I'm serious," he said. "There are so many holy mountains that no one uses. The place is infinitely big; it won't matter if one tiny part gets leveled."

He sat up and faced me.

"Tell you what. Why don't you come with me to Heaven for a bit? As my guest? We can check out the Peach Banquet together.

With you there, it might be tolerable. And if you don't like it, we can go break stuff. It'll be fun."

"Isn't there that time difference thing? If I'm in Heaven for a day, I'm gone for a year on Earth."

"So?" said Erlang Shen. "Maybe you deserve a vacation. A semester abroad. What people never tell you is that a day in Heaven is worth more than a hundred years on Earth. Earth sucks."

It was awfully tempting, I had to admit. Earth did often suck. Walking away from everything might have been just what I needed.

I sighed. But still.

"Not happening," I said. "My mother would—"

"To hell with your mother," Erlang Shen snapped.

It was an uncharacteristic flash of temper. When I looked at him, he withdrew immediately and shrugged.

"Thanks for the offer," I said. "But I think I'll pass."

I got up to leave. It was a long train ride back, and I was already late. Mom would be furious. "I'm gonna do a quick yaoguai check here before going home."

"Wait, wait," he said, suddenly alarmed. "You're just using true sight randomly now? Without Guanyin's warning?"

"It's my new paranoia in action," I said as I pressed my temple.

The park was all clear. Maybe demons preferred to sunbathe in less-trendy spots. I glanced at Erlang Shen, who seemed a little embarrassed at being laid out in all his godly glory.

He needn't have been. The pulsing waves of energy radiating off him would have knocked me to the ground, but I was used to the effect from Quentin. I gave him a reassuring smile.

"That reminds me," I said. "Quentin told me it'd be dangerous if I went to Heaven. Did you have a spell or something that would protect me?"

Erlang Shen said nothing.

"Or was he lying about it being dangerous? He said my humanity would be burned away, but he could have been making up an excuse to get out of taking me there."

Erlang Shen still said nothing. Not even a mumble.

I frowned.

I had only been speaking in a by-the-way manner, but something wasn't right. I gave Erlang Shen a closer look. There was an odd cold spot on his flank where the spiritual heat was completely missing, like he'd donated a kidney to someone. Given part of his godliness away.

"Hey," I said, ignoring the blistering sensation on my eyeballs. "I asked a question. How were you planning to bring me to Heaven without killing me? I'm talking about me as in Genie Lo, not the Ruyi Jingu Bang."

Erlang Shen puttered his lips in frustration. "You know it's really rude to ask someone a question with true sight on. Don't you want to turn it off before I answer? For the sake of good manners?"

"I don't."

"Then I suppose I have no choice but to tell the truth," said Erlang Shen. "I was planning on you dying."

■　■　■

No.

It couldn't have been.

I didn't want it to be.

"You really should have come with me when I offered," Erlang Shen said, his voice suddenly laced with venom. "Instead of being such an unpleasant girl. Humans can only be taken to Heaven if they're willing to go. There was no need for a fuss."

I tried to put the pieces together in my head as fast as possible. Why. How. Where. As if solving the greater mystery would make the immediate danger in front of me stand still.

But of course it wouldn't.

I slowly clenched my hands into fists. "Sorry to disappoint," I said. "Apparently I'm a well-known fuss-maker."

"You really think you're going to fight me?"

"I'm guessing I have a fair shot."

"You misunderstand. There was a reason why I approached you here, in a crowd."

He waved his arm across the field of sunbathers as if to wipe them all away. "Are you willing to sacrifice these people to deny me my prize?"

I didn't answer. I hadn't yet seen a god or demon perform deadly, offensive magic, but now was not the time to test whether Erlang Shen could throw lightning bolts.

I took a deep breath.

"Scream if you want," he said. "I don't care about the Jade Emperor's secrecy anymore. There's really nothing you can say at this point that will do you any good."

Sure there was.

"NA MO GUAN SHI YIN PU SA!" I shouted, dropping to my knees. "Salutations to the most compassionate and merciful Bodhisattva!"

Erlang Shen's eyes went wide.

Only a few people looked our way. This was the city after all; people screaming unintelligibly in public spaces were as common as pigeons.

But even still, there were some witnesses to Erlang Shen fritzing into thin air where he stood, his tail between his legs.

Their shocked expressions became their portraits. Every Frisbee stopped its journey through the air and decided to hover over the lawn like a UFO. A dog was caught mid-bound, a happy smile frozen on its face.

It occurred to me that I'd never seen Guanyin arrive with my naked eyes. A glowing fireball grew out of the air twenty feet up, like the way a child would paint the sun in the corner of the paper. It was like the brightness of a welding torch with none of the discomfort of looking at it. The sphere reached the limits of its containment and burst into a nova ring that spread over the entire field.

Guanyin stepped down onto the Earth as if she'd taken the stairs. She looked at me in my supplicant's pose, puzzled over why I'd summoned her. Especially after how poorly our last conversation went.

"I know where the remaining yaoguai are!" I shouted at her. "And I know who's responsible for setting them free! I need to talk to Quentin, *right now!*"

The goddess frowned, then reached into her back pocket.

"You know you could have just called him yourself," she said, putting her cell phone to her ear.

35

"I TOLD YOU HE WAS A PRICK!" QUENTIN SAID. "WHAT DID YOU think, I was saying it for funsies?"

He was shouting partly because he was still mad at me and partly because the wind rushing by this high up in the air made it hard to hear.

"I thought you were jealous or something!" I said. I felt my grip on him loosening as he made the turn on his somersault and clutched his warm body tighter to mine. I'd missed that feeling.

"Why would I be jealous? That'd be like you getting jealous of Guanyin!"

"Wait, you think I'm in the same league as Guanyin? Quentin! That's the sweetest thing I've ever heard!"

His skin flushed all the way up to his neck. "Focus! What are we doing here?"

"It'll make more sense once we land. Trust me."

The demons hadn't been appearing randomly. They'd been dealt out like cards from a pack. And to do that required a home base nearby, one that could keep them hidden if I swept over it with true sight. There was only one place in the entire Bay where my vision was blocked, ever since that first day on top of the bridge.

The wildfires burning in the remote headlands north of the city. They created shrouds of smoke—the only substance that Sun Wukong's golden eyes couldn't penetrate.

Quentin landed us on a hill upwind of the blaze. The scrubby ground, brittle from the drought, crunched beneath our feet. The greenery on the surrounding slopes was fighting a losing battle against the brown.

Pillows of smoke nestled over the peaks, only ascending with great reluctance. I couldn't use true sight in a place like this, which was exactly what Erlang Shen had been counting on.

Quentin and I rounded a bend and saw the flames. They weren't sprawling, but more like a patchy film of flickering orange over the landscape. Had they been any bigger the fire department would have attacked them in force.

As they were, it was a controlled burn. And the person in control was the shirtless, bright red man sitting on the ground cross-legged, with his back to us.

We flanked him as quietly as we could, ducking behind shrubs and rocks. The gentle roar and crackling of the flames masked our footfalls.

His skin was the same color as an artificially ripened tomato. I thought he might have been meditating, but it turned out he was engrossed in a handheld video game. Every so often he would inhale deeply and then blow out through his mouth. The entire fire-line glowed brighter when he exhaled, like one giant tinder puff he was keeping stoked with his breath.

He did this absentmindedly, without looking up from his screen. It was a chore he'd been assigned.

Quentin and I hunkered down behind a boulder.

"That's Red Boy," he whispered. "How did you know he would be here?"

"Process of elimination," I said. The way Erlang Shen had clammed up in the park under the influence of true sight made it clear—this was about what I *couldn't* see rather than what I could.

"You think there's more?"

I nodded. "I'm pretty sure the other demons who escaped Hell are hiding somewhere close by, using the smoke as cover."

"Why would they be doing that?"

"Because I told them to," Erlang Shen said.

We floundered around looking for him but couldn't spot him. We needed to look up. He was hovering gently in the air behind us, two stories off the ground.

Quentin lunged deep. I didn't hold him back. I'd learned my lesson with Tawny Lion to fight first and ask questions later. The Monkey King shot forth like a bullet, his big traveling jump weaponized.

Erlang Shen seemed to have expected this. He banked to the side, Quentin's wild charge clipping him in the foot. The impact spun him around in the air like a top, but that was it. He came to a halt as purposefully as a figure skater.

Quentin's arc was much less graceful. He went careening off at an angle, unable to control his motion once he was off the ground. He landed on the hillside, throwing up a puff of dust like a cartoon coyote.

The advantage that Erlang Shen had, being able to truly fly, was embarrassingly obvious. But to drive home the point, he swooped over to Quentin, grabbed him by the ankle, and flew back to me, using his speed to slam Quentin into the boulder. There was an awful cracking sound, a billiards break. It all happened before I could even move.

"Oh don't look so horrified," Erlang Shen said. "It takes more than that to put the ape down."

Quentin staggered to his feet. The wind had been knocked out of him, but hopefully nothing else along with it.

"What are you up to, you *hundan*?" Quentin spat.

"He wants the Throne of Heaven," I said. "He's sick of being under his uncle's thumb, so he's going to take it by force. And to do that, he needs the weapon that nearly conquered the gods once before. A full-power Ruyi Jingu Bang."

"The real version," Erlang Shen said. He bobbed on the air currents above us as if he were a buoy in a harbor. "The staff, that is. Not this human you're pretending to be."

"That's why you freed the demons from Hell and sent them after us, one by one," I said. "This was some kind of sick training regimen."

"Active recall combined with progressive overload," he replied. "The best way to remember old skills and develop new ones. I even took care to send yaoguai you'd beaten in the past, so that your body would 'remember.' Hence why I needed the jailbreak."

He'd been challenging me, ramping up the difficulty of my opponents bit by bit. I couldn't have come up with a better study plan myself.

"Granted, I didn't do a perfect job, since you don't have all of your abilities back. You seemed particularly determined not to change size or split into copies. But you've baked long enough. I'm done waiting."

"Oh, and speaking of baking," he said. "Shenyingdawang! Could you spare a moment?"

I didn't know who he was talking to until a voice rang out. "One sec. I'm almost at a save."

Quentin's face took on an expression I'd never seen on him before. Absolute fear. In one swift, fluid motion he threw me over his shoulder and started sprinting away. Fleeing.

Erlang Shen laughed at us instead of giving chase.

"What are you doing?" I shouted at Quentin.

He didn't even take the time to respond. He zeroed in on a ditch and threw me into it, hard. Then he dove on top of me.

The sky above turned into plasma. It felt as if we were trapped in one of those Tesla globes, blanketed by neon filaments that reached for human contact. Quentin pressed me down, away from the colorful display like my life depended on it.

The heat was so intense that it overloaded my nerves. The scale went all the way around again to cold, a frost-burn numbness that my brain had to take as a joke. There was no fire like this on Earth, ha-ha.

Then it stopped. I could see blue again.

"We have fifty-eight seconds before he can do that again," Quentin said into my ear. "Fighting a god *and* Red Boy—we're not prepared. We should run."

We should have. We should have fled and come up with a plan. We should have fled to the other side of the world and retired from the demon-fighting business.

But what rooted me in place, of all the random images that had to come to my mind unbidden right now, was that stupid book sitting in my room. The book of Sun Wukong's tales.

I couldn't shake the thought of how many unnamed villagers and peasants in those stories had to die just so that Xuanzang's deeds would look greater for it. Were they like the babbling, happy people in the park, completely oblivious to the end? Or did they see the demons coming for them, their last moments full of terror and pain?

Genie Lo, caring about strangers, bearing the weight of the world? No one was more surprised than me.

"We can't run," I said. "Erlang Shen's willing to blow his cover and start killing anyone he can get his hands on. We have to stop them here and now."

Quentin smiled at me. "Then we have forty-seven seconds to do it."

Maybe it was because we were in mortal danger, but he'd never looked more beautiful. I craned my neck upward and gave him a peck on the lips. "Let's go."

We sprang out of the ditch and ran straight at the source of the unholy flames. Red Boy greeted our attack with mild interest.

"Forty!" Quentin shouted. "Thirty-five!"

"Zero," Red Boy said. He inhaled through his nose, opened his mouth, and another vortex of color came out.

I wasn't fast enough to react. Quentin elbowed me to the side. I fell just in time to see the sun itself wash over him. He was completely engulfed in flame.

The pain from the True Samadhi Fire this close was a crisis of faith. It felt like my organs would never speak to each other again. The blood stopped in my veins.

Red Boy closed his mouth and the storm cleared.

"I've been training, too," he said. "I don't take as long to recharge now. I got a lot stronger on that island without anyone knowing."

I tried to crawl back to Quentin, my eyes barely working, the gravel stinging my skin. A rock formation with his shape stood where he should have been. I put my hands on it without worrying about the residual heat searing me to the bone.

He'd been tempered. His body didn't even feel like tissue anymore. This was a gray stone cast of Quentin, a mineral replacement.

And it had a crack running across the body from shoulder to hip.

"No," I said, trying to figure out how deep it went with my fingernails. *"No!"*

Quentin didn't move or speak. The expression that had been frozen on his face wasn't shock or anger. It was resignation. His eyes were closed, his mouth calm. It was too much of a goodbye, and I screamed.

36

ERLANG SHEN SWOOPED IN AND GRABBED ME BY THE BACK OF
the neck. He flew up, up, and away, taking me into the sky.

I thrashed in his vise grip, but he kept me at arm's length. I tried
to say that I'd kill him, but it came out as an unintelligible shriek
of rage.

Quentin should have been invulnerable. Immortal. Always by
my side. Maybe I was destined to lose, but I was never supposed to
lose Quentin, not even in the most tragic of possible outcomes. I
had been cheated down to my very soul. This was an abomination.

I screamed and screamed again, so hard that I tasted blood.

"It upsets me to see you mourn him," Erlang Shen said. "Wasn't
the whole point of your reincarnation to get away from Sun Wukong
and find a better owner? One who wasn't such a brute? One who
treated you with more dignity and respect, like a gentleman?"

"Shut up!" I howled. "Shut up shut up shut up!"

"I found your new human form first, you know. By all rights
you're mine, not the monkey's. The only reason I didn't reveal
myself was because I needed his unwitting assistance to draw out
your powers. Talent as big as yours can require multiple coaches,
you know."

He kept flying higher, but he turned us around to face the city.

F. C. YEE

"I have the feeling you didn't take my threat in the park seriously," he said. "So I'm going to take as many lives as the Great Fire of 1906 did, and make you watch. We'll see how willing you are to come with me to Heaven after that."

"Shenyingdawang!" He had to shout to be heard over my screaming. "I'd like a couple of blocks removed from the city."

"Which ones?" the demon asked, a contractor sizing up his quote.

"Any. Just make sure you get—"

Erlang Shen glanced at me and made a coy little face of trying to remember something.

"Make sure you include New Viscount Street and Second," he said.

My father.

Guanyin had put my town under her protection. But it didn't extend to the city, and I hadn't remembered to ask. I'd neglected my father. I'd shelved him outside my conception of "home."

I'd killed him.

"You know what?" Red Boy shouted back from the ground. "I think I'm just gonna level all of downtown entirely. I don't feel like going through the effort to be picky."

Erlang Shen laughed his consent.

Red Boy made two fists and began rubbing his knuckles together. His bright color became incandescent, the heat inside him forcing its way through his skin into the surrounding air.

"It's really quite fascinating, what you're about to see," Erlang Shen said to me. "The best way to describe it would be a human missile. A demon missile, rather."

Red Boy drew his legs up into the air, encased in a thick layer

282

of energy, his pose a mockery of an abbot in meditation. He began skimming silently over the ground toward the heart of the city in a straight line, slowly at first but accelerating, doubling and redoubling in speed. He wasn't a missile; he was the bullet in a railgun.

The demon reached the velocity where I knew there was no stopping him. The trigger had been pulled—the button had been pressed on my father and thousands of other innocent people.

I couldn't bring myself to look. I shut my eyes, shut my true sight down, shut everything down except for the tears streaming over my face.

■ ■ ■

"What are you doing?" Erlang Shen asked.

I didn't answer him. Then I realized he wasn't talking to me. I came back to the world of the living, steadied my sobs, and looked around.

Red Boy was no longer moving toward the city. He hovered where he was, the nucleus in a hot streak of light. A snapshot of a shooting star.

"Red Boy!" said Erlang Shen.

"He can't hear you," I said, sniffling. "He's trapped in a time bubble."

Erlang Shen had forgotten about the other divine being in my corner and smashed his head into a great big ceiling of impenetrable nothing. I could see the giant barrier spell hovering over us only because the wildfire smoke had stopped rising at that point. He dropped me, and I fell.

The air whistled past my ears. Erlang Shen shook off his daze and flew straight down to catch me, but he only made it a dozen yards before he hit another wall. He was caught in a smaller barrier, forced to play an angry mime in a real invisible box. The Goddess of Mercy had the aim of a cold-blooded sniper.

I plunged toward the ground. The wind stung my eyes, but the Earth taking over my view filled me with a sudden calm.

It's okay, I said to myself, a moment before impact. *I'm made of iron.*

The noise was greater than any Quentin and I had ever made upon landing. It was meteoric. Cataclysmic. But I'd absorbed none of the shock. The shock was heaped upon the rest of the world, and the planet would have to deal with it.

I stood up in the middle of a smoking crater. I was untouched. My lack of injury made perfect sense.

I saw Guanyin kneeling over Quentin's body, and I clambered out of the depression to their side. She was checking him with her hands, much as I'd done, but this time it meant something.

Guanyin looked up at Erlang Shen and then gave me a bitter smile.

"I sure can pick 'em, huh?" she said wryly.

"He had us all fooled. Can you heal Quentin?"

"I can try to restore Quentin, or I can help you end this," she answered. "But not both. It's taking most of what I've got to hold the two of them back, and I don't have enough karmic juice to go around. I'm already bewitching too many people right now to keep this fight a secret."

That she didn't talk about Quentin like he was dead gave me a thump of hope in my chest. "Fix him," I said. "Please."

"The two of you will be on your own afterward. You're asking me to put my faith in you."

"We can do it." I was ready to lie to her to get Quentin back, but this felt like the truth.

"Very well." She cleared a space around him and put her hands on the sides of his face.

A sphere of energy encircled them both. Quentin and Guanyin began twitching. Their movements weren't voluntary, especially not his. The little settlings of his stony form and her breathing were being played at higher than normal speed. And, I soon noticed, in reverse.

Dust around them that had risen sank back down to the ground. Errant stalks of dry grass cartwheeled backward, cleaning up their tracks as they went. A tiny beetle caught in the bubble moonwalked away.

A rocky splitting noise sent fear through my spine, but it was only the seam on Quentin's body sealing up. The gray pallor of his skin dissolved, and it became warm and touchable once more.

Guanyin was winding back causality itself. Undoing the passage of time.

She was so *powerful*. I had to fight the urge to fall to my knees and clasp my hands together in awe.

Quentin awoke with a gasp. He scrambled back from Guanyin in surprise. She staggered to her feet, breathing heavily.

"Well," she said, "that's everything I've got left in the tank."

"Are you okay?" I asked. The goddess looked pale and bloodless, as if she'd traded her very life for Quentin's.

"I'll recover once I'm back in Heaven, but I won't be doing that particular trick again for another century or three," she said, her voice already wavering like a ghost's. "Which means it's all on you to clean up properly. I don't even have the energy to maintain my grip on Earth right now."

She sounded like we were about to lose connection for who knew how long. I had to choose my remaining words to her carefully.

"Thank you," I said. *"Thank you!"*

"You can thank me by winning," she answered. "I'm not supposed to condone physical violence, but when it comes to those two *laan zai* . . ."

I raised my palms upward and then clenched my fists. "I promise to serve as your mortal intermediary."

Guanyin smiled. She fritzed once, twice. And then she was gone.

I couldn't escape the feeling that I'd been dropped off at the world's coolest party by the world's coolest older cousin.

"What just happened?" Quentin asked.

"You died and came back to life," I said. "Get with the program."

Even after all that, Guanyin had given us one last gift. Her spells were wearing off gradually instead of blinking out with her. In the sky, Erlang Shen pounded on the barrier, which looked to be on the verge of shattering, and Red Boy was only now picking up speed again.

I pointed Quentin upward. "Body block him," I said. "Don't let him near me for a minute."

Quentin glanced at Red Boy, his eyes full of worry for me. But he nodded.

The barrier above us broke. Quentin jumped straight up and met Erlang Shen halfway. This time he got a good grip. I could hear him whoop with glee at finally being able to lay his hands on that bastard. The two of them tussled in the sky, zigzagging over the hills.

I ran in front of Red Boy, placing myself right in his path. Even through the time bubble I could detect the spark of recognition in his eyes. He knew that in seconds I'd be taking the full impact of his speed.

I slammed my right foot down, embedding it six inches deep into the solid ground.

The smug air around Red Boy's face disappeared. Now he saw, like I did, that the next few seconds also meant that he was a sitting duck. A nice fat pitch hovering over the plate, and me with plenty of time to tee up.

It was time for drastic measures. Something I'd never done before.

Scratch that. I'd done it once before.

I thrust my arm at Red Boy, reaching out five feet, ten feet, twenty feet. Just like in the library with Quentin. I could feel my limb rubber banding, but it was merely reaching states that were perfectly natural to it. My arm was remembering.

I kept stretching it out, picking up more and more speed to the point where my hand was now a projectile. My palm strike smashed into Red Boy's torso, knocking the wind out of his lungs, and my long fingers wrapped around his body, hog-tying him.

The time bubble popped. I screamed from the pain of the True Samadhi Fires surrounding my prey, but I held my grip, and I kept flinging my arm forward. There were no brakes on this train.

Red Boy's aura hit critical mass and flared outward. Only it didn't reach me. I was carrying him away far enough and fast enough that I was safe. My arm was a pair of tongs, and the faster I stretched the less it hurt. My growing limb distributed the heat over a wider area.

Localized laws of physics are still laws of physics, I thought as I clenched my teeth. *Dickhead.*

I slammed his back into the hillside, squashing the remaining air out of him. But I wasn't done, not by a mile.

My arm went on, diagonally down, plowing Red Boy deeper and deeper into the base of the hill. Bedrock and boulders gave way to me as easily as the crumbling foundations of a sand castle. If he'd said anything or done anything before he disappeared under the rubble, I'd missed it completely.

Once it felt like I'd gone deep enough, I unclenched my hand and withdrew it. The impromptu mineshaft I left behind glowed orange, then red, then white. I threw myself to the side just in time to dodge a knot of flame so concentrated it looked like a giant worm escaping the molten core of the Earth. Fire in the hole.

Once Red Boy's detonation subsided, the mineshaft collapsed, bringing the surrounding earth down with a mighty *whump.* Some seismologist was going to have a confusing time working out what had happened.

As far as I was concerned, it was okay to leave Red Boy where he was. If he wasn't dead, he couldn't be sent to Hell where he might escape. And with an entire mountain crushing him, he wouldn't have any air to power his fire breath. If this kind of prison was good enough for the Monkey King, it was good enough for him.

My dust-covered arm slurped back into my body like a strand of extra-long linguini. The sight was nauseating. I should have kept my eyes closed like back when I was on the school roof.

Quentin slammed into the ground beside me, landing on his back. He scrambled to his feet.

"Son of a bitch keeps running away from me," he grumbled.

I looked up, visoring my eyes from the sun. Erlang Shen was

conjuring up something big, gesturing at us with his hands, and I finally remembered that he was a rain god.

"I, uh, think he only wanted a clear shot," I said.

Two manhole-diameter jets of water stomped us flat like elephant's feet. The Hoover Dam had opened a valve above our heads.

I knew how dangerous high-pressure water was. It was how they cut titanium. But still, I was surprised how hard the impact was. On a scale of one to Baigujing, this was like eating a dozen of her haymakers all over my body at once.

Quentin might have shouted after me but his words were lost amid the roar of the water. He was a flat blur. Neither of us could lift ourselves off the ground.

The downpour continued unabated. If we didn't do something fast, we were going to drown eight hundred feet above sea level.

My body screamed at me as I ran out of oxygen. It was screaming a message I'd been doing my best to ignore since I was young, if not little.

Grow.

I finally gave in to it.

37

THE ONLY SENSATION WAS THAT OF THE WATER STREAM getting smaller. My head was freed of the river, and I could breathe again. I put my hand up as a shield; it wasn't a completely ineffective gesture.

The view was like Quentin's skyward jump, slowed down to the extreme. Trees became smaller and smaller. The ground got farther and farther away. If we were in the city I might have been able to use the ascending floors of a nearby skyscraper like backdrop markers on a police lineup. As it was, I could only guess how big I was getting.

I got to my feet, unhindered by the square-cube law. I grew taller. And taller. Erlang Shen tried to shoot me down, and he even let up on Quentin to concentrate his efforts, but it was pointless. We were operating at different scales now.

I knew how big I needed to be. There was no need to go overboard. I just needed to grow to the size where the god hovering in midair was a little larger than the palm of my hand, relatively speaking.

Roughly the size of a volleyball.

I recognized the look on Erlang Shen's face. I'd seen it on my opponents so many times, up close, masked only by the loose weave of a net. The look that said, *Oh god, she can't be that tall. Who paired me against her?*

He turned to flee but caught a mouthful of Quentin's shoulder. His collision with the Monkey King kept him spinning in the air. Quentin had given me the perfect set.

"*MINE!*" I screamed out of habit. My voice thundered over the mountain, warning anyone and everyone not to take my kill.

I spiked Erlang Shen into the ground with so much heat that I could have made the dinosaurs go extinct all over again. I highlight-reeled him. It made me sad that scouts for the national team weren't watching.

And gods bounced, apparently. Who knew?

Erlang Shen dribbled away from my feet like a ball without enough air in it. Before he even came to a stop, he imploded around an infinitesimal point, some kind of gravity sucking his body inward into nothing, like a black hole. It happened without a sound.

Maybe when you were giant, everything seemed anticlimactic.

"Is he dead?" I asked. I winced after I spoke. I hated how loud I was.

"No," answered Quentin, who managed not to come across as tinny. "Gods get a sweeter deal when their physical body is busted. It's straight back to Heaven for him."

"That's BS."

"Not this time. He's committed blood treason against the Jade Emperor. There will be a quick hearing before he's punished. There's literally a special place in Hell for that crime."

Of course—the only thing the Jade Emperor would act quickly upon was a threat to his rule. If it meant Erlang Shen getting what he deserved, though, I wouldn't complain.

"Are you going to stay up there all day?" Quentin asked.

Shrinking down was easier and much less disturbing than drawing back an extended limb. Quentin and the ground came closer as if I were on a helicopter touching down. My body stopped naturally where it was supposed to. I could have tried to keep going and see what life would have been like as a size small, but there was no way I was ready to unpack all of that baggage right now. Regular, tall-ass Genie would suffice.

We were both still soaking wet. I figured watching Quentin shake the water from his hair like he'd emerged from the pool in a cologne ad was my reward for a job well done. His now-transparent shirt lapped at the muscles on his torso.

His eyes caught mine before doing a double take. "Holy crap," he said. "Look at your arm."

I yelped. The limb that Red Boy burned had been washed clean of rock dust. Now it was shiny black from my fingers up to my elbow. The color of polished iron.

My nails were as golden as my true sight eyes. They glittered expensively in the sun, like unburied treasure.

I wiggled my fingers. There was no loss of motion or sensation. The transition between the iron and flesh was a fine ombré.

Hoo boy.

Rather than process this like I needed to, I let my mind slip away. It might return to me later. Right now my thoughts were as free as a bird.

"Hey, tell me something," I said. "I never made it to the end of your book. What did your traveling group get for completing their quest?"

Quentin rubbed his chin. "Xuanzang was given Buddhahood.

Sandy became an arhat. Pigsy got to be a shrine cleaner, which meant he could eat all the offerings of food people left for the gods. He couldn't have been happier. Why?"

Xuanzang might have gone all the way to the West and back purely out of noble intentions, with no expectation of a reward. But it sounded like everyone still got what they wanted at the end.

That settled it then. I happened to want *this*.

I grabbed Quentin by the collar, leaned down, and kissed him.

He was a little startled at first, but then he kissed me back, hard. Like real hard. Like he'd been waiting for this moment since the day we met.

I felt his strong arms circle my waist and cinch tight, lifting me off the ground. I grabbed fistfuls of his hair, which I'd always secretly dreamed about doing, and crushed his lips to mine. Kissing Quentin was as rough and as confrontational as any of our other interactions, and I loved it.

"This is so wrong," he said, his words slightly muffled as I bit him in the mouth. "It's like King Arthur having feelings for Excalibur."

Eh. From my perspective it was more like Jane Goodall hooking up with King Kong. You know, if King Kong were hot and infuriating and oddly supportive of Jane's feelings over time.

Quentin went for my neck in a way I was highly looking forward to, but then he suddenly stopped.

"Uh, Genie," he said, pulling away. He peered over my shoulder at something.

"Do not give me bad news right now," I snapped. "Don't you dare."

"All right," said Quentin. "Good news, then. We found what we were looking for."

"What do you mean?"

"You know how there were one hundred and eight escapees from Hell? And we only took care of a handful at most?"

I groaned. "And I said that the rest were probably hiding here under the cover of the smoke, waiting for Erlang Shen to call upon them as needed."

"Yeah," said Quentin. "The good news is that you were right, as usual. Yaaay."

The wildfires had receded without Red Boy there to sustain them. They mostly just disappeared instead of burning out, leaving behind brush that didn't even appear scorched. The smoke that had been clogging my true sight rolled up and left, drawing back the curtain on . . .

Demons. Lots and lots of demons.

"There's the Black Wind Demon," said Quentin. "Lingxuzi as well. The Golden Horned King. Xiong Shanjun. The Scholar in a White Robe—"

"Quentin, I get it."

They could have been a crowd sitting around an outdoor concert waiting for the band to appear. The smoke clearing up got them on their feet. Maybe the show was about to start.

A few of them tapped tentatively at the air, expecting there to be a barrier of some sort. If Erlang Shen had been using one to contain them, it was gone now.

I could tell the figures were all yaoguai without true sight. They fit the profile—human forms, with one or more monstrous aspects. Clothes that were just slightly off-kilter somehow. An expression of intense hatred once they spotted Quentin.

I seethed right back at them.

"This is bull crap!" I shouted. "I'm tired! I don't have the energy for this!"

"Genie," Quentin said. "Please stop telling the swarm of yaoguai how weak you are right now."

"I don't want to deal with you!" I hollered at the demons from afar. "Screw everything! Evil wins, are you happy?"

"You know, if you're not up for another fight, you could let me take care of it. Like in the old days."

And here I thought our make-out session had signaled progress.

"Oh my god *fine*," I shouted, throwing my hands in the air. "I will let you use me as a stick. I'll be the Ruyi Jingu Bang again. Get it out of your system just this once, and then shut up forever about it."

I was even more disappointed than I was letting on. Getting closer to Quentin didn't mean much if he'd been simply playing the long, long game to get his staff back. I didn't know what the process was for turning into the iron staff of yore, so I shut my eyes and held out my arms angrily as if I was demanding a hug.

"That's not what I'm asking for!" Quentin said. "I was talking about something else! I know how much you hate that idea!" He looked deeply hurt that I would even imply that.

I opened my eyes so I could roll them at him. "Okay, then what *is* your plan?"

"This." He reached around my back and grabbed the end of my ponytail, which had miraculously held together throughout the whole ordeal.

"Ow!"

"Relax, I'm using my hair, too." He showed me the two dark strands in his fingers, one plucked from his head and one plucked from mine. Long and short, just like us.

Then he did something gross and popped them into his mouth.

The action meant something to the yaoguai, beyond being disgusting. Their eyes grew wide and they stopped in their tracks, afraid to come any closer.

He chewed the hairs with the front of his mouth instead of his molars, chopping them into little bits. Then he stepped forward and spat an army into the air.

■ ■ ■

I assumed that the pieces of hair were turning into clones. Like the trick he'd pulled with his parents. That was the only way I could explain the horde of Genie Los and Quentin Suns that spilled out of his mouth onto the hillside.

The doppelgangers started out small but then grew to full size as they scrambled to their feet and blinked in the sunlight. They were like baby foals, able to walk and see only moments after being born. They looked exactly like us, right down to the burns and tears on our clothing.

Once he was done hocking the world's weirdest loogie, Quentin wiped his mouth and pointed toward the assembled yaoguai.

"Sic 'em," he commanded.

The assembled legion of us took off for the yaoguai with a delighted roar. The demons were outnumbered, a clone-Genie and clone-Quentin for every one.

"See?" the real Quentin said to me. "We're on perfectly equal footing, technically. Full partners."

"I . . . uh . . . sure?"

The brawl that ensued once the two sides made contact was ugly, lopsided, and quick. The yaoguai had no chance, and some of them even tried to preemptively flee, only to get tackled from behind.

But despite the savage beatdown our side was raining upon them, there were no telltale whorls of ink that indicated the demons were being slain. In fact, you could have argued that the little clone army was being relatively merciful. They grabbed and pinned their enemies, forcing the demons to look at Quentin and me.

Real Quentin leaped onto a boulder.

"Hear this!" he bellowed. "If any of you even look funny at the human world again, I swear on every god who ever sits upon the Dragon Throne that you will regret it. Harm a human and I will turn you into *puppets* of suffering and regret. Do you understand?"

I saw a few demons nod as much as their captors would allow them to. The general look of terror on their faces told me that this bunch wasn't quite as nasty as Red Boy or Baigujing. They might have been rounded up by Erlang Shen to fill out the B-squad.

"Swear it!" Quentin shouted. "Swear on your very spirits!"

The demons bowed as hard as they could before the clones let them go. They scattered into the hillsides, leaving with some kicks on the backside for good measure.

"That was lenient of you," I said.

"My earrings still work. If they threaten humanity, we'll stop them. Like we always do."

Once the demons were gone, Quentin let out a pinky whistle with the proficiency of a football coach.

"Okay," he said. "Let's pack it up."

The clones began poofing into white smoke. I watched, dumbfounded. I was wrong about Quentin before. Somehow, even after everything that we'd been through, he could still show me things that screwed with my head.

Quentin plopped back down next to me and sighed. "Man, that trick takes a lot out of me."

"Probably for the best that you don't do it too often. It's kind of unsettling and . . . hey! *Hey! You two!*"

A delinquent Genie-clone and Quentin-clone had ignored the order to self-destruct and were instead getting busy with each other, right there on the ground. Sure, Quentin and I had kissed, but this was escalating to a higher MPAA rating.

I couldn't believe I needed to chaperone my own clone. "THAT'S OFF LIMITS!" I shouted at them. "NOT UNTIL YOU'RE NINETEEN!"

"Aw, come on," Quentin said with pure dismay on his face. "Nineteen?"

"Go wait it out in Heaven if you don't like it."

◾ ◾ ◾

We were almost home before I remembered I'd forgotten something.

"Crap!" I said. "My arm!"

I wasn't *too* worried, because I figured Quentin had a spell to hide it. But his face told me otherwise. It said I should worry.

"I'm not sure what I can do about that," he said. "The True Samadhi Fire burned away anything that masked your inner nature."

"Well, you better friggin' try."

Quentin grumbled and took my iron hand. His skin felt extra-warm against the metal. He hummed to himself and swayed with the effort.

Slowly but surely the iron color receded, leaving my skin behind. It drew out of my fingertips, removing the gold from my nails.

"There," Quentin said. "Done."

"Uh, no. Not done."

Most of the metallic hues had disappeared, but there was still a halo around my wrist. A swirl of gold pinpoints on a black background circled my arm. It looked like a beautiful tattoo of the Milky Way, the kind that I would see shared in an online photo feed.

"Get rid of it," I said.

"I can't. This is the most I could reduce the perception of your inner self. Like how I can't hide my tail."

"Get. Rid. Of. It."

"It's fetching," he said.

"It's a *tattoo*. Do you know what my mother will do when she sees it?"

Quentin gave a helpless shrug. I started panicking more than I ever had in any of the demon battles. Forget my mom. Not even my dad would be cool with this, and he couldn't get worked up over anything. Disowning me would be their first agreement in years.

"Quentin!" I shouted.

He threw his hands in the air. "I could always bewitch your mother so she permanently overlooks whatever's on your wrist?"

"Do it!"

He frowned. "I wasn't being serious."

I was, despite the hypocrisy of it, after having told Guanyin not to magic my mom.

"Trust me," I said, gripping him by the shoulders. "This is the lesser of two evils."

38

I WAS TAKING A BREAK FROM STUDYING IN MY ROOM WHEN I first saw the video on the evening news.

Some hiker had caught distant snippets of our rumble with Erlang Shen. There I was, growing taller and taller until I swatted something that couldn't be seen out of the air. That's when the clip ended. A freeze-frame of me in all my titanic glory.

I looked like a giant robot in a skirt. In what I could only assume was yet another favor from Guanyin, an unnaturally cloudy mist obscured my face from view.

"Witnesses are calling it a CGI marketing stunt, most likely for an unannounced reboot of *Attack of the 50 Foot Woman*," the news anchor said. "Which begs the important question—*is Hollywood out of ideas?*"

I groaned into my palms. I would have to burn that outfit and pray Yunie didn't have my wardrobe catalogued in her head. I didn't want her suddenly remembering the magical crap she'd been exposed to.

Not before I could tell her about it.

I had decided. Yunie was going learn everything that had happened to me regarding gods and demons, down to the last tooth and claw, and she was going to hear it from me, face-to-face. Quentin's long-lasting forgetfulness spell had given me the chance to make a proper confession to my friend, and I wasn't going to waste it.

There was a tapping at my window. I ignored it. Quentin could let himself in.

"The Colossus of the Headlands," he said. "You have so many likes."

"You're going to have to cast another spell on my mother. Being online famous is her worst nightmare for me. More so than being eaten by demons."

"How's your arm?" he asked. "No one else thinks you have a new tattoo?"

I raised my wrist. "I haven't taken off this sweatband in three days," I said. "I'm going to be known as Sweatband Girl. You've cursed me to that existence. I hope you're happy."

I heard Quentin sit on my bed, the springs creaking up and down. The pages of a book riffled open. He'd probably helped himself to the contents of my shelves.

"What are you going to do now?" I asked.

"What do you mean?"

"You cleaned up the worst of the demonic incursion. You beat your oldest enemy. There's no reason for you to stick around."

"Of course there's a reason. The yaoguai could always go back on their promise to stay out of trouble. New ones might arrive. I'll have to remain on Earth to keep watch over the whole situation."

I'd been biting my lip the entire time in anticipation of his response. But he said he was staying. I could stop chewing on myself now.

"I'll flesh out my background," he said. "Set up clones for my parents on a long-term basis. I sort of miss having them around. Even if they were overly strict."

"Don't change their personalities," I said. "I like your parents. In fact, I have them penciled in for dinner with my mom next week."

"Sure," Quentin said. "What about you, though? What are your plans now that Heaven and Hell are out of your hair?"

"It's back to the grind. I'll be a junior soon. Application season is going to start for real."

"Still aiming for the promised land, huh?"

"I've got no reason not to. I don't care what Anna said. I'm gunning for every top-tier school out there. If they want to say no to me, I'll make them go through the effort."

"Bash on the gates and see what happens," Quentin concurred. "I can't argue with that logic."

"And in the meantime, I'm hitting the programming books. I'll learn what I can on my own, and Rutsuo offered to mentor me for the rest. My goal is to make my own app by the end of the year."

"I thought you weren't into computers."

"I've recently learned that what I *am* into is having skills," I said. "Skills that no one can deny or take away from me. People can always say I don't look impressive enough, but they can't argue over how strong I am once I punch them in the face."

Quentin chuckled.

"With an app," I corrected. "Once I metaphorically punch them in the face with a really slick, well-made app."

"You should be careful," Quentin said. "If you go too far down that route, you could end up making a life in the Bay Area."

I let the statement hang as I went back to my notes. Sometimes

F. C. YEE

you just had to accept that you might never change as much as you want to.

Quentin smiled, flipped a page, and began reading.

■ ■ ■

Half an hour passed before he got bored and stood up.

"Want to go make out while flying through the air?" he asked. "We can land in Wine Country."

I spun around in my chair to face him. "I don't know. Any higher than a thousand feet up and I only kiss the ancient legends I'm in a proper relationship with."

Quentin immediately dropped to one knee. "Eugenia Lo Pei-Yi, will you—"

I knocked him over with a kick before he could finish the sentence.

"Okay, too fast." He sprang back up and grinned, undaunted. "How about a date then?"

That was acceptable. I took Quentin's hand and left all my plans, all my fears, all my worries behind me. They'd be there when I got back.

■ ■ ■

"This looks like the stuff that comes with bubble tea." Quentin prodded the tapioca pearls that garnished his oyster.

"That's because it is," I said. "Give me that if you're not going to eat it."

I wasn't going to let the food go to waste. We were sitting at a table inside the best restaurant in the country.

We'd lost track of time during our jaunt to Wine Country and gotten hungry. Quentin had asked me where I wanted to eat, and I'd said the name of this place as a joke. But after a quick search on his phone, he'd jumped us to the unassuming, renovated saloon that served as the premier culinary destination in the western half of the United States.

The inside of the restaurant was pretty unassuming for a fancy place, mostly white wallpaper and white tablecloths and dark wooden leather chairs. But the other diners had the nervous air of competitive high-divers on the ledge, about to take their last shot at the gold.

Magic and hexes must have gotten us past the door and into our seats. That, or Quentin bribed the crap out of the staff with more gambling winnings than I could have hidden under my mattress. I let the details slide. I deserved a nice meal after everything I'd been through.

A waiter set down the next course as gracefully as a ninja in early retirement. It was something made out of cucumbers, which was much more Quentin's speed. We both wolfed it down in an instant.

Quentin swallowed his portion first, which gave him time to laugh at me.

"What?"

"You're the only human being here who isn't taking pictures of the food before eating it," he said.

"You mean *we're* the only human beings. As far as I'm concerned, you're one of us. Help as many people of Earth as you have, and you're part of the club. Past the gate."

Quentin's eyes softened. "I don't think it works like that. I haven't been reborn as a human. I didn't earn it like you did."

"You did in my book. Besides, I'm not open-minded enough to have a boyfriend who isn't at least part human."

He grinned and shook his head at me. "You're crazy, you know—"

BONGGGGG.

Quentin was interrupted by the sound of a gong. A big brass gong. A big brass Chinese gong, right here in a French restaurant.

Dozens of pairs of feet tromped over the wooden floors. Two columns of hatted, robed men shuffled into the room, making use of all the space in between the tables. Someone who was better than me at being Asian could have said what dynasty their colorful silken dress was from.

Judging by their subservient posture, they weren't a threat. Quentin hadn't leaped out of his seat, ready to fight. In fact, he was leaning back and slumping over like he did when he was bored in class.

The men all took a knee simultaneously, forming a human walkway that led straight to our table. A sedan chair entered from the other end. The golden, lacquered palanquin was borne by silent armored guardians who coordinated their steps like ballet dancers so as not to jostle the occupant.

Ever so slowly the chair made its way across the room to our table. Once it finally arrived, a servant pulled the embroidered silk curtain aside.

Out stepped a fuming, red-faced bank manager. Or a summer camp director. That was the impression I got of the man, even though he was decked out in fineries that could have stocked the Met's exhibition halls for ten seasons straight.

A servant cleared his throat. *"All hail His Imperial Majesty, August Ruler of Heaven and Divine Master of—"*

The Jade Emperor waved off the announcer so violently that he backhanded the poor schlub in the mouth. I hadn't expected to meet the king of the gods under these circumstances.

"*You,*" he hissed at me.

"*Moi?*" I said as innocently as I could. Quentin snickered. This was going to go poorly if he kept egging me on.

"Yes, you! Flaunting your powers where any human can see them! How dare you!"

I looked around the room. The other diners were frozen mid-bite. Guanyin stepped out from behind the palanquin, being her gorgeous self in a plain *qipao*. She gave me a smile and a finger wave behind the Jade Emperor's back.

"Look, nothing stays hidden for very long these days," I said. "Everyone's got a smartphone. Your big masquerade was going to fail at some point. You might even have to—and I know this is a big shock—manage your own affairs in the mortal realm."

"*Ooooh,*" Quentin mooned.

"Shut up, you damned ape!" the Jade Emperor shrieked. He apparently had as little control over Quentin as Mrs. Nanda did. "You're part of the reason this mess is spiraling out of control! The two of you have let yaoguai run free on Earth for the first time in more than a thousand years!"

"Okay, that is on us," I said. "But what did you want me to do, slaughter them all?"

"Yes!"

I narrowed my eyes. Killing every single yaoguai would have meant a convenient cleanup of Erlang Shen's misdeeds, and a lot of face saved for his uncle. The Jade Emperor would have wu wei'ed himself into another moral victory.

"They were living beings that hadn't done anything wrong yet," I said. "They deserved a chance to do better. Who knows, maybe with enough time they'll become human."

"Of course *you* would think that the scum of the universe could ever improve their lot," the Jade Emperor scoffed. "Just because the Ruyi Jingu Bang managed to worm its way around its karmic betters doesn't mean the rest of the gutter trash—"

I interrupted him by draining my glass and slamming it on the table upside down. I'd read somewhere that in Australia, it was a signal that I could beat up anyone in the room.

"What are the odds that you want to finish that sentence?" I asked.

It took a little while for the Jade Emperor to gather that I was threatening him, probably out of sheer unfamiliarity with the sensation. But the payoff was worth it. His eyes goggled out, and he spat into the air like a trumpet player with no trumpet.

"No, please, continue," I said. "You were in the middle of insulting the living weapon your nephew wanted to use to destroy you."

Quentin hooted and clapped his hands together. There was no popcorn, so he took a big chunk of bread and tore into it with glee as he watched us.

The Jade Emperor tried to recover from his tailspin. "You impudent—wretched—disrespectful . . ."

This was getting sad. "You didn't come here solely to wag your finger at us. Say what you really wanted to say."

The King of Heaven huffed and puffed until he calmed himself down. I waited patiently for him to compose himself.

"I am here to make a proclamation," he said, finally. "Because you have so thoroughly violated my policies of discretion, an official Judgment of Heaven is necessary to handle the fallout."

"Well hey—haven't seen one of those in a thousand years," Quentin chimed in.

The Jade Emperor shot him a dirty look before continuing.

"This region of Earth has degraded to the point where it requires more direct management than the celestial pantheon can provide. Therefore, the great Kingdom of California will be cut loose from our jurisdiction."

I mashed my nose into my palm. "California's not a—never mind. Go on."

"Any spirit or yaoguai may henceforth set foot in these borders, enjoying the *freedom* you value so much," he said with a sneer. "Accountability for what happens will fall squarely on the shoulders of a specially appointed Divine Guardian, who will manage all non-terrestrial interactions inside the protectorate."

Guanyin came up to the table and lowered her eyes.

Finally. The Goddess of Mercy and Gettin' Stuff Done deserved to be in charge for once. Governing a chunk of Earth would be right in her wheelhouse.

But something about the situation didn't sit right. The smugness in the Jade Emperor's tone made it sound less like he was giving Guanyin a promotion worth celebrating and more like he was washing his hands of an impossible task. The lengths to which he'd go not to do any dirty work astounded me.

"Non-terrestrial interactions," I said. "Let me guess. What you really mean is demon fights, rogue gods, and magic spells exploding in people's faces. Pure chaos. California is going to turn into a big hot mess of spiritual shenanigans that nobody in their right mind would want on their plate."

The Jade Emperor smiled and then bent his head.

Quentin and I shared a confused glance at the gesture. Surely he couldn't—

No. No way.

The ruler of Heaven was bowing. To me.

I thought maybe he'd fallen asleep on his feet, or suddenly lost the tendons in his neck.

But Guanyin had dipped even further, fixing me with a pointed stare. And all the other attendants kneeling on the floor had pivoted toward me, kowtowing.

No way no way no way . . .

"Well stated, Madame Divine Guardian," the Jade Emperor said. "Your very own big hot mess indeed."

ACKNOWLEDGMENTS

I'd like to thank my entire family, especially my sisters Melissa and Blythe. I'd like to thank my wonderful editor, Anne Heltzel, for giving my work a home, and my fantastic agent, Stephen Barr, for showing me the way. I'd like to thank Nancy Sondel for putting me in the right place at the right time. And I'd like to thank Karen. She knows what she did.